Praise for the Megan McGinn Novels:

Never Alone

"NYPD detective Megan McGinn plays fast and loose with the rules in this fascinating debut."—*RT Book Reviews*

"A promising debut."—*Kirkus Reviews*

"*Never Alone* ... has all the ingredients of a blockbuster police thriller and it delivers on every level."—*Suspense Magazine*

HIDDEN VICES

— A Megan McGinn Novel —

C.J. CARPENTER

MIDNIGHT INK
WOODBURY, MINNESOTA

FIRST EDITION
First Printing, 2015

Book format by Bob Gaul
Cover design by Lisa Novak
Cover art: iStockphoto.com/26384891/©Jean-nicolas Nault
        iStockphoto.com/36305010/©shaunl
        iStockphoto.com/34769362/©Paolo74s
Editing by Nicole Nugent

Midnight Ink, an imprint of Llewellyn Worldwide Ltd.

Library of Congress Cataloging-in-Publication Data
Carpenter, C. J., 1969– author.
  Hidden vices: a Megan McGinn novel / by C.J. Carpenter.—First edition.
      pages; cm.—(A Megan McGinn novel; #2)
  Summary: On leave following her last case and her mother's death, Detective Megan McGinn finds herself drawn back into an investigation when a judge in the New Jersey town where she is staying is murdered and his secret vice is exposed—and someone attempts to kill her.
  ISBN 978-0-7387-4198-7 (alk. paper)
  1. Murder—Investigation—Fiction. 2. Judges—Juvenile fiction. 3. Women detectives—New Jersey—Fiction. 4. Child sexual abuse—Fiction. 5. New Jersey—Fiction. I. Title.
  PS3603.A76855H53 2015
  813'.6—dc23
                        2015007163

Midnight Ink
Llewellyn Worldwide Ltd.
2143 Wooddale Drive
Woodbury, MN 55125-2989
www.midnightinkbooks.com

Printed in the United States of America

For my grandfather John J. Daly and Joseph Chanecka, the best bonus dad I could have ever hoped for.

This book is about surviving, and you both gave me the strength to endure any circumstance.

With love.

ACKNOWLEDGMENTS

Thank you to my supportive family and friends. I could not have gotten through *Hidden Vices* without all of you. A special shout-out to Alexandra Cohen and Deborah Picone, two fantastic friends I don't get nearly enough time to share laughter and great food with!

Last, but certainly not least, to the readers of *Never Alone*. You took a chance on a new author and I am deeply grateful to you. Your support is just as important in the process as the words I put down on paper.

PROLOGUE

I PLUNGED THE KNIFE *into his chest using both hands, hoping I hit his cold dead heart. There were two other wounds on retired Judge Monty Campbell: his neck was slashed and blood poured from his crotch. It was a damn mess. I knelt beside him and stared into his hazel eyes: just as lifeless in death as they were to me in life.*

Not anymore.

If it weren't for the two diet sodas I'd drank last night, I might have missed this opportunity. I'd fought the urge, turned over in bed, silently pleaded with my bladder, "Don't make me get up and walk across the cold wooden floor."

Two more pangs of pressure built and I was forced to concede. I kicked the comforter off and hurriedly tiptoed over to the bathroom. As predicted, it felt like the balls of my feet were inching over ice cubes.

Damn diet sodas.

I was going back to bed when a light flickering from the main house caught my eye. It came from the great room. I always thought that was a pompous name for a living room. Not that I was ever invited into that sector of the home even when I was living in one of the wings. My things were moved without my consent into the gatehouse a stone's throw away, only one day after the funeral of my mother. Grieving wasn't the Judge's strong suit. I didn't mind it so much, and, to be honest, I half expected it.

Judge Campbell walked past the window with something in his hand, most likely a glass of booze. A shadow roaming against the wall was what told me someone else was there with him. I looked down the driveway. Only the Judge's car was parked outside. Suddenly the Judge threw his glass against the window, leaving a watery blur. The most I could make out were two figures weaving around one another like boxers: one waiting for the other to launch the first punch.

Perhaps my grogginess was responsible for my next decision. Though, more likely, the malevolent events taking place one hour into the new day were the deciding factor that lured me back to Judge Campbell's house.

That's what I called him: The Judge. Dad seemed too intimate.

ONE

SITTING IN BUMPER-TO-BUMPER TRAFFIC on the FDR allowed for far too much rumination over her decision to leave Manhattan. She turned the radio on, scanning for a weather report. The days' headline news had just started. When the announcer mentioned her by name, Detective Megan McGinn promptly turned the radio off. She caught a glimpse of herself in the rearview mirror. A wounded expression reflected back.

"Time to buck up, little soldier," she said to the reflection. It was a sentiment her father, Pat McGinn, had expressed to her countless times, always accompanied with a shoulder squeeze and a finger pointing at her lower neck just to flick the end of her nose when she glanced down. The memory produced a reluctant smile, and a wink into the mirror reminded her of the strong Irish stock she came from.

With the radio off limits and frustration mounting due to the gridlock, she turned her cell phone on to check for any messages. It read three new voicemails, and one saved. She knew what the archived message was: the last message her father left her before he died. Sometimes in the middle of the night she'd play it. It soothed her the same way a closet light comforted a child at bedtime.

"Nothing there in the dark that isn't there in the light," Megan's mother, Rose, would say to her when she was a little girl. If only Megan had known six weeks ago how inaccurate that statement truly was.

She switched her phone to speaker as the first message began to play.

"Ms. McGinn, this is Cheryl from the Woodlawn Cemetery. I just wanted to let you know that the headstone you ordered will arrive at your mother's site within the next two weeks. Everything is an exact match to your father's stone. And also, if you're interested, there is plot availability on both sides of your parents if you want to make any future arrangements for yourself or other family members. I can be reached at—"

"Un-fucking-believable." Megan shook her head in disgust in response to the tacky sales pitch. Annoyed, she moved to turn the cell off when the second message began.

"Meganator McGinn. It's Uncle Mike. Haven't heard from you in a while kiddo, we're worried about you. Give us a ring. I know it's a few weeks away, but it's our place for Christmas this year. Your Aunt Maureen and me and the rest of the gang don't want you on your own. And for Chrissake, you have to come. Someone has to knock back a few shots with me so I can deal with Maureen's sisters. Love ya, kiddo."

She smiled, happy she'd kept the phone on. She whispered back, "Love you too."

Retired Homicide Detective Michael Murphy, Uncle Mike, was her father's partner on the job. The two were thick as thieves.

4

Besides Megan's brother, Brendan, who lived in the Midwest, Uncle Mike, his wife Maureen, and their large clan of sons and daughters were now the only semblance of family Megan had left.

It was the next message she should have deleted without listening to.

"Ms. McGinn, this is Peter Carr. I'm working on a story for The New York P—"

That was all Megan needed to hear. She punched the pound button, wishing it were her index finger poking out Peter Carr's retina and that of any other reporter attempting to score an interview with her.

All of them are assholes, she thought to herself. She tossed her phone into the back seat.

The traffic started moving, albeit slowly, but any gesture forward was better than idling in the same spot for fifteen more minutes. She'd been concerned about having enough time for the last stop on her to-do list before leaving Manhattan. It was the most important item on the list, but hardly an enjoyable one.

———

"Hey, Ginty." As in the past, Megan placed the can of Guinness on top of her father's headstone and knelt down. Her black leather gloves protected her hands from the wet snow as she cleared off the area covering his name. Patrick Joseph McGinn. Written below was *Fidelis Ad Mortem,* Latin for the New York Police Officer's motto: "Faithful Unto Death."

"That's better." Every time she visited his grave, Megan was unfortunate enough to find herself replaying the day she'd found her father at home, slumped over in his chair, his dog in a frenzy at his feet. Megan's mother had been staring out the window through her foggy Alzheimer's state.

Megan kissed the tips of her fingers and gently touched the stone. "Miss you, Gint. Miss you lots. Take good care of Momma, okay?" She sat a moment in awe of the fact that six months ago she'd never imagined the start of winter would include visiting both her parents in Woodlawn Cemetery. Some nightmares live into the daylight, and this was Megan's.

Moving over to her mother's final resting place, she knelt down, not caring about the dampness bleeding through her black jeans or the cold air blowing the ends of her auburn hair around from under her black knit hat. She tidied each corner of the plot as meticulously as her mother would have preferred. A reluctant grin emerged from the memory of the well-meaning, yet fruitless efforts toward a tutorial on bed-making etiquette.

Ten-year-old Megan stood next to the bed wearing purple high tops and ripped jeans, a softball glove on one hand, a ball in the other, smacking it into the palm while she protested Rose's instruction. "What the heck is the point of makin' the bed if I'm just gonna sleep in it again tonight? I mean, how am I gonna move my feet if the sheet is that tight under the mattress?" She pointed at the sharp-edged corner of her Bionic Woman sheet set. "My toes will fall off in the middle of the night!" She lowered her Yankees cap to emphasize her brooding mood.

After a deep breathe in which Rose surely wondered if her true daughter had been switched at birth and someone, somewhere had the doll-playing, dress-wearing, *yes, ma'am* child by mistake, she answered in exhaustion: "Just do it." Which was followed by the *jeez* every parent hears a few thousand times during their tenure as provider and role model.

"All corners tight, Momma." Megan placed the long-stemmed pink rose she'd brought along over her mother's grave. She sat in silence, one hand over the fresh plot, the other picking at the dead grass in front of her, flicking it in the air, indifferent to its direction or landing. As long as she could hear the rip of the grass, it was enough to keep her from breaking, for a minute or so. She blamed the chill of the wind for her watery eyes and continued yanking dead blades surrounding her so that they outnumbered the tears streaming down her face.

Then Megan stood, her back facing her mother's final resting place, and in a voice that began to tremble with each word said, "I'm sorry I wasn't able to protect you, Momma. I should have done better. I should have known." She shook her head. "But I didn't."

She walked back to the Range Rover knowing it would be quite some time before she would be able to face their graves again.

She sat in the truck giving the engine time to warm again and herself a chance to regain her composure. She flipped the visor down to view the fallout of the cemetery visit. Her eyes were bloodshot, puffy. Her nose pink, both from the crying and from the cold air, which she attempted to convince herself was the root cause. Mascara smudges over her pale face gave her the heroin-chic look of the nineties. The only thing that didn't look like a train wreck was her long auburn hair, thanks to the black cap.

"So much for waterproof makeup." She dabbed a tissue in the bottled water she'd brought with her for the trip and began the restoration. She could feel the vibration of her cell phone against the seat belt. She checked the caller identification and forwarded the call to voicemail, waiting out a rush of guilt for not answering.

Damn Irish Catholic guilt.

"Hey, McGinn, it's Nappa. I just wanted to check in and see how you're doing. I haven't heard back from you and was getting a little worried. I stopped by your apartment, but I guess I missed you. Anyway, give me a call."

She could hear the hesitation in her partner's voice. Or maybe she was confusing it with frustration. Either way, there was nothing she could do at the moment to remedy it. She'd made her decision the day they turned off her mother's life support.

Megan got on well with her partner, Sam Nappa. (One night they almost got on extremely well.) Right out of the gate they'd been a good team. And as a fringe benefit, it didn't hurt that he was easy on the eyes. Tall, dark, and built sure beat working with a balding potbelly all day long. They'd witnessed a lot in their time together in Homicide, but in recent months they'd seen too much that hit too close to home, and Megan needed space.

The frustration in Nappa's voice was now obvious. *"Listen, I didn't want to say this on a voicemail, but I guess I'm going to have to. I know you need time away. Take it. I'll be here when you come back. But, McGinn, you need to remember one thing: you are a cop. One of the best Homicide detectives I know. I still have your badge, so let me know when you want it back."*

Megan tilted her head back onto her seat. "Not any time soon, Nappa. Not any time soon."

TWO

THE FEMALE VOICE EMANATED from the GPS in a smooth, somewhat patronizing tone. Megan pictured the female voice wanting to say, "Jackass who is too lazy to read a map, get the fuck off at the next stop." Instead, she heard an intelligent, borderline sexy voice instructing her with the allurement and self-confidence of a woman soliciting phone sex. "You have now entered New Jersey."

"What the fuck am I doing?"

Megan stared at the car in front of her with one elbow cocked up against the window, a knuckled fist resting against her temple. "I cannot believe I'm going to New Jersey in the beginning of winter." The Beach Boys played on the car radio, singing something about beaches and girls and the sun. With flurries blanketing the windshield and the sound of the wipers squeaking against the glass, the last thing she wanted to listen to were fun-in-the-sun classics.

"I'm going to a lake house at the start of winter, in New Jersey?" With raised eyebrows and a small grin mocking her peculiar choice, she asked herself, "What in God's name are you thinking, you wing nut?"

Megan didn't drive much, living in New York City, and she loved how high up she sat in the Range Rover, regardless of the false sense of security it gave her. She'd bought Arnold, her SUV, over the Internet. Megan gave everything she owned a name. It was a quirky thing she'd been doing for as long as she could remember. Everything important had a human name, not like naming a dog Spot. She'd name her dog Will or Dave—if she ever decided to tie herself down with a pet.

The day she got Arnold she'd bought the car insurance online as well, completed a registration form and made an appointment at the DMV, and *cha-cha-cha*: she was the proud owner of an environmentally incorrect vehicle that had balls of steel and four mounted headlights that were so bright it looked like the war of the worlds had started. The seats in the Range Rover had warmers, much to her delight. She pressed a button and her backside was as warm as tight buns during a smack and tickle session. Her previous vehicles didn't come close to such luxuries.

Buck, the used car she'd saved up for and bought for six hundred dollars, was no exception. She'd decided on the name as soon as she left the lot. At every red light, the car would buck forward, nearly colliding with the vehicle in front of her. But Megan had been determined to buy a car. She was about to leave for her freshman year of college and wanted to have the freedom to get around. Pat knew it would be used to go to parties and gave Megan the "do not drink and drive lecture" more than once before she left for school, but he also knew she didn't need it. She was an old broad in a young girl's body.

The first time she drove into the college parking lot for freshman orientation, well, let's just say Dorothy was a few light years away from the yellow brick road, let alone Oz. She parked between a red Porsche and a black BMW that afternoon. Both had colorful bows hanging from the rearview mirror, a vomitus display, in her opinion, by an overindulged brat. She was proud of how scrappy Buck looked; the eleven-year-old Chevy Cavalier with red faux-leather interior would be the most recognizable car in the freshman lot. The rusting rear bumper and white scratches on the doors probably had something to do with it, but Buck was hers, paid in full with her own money. Megan held her head high, and when the rich kids realized the cop's kid there on a partial scholarship had fake identification to buy booze, it got even higher. In more ways than one.

———

Of all the places Megan researched in planning her hiatus from Manhattan, she could hardly believe her choice. She'd contemplated beachfront packages in Mexico, Hawaii, the Caribbean; apartment rentals in Barcelona, Paris, Rome. Each would have been a wonderful choice, but she didn't feel she deserved such a vacation. Not after everything that had happened.

Then there was that pivotal trip down to the laundry room one night. While waiting for the elevator back up, she read the tenants' message board. Apartment 2F had a bedroom set up for sale. 9F sought a roommate—a non-smoking, non-drinker, responsible, and exceptionally tidy. Translation: please be boring, undersexed, and have the social calendar of a nun working in Calcutta.

Then her phone alerted that her she had an email. She wasn't familiar with the sender, but when she opened the message and saw the photo of the lake and the house and the capital letters: HOME FOR RENT, she figured it was fate of some kind. Or the result of one of her vacation-website registrations. The following days were filled with phone calls flying back and forth, and a check for the deposit was sent via overnight delivery. A few days later, Megan was en route.

Lake Hopatcong in New Jersey was the venue for Megan's self-imposed exile for what she considered an emotional downward spiral. She couldn't shake the feeling the locals knew she was on her way. It was a detective's gut feeling, but she didn't trust hers anymore, so she chose to ignore the pangs in her solar plexus.

One hour later the navigation pronounced another direction. On the spot, Megan named the GPS Sheila. The smart, seductive voice reminded her of a girl in college, Sheila Sanders, better known as Downtown Sheila. Sheila was crazy smart, the kind of kid who could hear or read something once and that's all she needed. She had a true photographic memory, or rather, a pornographic memory; she said she never forgot a cock. Sheila would party like a rock star the night before a midterm and still get all As. She'd snort anything from coke to Splenda to flour off of a loaf of bread—whatever got her off. But what got her off the most was ducking out of class with a guy and giving him head in the janitor's closet.

Megan never judged, but she'd seen enough as a Homicide detective's daughter to know that Downtown Sheila was on her way down—and not in the way she enjoyed.

Megan's trip through memory lane was interrupted by Sheila's intelligent but too-smooth voice: "Exit 30 is point-five miles away. You are two-point-three miles from your destination."

McGregor Avenue in Mount Arlington was the final destination on the GPS. The town spanned a little over two miles of the forty-five miles of shoreline on Lake Hopatcong, the largest lake in northwest New Jersey. The main thoroughfare in Mount Arlington was Howard Boulevard. It was two miles of winding road, a few homes, an Elks Club, and a restaurant named Pub 199. The main street would fill one Manhattan block with space to spare, and the closer she got to the house, Megan became quite sure there wouldn't be any taxi cabs or traffic jams. A mini-mart, post office, and barbershop were stationed on the left. A small green establishment that resembled a back yard shed more than a watering hole was located directly across the street. Pete's Bar looked as though it had groomed plenty of future AA members. This was the center of town. Not exactly 57th Street, which was fine by Megan, for now.

In deep need of a caffeine jolt after the drive, Megan pulled into the parking lot of the mini-mart. She got out of the Range Rover and looked back toward the bar. Seven vehicles, all pickups, were parked outside. Two men in sweatshirts, jeans, and tan work boots smoked cigarettes near the door. One wore a blue and white do-rag, his long black hair extending over his shoulders. Neither wore coats in the sub-forty-degree weather. Both stood staring at Megan as she entered the store.

An Indian man stood behind the counter, and she offered a smile. In return, he gave her as frigid a response as the townies across the street.

Friendly place.

"I'd like to get a cup of coffee," she said and pulled out cash from her back pocket.

"Back of store."

"Oh-kaaay." Megan walked to the back only to find that the coffee was located next to the newspaper/magazine aisle. She glanced down, immediately catching a glimpse of her last name. As she poured the coffee, she could feel the owner watching her every move, as if he were on surveillance. Anxious to leave the store and the vicinity of any newspaper, she paid and opened the door. The

13

wind swirled inside and caught one of the many fliers taped to the glass. One sheet flew up, detaching from the door: MISSING. A young boy's picture dominated the sheet. The notice was aged, torn at the sides.

Refusing to engage her curiosity, Megan climbed in her Range Rover and drove away.

———

A young woman who'd been standing two aisles away as Megan got her coffee walked over, picked up the paper with great care, and placed it back on the door, pressing the tape against the glass.

She watched Megan drive away then promptly bought the last newspaper on the stand with Megan's picture on the front page.

THREE

Lake Hopatcong was on her left, and McGregor Avenue was within sight. Megan slowed, pulled over to the side of the road, rolled down her window, and killed the engine. She relaxed back into the headrest, closing her eyes. With the concentration of a Buddhist monk in prayer, she took a deep breath of the lake air. It was cold and fresh with a hint of pine. Pure silence fell over her, outside as well as within. The voices of guilt, sadness, and anger were muted. And if it lasted for only a moment, it was a start—anything to keep her from the memories of her last case and its fallout.

But the first few lakefront homes on McGregor raised a flag in Megan. They were shacks with junk covering the yards, roofs that looked five minutes away from buckling, and porches that should have sported a kid playing the banjo. Worried, she checked the house number on her printed-out short-term lease again.

"Thank God," she said, relieved there wasn't a match. Driving around the bend, the street turned from broken-down lakefront homes to mini-mansions. Megan whistled. "Now we're talking."

Most of the homes on the street were lakefront. A handful of residences were built into the landscape, but the waterfront views demanded all the attention. She neared the end of McGregor, where two older couples were packing up their cars.

"Jesus, what is this, a casting call for the remake of *Cocoon*?" Then Megan cracked a smile as she pulled up alongside them, rolling down the window. "Mr. and Mrs. Mack?" She was unsure which couple were to be her temporary landlords.

"Hello, there." One man stepped forward. William Mack had a sturdy, muscular build for a man in his sixties. "You must be Miss McGinn," he said, offering his hand.

And you must have cataracts to call me miss *anything.*

"Why don't you park in front of the garage." Most of the lakefront homes had street-level garages. "It's the white one with black trim."

Megan did so and climbed out of Arnold.

"Hello! I'm Elizabeth Mack." Mrs. Mack was tall, thin, and probably in her sixties, but she could pass for early fifties with her porcelain skin. She wore a gold Burberry coat, black pants, and laced black boots, and she walked with as much grace as Audrey Hepburn in a ball gown as she approached Megan. "I'm so glad we were able to connect before we start our trip."

Megan smiled.

"Meet Mr. and Mrs. Morse. We drive down to Florida together every year at this time," she said, hugging her jacket closer.

Megan peered at the couple behind the Macks. Mr. Morse had more hair coming out of his ears than over his head. And the little he did have was dyed shoe-polish black, clashing terribly with his bushy white eyebrows.

"Pleasure. I have to say, we're not used to having a celebrity here, especially in winter."

Celebrity?

"Jesus, Al!" Mrs. Morse hushed her husband by elbowing him in his side.

Mrs. Mack placed her hand on Megan's shoulder and gestured toward their home. "Let's get you familiar with the house." She gave Mr. Morse a cold, fixed stare that moved him to silence. Based on Mr. Morse's reaction, Elizabeth Mack didn't dole out reprimanding scowls often. He stood at the top of the driveway and looked down at the ground, moving broken gravel around with the tip of his boot like a Catholic schoolboy caught performing a lewd prank.

Mr. Mack pointed at the garage and offered, "You'll probably want to park in the upper level. There's a set of stairs that come out at the bottom. That driveway is impossible to get up even in the smallest amount of snow."

"Even with a Range Rover?" Megan asked.

"You can try, but you better hope you have plenty of salt and don't lose power in the house to light your way; otherwise you're damn out of luck."

"Do you lose power a lot during the winter?" Megan asked, trying not to sound too concerned in a *I'm a city girl who calls the super for anything and everything under the sun* kind of way.

"Don't know. We're never here." He laughed again, but the humor fell short for Megan.

"Uh-huh," Megan said warily.

He held the side door open. "Welcome to Chez Mack, or as we some times call it, The Macks' Yacht Club."

Jesus, Mary, and Joseph Christ.

Megan wasn't sure if she said the sentiment aloud or not.

17

"What do you think?" William and Elizabeth glanced at one another with a smile.

"Ah…" Megan was trying with all of her heart not to utter any profanities. With her Irish heritage and a Greek sailor's mouth, it was a challenge. "It's…" She raised her hands in the air, wondering if she'd lost all verbal capability.

"Pretty fucking awesome, wouldn't you say?" Mr. Mack blurted out.

"Yeah." She nodded. "Pretty fucking awesome." On first look out at the lake, Megan felt like she'd just won the lottery.

The panoramic view was equivalent to a private screening of an IMAX movie titled *Lake in Winter*. The Macks explained they were on the center of the lake, aptly named the Great Cove. Lake Hopatcong was mostly frozen over with the exception of the area surrounding their boathouse. It's not that Megan was expecting a pond; she was just surprised at the vastness of the lake: nine miles long. Facing the Macks' home on the other side of Great Cove were homes and boathouses scattered throughout the landscape surrounded by leafless trees and an air of silence as if they'd entered hibernation. Wind blew over the lake, pushing wintery dust into the air. As Megan soaked in the silent vista, the water surrounding the boathouse began to move.

"Oh, don't mind that. We have a bubbler system on timer in the water. It's to keep the dock from freezing during the winter," Mr. Mack said casually.

Megan nodded. "This must be gorgeous in autumn."

Mrs. Mack walked over to remove a picture frame from the fireplace mantel. "Here, this was just a few months ago."

New England in autumn on a New Jersey lake, Megan thought.

Brazilian cherry hardwood floors, warm green walls, and white wainscoting reflecting all the earth elements that winter didn't allow to be seen comprised Chez Mack's interior. Megan had, wrongly, shown a bit of ageism toward the Macks prior to arriving. She'd envisioned a house overflowing with tchotchkes and pillows with *Life Is Where the Lake Is* embroidered on the front. Faux flower baskets and countless candles that would make Yankee want to become Canadian. But while the kitchen was retro, it had a double oven mounted in the wall. From 1953, General Electric, Mrs. Mack mentioned during the tour, which was then followed by a "God Bless America" comment from Mr. Mack in the next room, winking as he brought the last of their luggage into the main room.

"You like it though, don't you?" Mrs. Mack asked.

She was flabbergasted that anyone wouldn't. "Like it? It's incredible."

"We've owned this house since nineteen-fifty-three, used it as a summer home for years, then decided to live here full time when all the kids moved out. But the winters are getting to William, with his back and all, and well, wasn't it Bette Davis who said aging isn't for sissies?" Mrs. Mack hesitated. "I'm sorry about what Al said before. He's, he's … "

"He's a blow hole," Mr. Mack added.

Megan laughed at the blunt observation.

"William, please." Mrs. Mack's attempt to correct her husband not only fell on deaf ears, but she broke into laughter herself.

"We've put together a list of numbers and contacts for you, just in case of emergencies, or you lose power," he mentioned.

Megan was still stymied that the thought of losing power had any humor attached to it. "Great."

Mrs. Mack stopped short. "I just realized, I never asked you how you heard about the house being for rent."

"I received an email regarding a winter rental."

The Macks looked at one another, eyebrows raised. "I didn't realize our realtor was sending emails." She shrugged. "Well, I'm glad she did."

"Elizabeth, darling, it's time to hit the road with Mr. and Mrs. Blow Hole."

Elizabeth shushed him, then reminded Megan, "If you need anything, our number is on the bottom."

"Thank you. I appreciate it."

Mrs. Mack looked at Megan with sympathetic eyes. "I hope you find what you're looking for here." She was getting misty-eyed. "I know that ... Well, I hope your time here helps."

Megan offered a faint smile and nodded. She walked the Macks out to their car, waving goodbye as they drove off. For the first time in months, Megan was truly alone. She stood a moment, staring into the woods. The Macks' emails had explained it was a green-acred protected section, and nothing was allowed to be built in the area. For a moment she felt she was being watched. She shook her head. "Get a grip, McGinn. You're finally away from crowds and you start imagining people everywhere." She turned toward the lake, deciding she'd sit by the lake before the big unpacking of her one large suitcase. Semi-frozen or not, it wasn't Manhattan and it was where she'd call home for now.

The Macks had left two Adirondack chairs down on the dock. Megan poured a large glass of the red wine the Macks had left on the counter for her and grabbed a blanket, both offering their own kind of solace in the cold afternoon. She used one chair to sit in and the other to prop her feet up on. Sitting lakeside, even if it was more tundra than lake, could not help but bring Megan's memory back to the last time she'd been at a lake. The Murphys owned a camp in upstate New York, north of Albany. Megan was ten years old when her father explained that she and her brother would be spending most of the summer with the Murphys. He said he was going to be working a long case and her mother was planning on spending time with relatives in Philadelphia.

Her father was always such a bad liar when it came to Megan. The future detective learned early how to make someone crack under pressure, and to her dismay she had a lot of practice in her youth. Post-lie, preteen Megan had regarded Pat with silence and an icy stare. "Now tell me the truth," she demanded.

Pat knew when Megan was on to him. He explained further, still editing his response to a certain extent: Rose was "exhausted."

"She sleeps all the time." Megan's response was far from an exaggeration. Rose did, periodically, take to her bed for days on end. Megan, precocious as she was for her age, was still too young to understand manic depression. She only knew her mother to be either very happy or very sad.

"It's a different kind of exhaustion, sweetie," her father had responded, choking back half the sentence.

Days later Megan and Brendan joined the Murphys up at their camp on Lake Galway. Swimming, fishing, and canoeing filled the days. At night, board games and campfires were the norm, as was Megan sneaking as close to the adult conversation as possible without being detected. While the adults drank their highballs and Manhattans, she'd hear their comments.

"Pat is holding strong. Do the doctors think she'll make a full recovery?"

"It runs in her family. They're hoping she'll be back to herself in no time."

The phrase "it runs in her family" was never far from Megan's mind. But in her heart she knew there were more of her father's attributes ingrained in her than her mother's. As she grew up, she made certain that was the case.

Megan had only taken three sips of wine before she pulled the blanket up to her chin and felt her eyelids become heavier with each blink.

———

Rose stood in front of Megan, her lips moving. But there was nothing but silence, as if the volume had been turned down on her vocal chords. She wore a hospital gown. Her hair was matted and there were black and blue marks around her neck. Her ruby red lips and bloodshot eyes seemed to glow against her drab skin. She stood barefoot on the dock, her frail arms by her sides. Still mouthing words that went undetected, Rose held her frail arms out to Megan. With a flick of a switch, her words amplified, like a freight train running through Megan's mind.

"Why, baby girl? *Why?*"

Megan flew forward in the wooden chair, her heart slamming against her chest. She dropped the wineglass, shattering it.

"Momma!" Megan forgot where she was, frantically looking around. "Where…? What…?"

She closed her eyes, swallowing what saliva remained in her dry mouth. Somehow she'd managed a sweat over her brow in the chilled air. "Jesus Christ."

So much for the first hour of respite, she thought to herself.

FOUR

I GLANCED OVER AT the main house. Of course no lights were turned on. I hardly expected there to be. I must have read through the newspaper ten times before I searched the Internet about the woman in the store who was on the front page of the day's paper. Only then did I realize she'd been in the newspaper quite a bit recently. I felt quite badly for her. Her eyes were sad. They matched her somber demeanor. I found myself thinking that we all go through hell at one point or another, suffering. But hers—hers seemed a unique torment. And now I knew why.

———

Megan's nightmare on the dock hit too close to home. Figuring she wouldn't get to sleep again soon, she decided to unpack. The first item she took out she placed on the bedside table. It was a photo of her parents before the Alzheimer's, before the incidents. Unpacking one large bag doesn't take long, and when the task was completed,

Megan found herself exhausted. She closed the day by collapsing in bed. Amazingly, it was mere seconds before she fell asleep.

When Megan turned over, she thought the clock would read nine or ten in the morning. Not one in the afternoon. She hadn't slept that late since college. And that was usually due to an evening of good ol' freshman college debauchery. She felt slightly hungover but was sure it was from transition and not self-indulgence. She could have stayed in bed for another few hours, and would have if her stomach hadn't reminded her she'd missed a few meals.

Reluctantly, she got up, showered, and decided to buy the bare necessities at the store she'd passed when entering town. Megan had walked up through the garage and started the Range Rover when she saw a young female jog by. She was only feet behind the truck when Megan looked in the rearview mirror and noticed the jogger dropped something. She quickly got out and picked up a cell phone. "Hey! Hey! You dropped your phone! Miss! Your phone!"

"Hey, who are you?"

Megan turned. There was a teenage girl standing at two o'clock leaning against the mailbox, one dangling earbud blaring music, carrying a backpack.

"Lady, you can yell all you want, she's not going to respond."

"Why?"

"Apparently Mensa missed your application," Rude Teenage Girl responded.

Rude little shit, Megan thought.

"She's deaf. The phone is for texting." Rude Teenage Girl had medium-length hair, the perm nearly gone, rings on every finger, and

24

multiple bracelets lining each wrist. She was pale, lean, and made every teenage girl's mistake: blue eye shadow and thick dark mascara.

"Oh. I didn't know," Megan answered.

"Obviously."

Megan took a deep breath. "Well, *lovely young lady*, do you know where she lives so I can get it back to her?"

"Maybe." She folded her arms, speaking to Megan in a suspicious tone, with a stare that implied she was going to need some questions answered first. "You related to the Macks? It's their house ya know."

Megan gave as bratty of a tone back. "*No, I'm not related to them*."

"That your truck?"

Now this kid is getting on my nerves, Megan thought. She held the girl's gaze and kept silent.

"Just you here?"

Megan snapped her head back and forth looking up and down the street. "I hope you're not the welcoming committee."

Rude Teenage Girl stood unimpressed, rolling her eyes. "Answer, please."

"Who wants to know?" Megan asked in the surly detective tone she was so accomplished at.

Rude Teenage Girl brought it down a few notches. "Sorry. I'm Billie. I live down about fifteen houses."

Megan nodded. "I'm Det—I'm Megan. I'm renting the Macks' house for the winter."

Billie raised her eyebrows in that wiseass teenage way. "You're *Det-Megan*? Don't you know your own name?"

Megan didn't have children, and, in this moment, she most certainly didn't want any. "Good to know rudeness travels tri-state. I'd hate to think Manhattan was being blamed for the whole brunt."

Billie rolled her eyes and pointed down the shoreline to a large estate. "See that house? She lives in the gatehouse on the property. I'll write down the house number for you. It's like two minutes away."

"Thanks," Megan replied.

As she was getting into the Range Rover, Billie yelled down the street, "Hey Det-Megan?"

Megan turned, knowing she was in for a smart-ass comment.

"*Welcome* to the neighborhood." Billie bowed, opening up her arms.

Megan shook her head and whispered to herself, "That girl is my birth control for the next three years."

FIVE

MEGAN USED BILLIE'S DIRECTIONS and found the location of the deaf woman's house, or rather gatehouse. There were no cars in the driveway. The property felt like a cemetery: cold, quiet, void of life. She rang the doorbell, feeling a bit stupid, since a deaf woman couldn't hear it, but flickering lights from inside the home explained that. When she got no answer, Megan assumed the woman was still on her run. She tore off a sheet of paper from a pad she'd kept in the glove box and wrote a note explaining that she'd found the phone when the woman jogged past her, and Megan wanted to return it. Megan signed her name and then left the page on the doorstep under a stone from the lawn edging.

As she turned back from the door, a feeling tugged at her. Her gut told her something wasn't quite right here. *Not your job to follow that instinct anymore, Megan.* She chose to ignore it. As she opened the car door, she glanced up and realized she wasn't actually alone. Perched on the top of a phone pole was a hawk. The way it peered down at Megan made her feel challenged. The predator possessed an air of self-confidence that bordered on arrogance.

Like looking in a mirror, she thought to herself.

Megan climbed into the truck, refusing to break eye contact with her contender. When she closed the car door, the hawk took flight. She stared until it was out of view, then started the engine and flicked on the seat warmer. Best invention in the world. If the heat in the lake house ever gave way, she'd sleep in the Range Rover. It would cost more than a room at the Four Seasons in gas, but it was an option, if in dire need. The gas light lit up on cue as she pulled out of the driveway. She remembered passing a gas station a little less than a half-mile from the gatehouse.

The station looked as deserted as the property she'd just left. The garages were pulled shut and there were no cars or even an attendant within sight—not that she could blame them. She glanced at the Range Rover's temperature display. *Nineteen degrees isn't an enjoyable temperature, unless you're a polar bear.* She caught a glimpse of movement in the main office area. Megan climbed out of the Range Rover with as much grace as a pig skating on ice holding a glass of champagne.

A woman in her fifties emerged from the station. She walked out to the car with a small smile on her weathered face, having seen Megan's dismount of the truck. She wore tan work boots, faded jeans, and a denim shirt underneath an army jacket. Here was a woman in touch and incredibly comfortable with her masculine side.

"Looks like a parachute might come in handy next time you get out of that truck." She smiled. "Going on safari with this monster?"

Megan raised her eyebrows looking back. "Not a bad idea, actually."

"What can I get you?" The woman reached for the gas pump.

"I can do that," Megan assured.

"Sorry, hon, not in New Jersey. Only attendants can work the pump," she answered while unscrewing the gas cap.

"Why?" Megan asked, though she was more curious why the woman referred to her as *hon*. Megan would be lying to herself if she said introducing herself as *Detective Megan McGinn* didn't stroke her ego a bit. After all, she'd worked damn hard for that title. Being referred to as *hon*, especially by another woman, felt belittling. It was too familiar.

The attendant waved off the question. "It's a state thing. Been that way ever since I can remember. So, how much?" she asked again.

"Fill it, please. Regular."

"I half expected a Navy Seal to come flying out of this beast, not a petite thing such as yourself."

"Yeah, I didn't realize the previous owners put on such large tires before I bought it."

"You're not from around here, are you?"

"How can you tell?" Megan asked.

"You have all your teeth," she said with a hint of sarcasm. "I'm just kidding." She pointed to the rear of the truck. "New York plates."

Megan nodded.

"What brings you out to a New Jersey lake town this time of year?"

"I love the winter." It was a partial truth. She did enjoy the change of seasons; it just wasn't her reason for being there.

"Well, you'll get a lot of that around here. You have the right vehicle with the amount of snow we get. You're in pickup-and-plow country. Gets real quiet over the next few months."

Thank God.

"Did you buy a place nearby?"

Jesus, what is it with the people around here? Are you ex-Stasi?

"No, I'm just renting. Down the street." She nodded in the direction she'd come from. "McGregor Avenue."

"McGregor. That wouldn't be Will and Elizabeth Mack's place, would it?"

"Yes, it is."

"The Macks are good people. I run into them once in a while at the pub down the street. You passed it if you came in off Route 80."

Megan nodded. "I remember that place." As if she could have missed it. The only other buildings in the small stretch of town were the mini-mart, the post office, the bar, and an Elks Club with the sign informing the town of the pot roast dinner at the end of the month. Oh, and the town municipal building, which was slightly smaller than the mini-mart. Megan envisioned the same person working at all the places, running from door to door with a mere change of a hat depending on which building they serviced at the time.

The gas pump finally clicked off at $75. Jesus. Megan could have used a small sedative before paying that tab. Naming the truck Arnold wasn't a bad idea, given it seemed to terminate all the money in her wallet.

"Need help getting back in?" The woman smiled while watching Megan climb into the driver's seat using effort similar to rock climbing.

"I'm good."

The attendant walked up to the driver's side window and handed Megan a receipt and a slip of paper. "Here, it's a coupon for twenty percent off your next oil change."

"Thanks."

"I'm Lynn. If you need any help maintaining this monster while you're here, my son does a lot of work on 'em."

"Great, thank you." Megan rolled up the window and made a quick U-turn out of the parking lot, noticing in the rearview mirror Lynn standing, staring at the back of the truck as she drove off.

———

A man stood a few feet back from the windows in the garage. He'd stopped working on the carburetor he'd been in the process of rebuilding when the woman pulled in for service. He lit a cigarette and finished the beer he held, then chucked the empty can into the corner bin. Like the owner of the station, he'd noticed the New York license plate. Her looks definitely interested him, but her purpose for being there interested him more. After all, he did pick up a newspaper once in a while and had recognized her immediately.

The man walked up to the window, exhaling his cigarette smoke against the dirty glass and watching the truck until it was out of sight, and then dialed on his cell phone.

"Hey, someone new in town. I'm pretty sure it's her."

SIX

MEGAN BOUGHT MORE SUPPLIES at the mini-mart before returning to the lake house: milk, bread, frozen pizza, two pints of ice cream, chocolate chip cookies, more wine. All the elements to a new diet quite possibly called Food Baby Coma. She noticed a tiny Chinese take-out restaurant on a side street and decided to stop and order. The decor was not even close to minimal and she wondered if the health department made even annual inspections, but it smelled incredible. Again, not adhering to a let's-fit-into-those-skinny-jeans-by-spring regimen, she ordered barbecue ribs, two egg rolls, and General Tso's chicken with fried (not steamed) rice, and chicken lo mein.

Once back at the house, she changed into a pair of loose-fitting pants and made herself comfortable on the couch. She turned on the widescreen television, ignoring any and all news channels.

Let the hermitic evening begin.

Megan channel surfed and, oddly enough, ended up on a channel she had zero respect for in her state of gluttony: a fitness channel. She raised her glass of Cabernet. "Here's to you ladies. C'mon, work it. That looks pretty fucking tiring, if you ask me. You're probably a size zero, but who is having more fun? Me or you?" She was halfway through her dinner and wine bottle when her cell rang. She glanced down. She let it ring three times before answering.

"Yeah."

"McGinn, I'm surprised you answered," Nappa said.

"Yeah, so am I." Megan threw back another sip of wine, truly not wanting to have this conversation. But her Irish guilt over dodging his calls had reached critical mass.

"How is lake living treating you?"

"Nappa, I must get over eight hundred channels on this television."

"What are you watching on your eight-hundred-channel television?"

"Some fitness show." Megan started to channel surf again, finding a boxing match. She thought it was fitting, for she was sure the conversation was about to take a turn. "Why haven't I ever made time for this before?" She began to gnaw on a rib.

"Maybe because you were working?" Nappa offered. "Remember work?"

"Yeah, it's that thing that eventually killed my father and is responsible for a sick fuck attempting to murder my mother. You mean that work, right? Did you call me for a reason? And by the way, I *just* got out here; why are you pressuring me?"

"That wasn't my intention, I'm just checking in on my partner during her time off."

"I'm not your partner anymore."

"Right now, sure. But you'll bounce back, and if you keep eating whatever it is you're devouring on the other end of this phone call, you'll probably be able to bounce to a few other places."

Megan threw the sucked-to-the-bone rib on the paper plate. "Funny. Very funny, Nappa."

A moment of an uncomfortable silence led to Nappa clearing his throat before saying, "Doing a lot of background on the Worth case, still looking at cold cases that might be connected."

The last thing Megan wanted to hear about was the Worth case. That case landed her at the top of her game as an NYC Homicide detective, but it was also the beginning of the unraveling of her life.

"I also called because you received a letter from Mrs. McAllister." Mrs. McAllister was the mother in Megan and Nappa's last homicide case. "It looks personal. Do you want me to forward it to you?"

Megan clicked the remote a few more times and an angry man with slicked back hair waving a Bible stared into the camera. Veins popped out of the side of his temples as he shouted. She was happy she'd had the television on mute.

"Yeah, sure."

"Give me your address."

She did and then quickly ended the call. "I have to go, Nappa."

After her gluttonous evening was over, Megan found herself unable to sleep. She sat up in bed with her arms wrapped around her knees. She listened to the wind as it came off the lake, blowing through the trees on the property and setting off the sensor lights positioned on each side of the house. Their shadows moved across the bedroom walls. The sound of water having yet to freeze slapped against the lake wall and echoed her inner state. She was attempting to transform her pain into healing, but it felt as though she'd just begun the 500-mile Camino de Santiago pilgrimage. She wondered if she'd ever see the end in sight. Because right then, she couldn't.

A strong gust blew up outside and Megan heard something crash down on the deck. Her detective instinct prompted her to grab her gun from the bedside table. She leapt off the bed and slowly walked to the front of the house, her gun at the ready. Megan didn't need to turn any lights on; the sensor continued to light up the front deck. She first positioned herself to the right of the room and peered out. Nothing. She moved to the left of the bay window. A large ceramic garden pot filled to the brim with old dirt lay smashed in front of the glass.

There is no way the wind could knock over something that large, she thought to herself.

Megan double-checked the locks and windows of Chez Mack, as well as the alarm. All was secure with the exception of her peace of mind. The rest of the night she slept with her gun beside her and her senses heightened.

———

There was very little light illuminating McGregor Avenue as the figure walked away from the steep driveway. Only the burning end of his cigarette and a street lamp a few yards away guided him to his car. He walked by the Range Rover with a grin on his face.

SEVEN

THE NEXT DAY STARTED earlier than Megan had planned on. She attributed it to the odd occurrence in the middle of the night. Feeling restless and quite frankly bloated from the amount of Chinese food she'd gorged on, she decided to take a hike on a trail in the back of the lake house. Cold, fresh air and a quiet atmosphere would be her solace for the morning. The Macks mentioned it was a nice twenty-minute walk and pointed out where they kept their walking sticks. Megan assumed the sticks were due to their age—right up until ten minutes of the hike felt like fifty.

I should have brought one of those fucking walking sticks. God I hate when I'm wrong.

She had to smile at her city arrogance yet again. Megan was accustomed to walking on pavement or up and down subway stairs, not frozen ground up a quite steep hill. Once she reached the top, she found an ass-chilling boulder to sit on. Staring out at the leafless trees standing like skeletons in the wake of the increasingly declining temperatures somehow made her feel at home. The vast space pulsed with a natural power she didn't want to disturb, like a sleeping bear or her father when he was watching a baseball game. She knew they'd have life again come spring, and it made her wonder if she'd ever feel a level of vitality in her own soul once more. At that moment she could hear her father's voice. When she was down—when the boy didn't call back when he said he would, or she lost a softball game, or when she was working her way up the ranks of becoming detective—Pat McGinn would utter, "Meganator, time to put your big girlie pants on. Buck up, kiddo."

It was an odd sentiment that held so much truth, even she couldn't deny it. She held on to it until the ice-cold rock she was seated on became untenable to her numb buttocks. Megan began the trail back down the hill she'd climbed and noticed a pit she hadn't seen on her ascent. It looked as though bonfires were held there, based on the number of cigarette butts, empty beer cans, and a broken bong.

"So, this is where the high school kids hang out," she laughed, continuing on her trail, basically holding on from one branch to another until a slippery spot provided the right conditions for a fall on her ass. "And this is why my parents didn't name me Grace." She hoisted herself up and noticed the hawk one tree away. "You're a little too close for comfort, my friend."

He peered down at Megan, completely unflinching.

"Didn't I see you yesterday? Are you following me?"

Great, Meg, now you're talking to birds. What the hell?

Megan continued down the hill, feeling the hawk watching her every move. It matched the feeling she'd had on her last case before arriving in New Jersey, though not as menacing. Not by a long shot.

———

The reflection off the snow-covered lake was so overwhelming, Megan donned a pair of sunglasses to sit on the couch while drinking her second cup of coffee and reading through the three-ring binder the Macks had left for her. A leisurely second cup of coffee—not something that happened much in her Upper East Side apartment. The last few days of smoky skies and the somber feeling that the sun and the color blue had entered hibernation hadn't been a help to her mood. But it was the beginning of winter in New Jersey, she reminded herself.

She recalled Elizabeth Mack mentioning the scenic drive circling the lake and decided there'd likely be few sunny days like this one. Megan climbed into Arnold and turned off Sheila, the slutty-voiced navigation system. It was a day to enjoy a quiet drive and the light filtering down through the sunroof. She didn't even turn on the radio for fear of hearing about whatever horrific event had happened in the world since last night.

Megan drove the winding path circling Lake Hopatcong, curious as to what the rest of the lake had to offer. She was lulled into random speculation. When her phone rang, she answered without checking the caller identification. As soon as she said hello, she regretted it.

"Detective McGinn, where in hell are you?" Lieutenant Pearl Walker bellowed into the phone. Walker, unlike Nappa, didn't have a phone voice that matched her looks. She was a stylish, milky-brown fifty-something who looked more like a thirty-something. She was tough, compassionate when she needed to be, and, most of all, still considered herself Megan's boss. Candid comments replaced the more humorous aspect Nappa displayed. "Nappa told me you're in New Jersey. Are you out of your ever-loving mind?" No breath was taken before she added, "I thought you needed time off to get away, as in away, away. As in, um, I don't know, maybe Mexico or Ibiza, having your way with a few cabana boys—not in New Jersey in the wintertime at a lake house. That's not a vacation, that's a damn asylum."

Megan interrupted with sarcasm. "I'm fine. How are you?" She heard Walker sigh loudly into the phone, her version of an apology for striking out so strongly in the first conversation the two had shared since her mother's funeral.

In a more passive, motherly tone, she went on, "I'm missing my best detective but other than that, taking things day by day. How are you holding up?"

"I'm fine. Good. Okay."

"Nice buffet of an answer. When do you think you can come back?"

Megan shook her head. "Lieutenant, I just got out here. It hasn't even been a week."

"I know, but I also know work is the best thing for you right now," Walker answered, knowing Megan would contradict her.

Pearl Walker and Megan were birds of a feather where work was concerned. They both were driven, hard-working, not the type to sit home watching bad television and wondering who would get voted off whatever island or weight loss show. But for now, Megan needed a vapid experience, which she assumed the days ahead would provide.

"You're right, most of the time—but in this case I need some space."

"So you are planning on coming back?"

Megan raised her eyebrows, exasperated by her boss's Jack Russell terrier sense of interrogation.

"Give me until after the holidays and we'll reassess the situation."

"*Reassess the situation.* Now you're talking like *my* bosses," Walker responded in a huff. "If you need anything, you know to call, right?"

"Especially if it's going to be as pleasant as this conversation has been." Megan smiled.

"I'll check back again soon, detective."

"It's Megan."

"All right, Detective Megan." Walker hung up without a good-bye, again adding to the idea that perhaps some sensitivity phone training may be needed in the future.

———

Refocusing on her drive, Megan found herself entering a small town called Sparta in New Jersey. It was quaint with wreaths donning every streetlamp. It was a little early for that, in her estimation, but she tended to want to ignore this year's holiday season. A sign read LAKE MOHAWK. It consisted of a small street one would expect carolers to be strolling down when Christmas actually came. The hamlet-sized town was intriguing, if even sweet, mainly because she saw more people in the few shops and restaurants than she had in the entire last two days. Apparently not everyone was at home overindulging on Chinese food and self-pity.

One restaurant, Krogh's, caught her eye for a late lunch. They had valet parking, which was helpful given she couldn't see a spot big enough for the Range Rover.

The gentleman who took her keys was kind and a little shocked when Megan lunged out of the truck. Megan said, "Hope you have room for this baby."

"I hope I can drive it, but don't worry, hon, I'll take care of it."

Again with the hon *thing?*

Megan thanked him and asked if she needed a ticket, to which he laughed and said, "No, we just hold on to the keys till you want to leave or we close."

Krogh's interior was more like a log cabin than a restaurant brewpub. Dark ceilings with beams and faux Tiffany lamps covered each booth. The large brass microbrewery had floor-to-ceiling glass doors. Megan found an empty seat at the horseshoe-shaped bar. The stool was too high, so she dangled her legs as if she were ten again. It made her smile, thinking back to the days when her Grampie, her dad's father, would babysit. That was back in the days when children could sit at bars. He'd buy himself a beer, and Megan was allowed as many Shirley Temples as she wanted, or until she got a stomachache. Which was usually the case after a pile of fries or onion rings and a hot dog.

She decided to forget the fact her legs couldn't touch the floor and ordered the house brew of the day. When she reached for a menu, she noticed the local newspaper on the bar: LOCAL JUDGE STILL MISSING, PRESUMED KIDNAPPED. She'd just started reading the article when a familiar voice spoke behind her.

"Oh my God, is that *Trouble* I see on the barstool?"

EIGHT

At first Megan cringed, thinking someone recognized her from the newspapers. Then she recognized the voice along with the nickname Trouble. The voice had changed a bit, as all voices do after years of cigarettes and booze. Few men could make her blush—it had happened once with Nappa, on a lonely night working her last case—but this man made her blush years ago. More than a blush, actually; it was the first time she'd felt yearning.

Megan turned and saw Christopher Callie.

Callie, as he was referred to during college years at Marist, stood only feet away from Megan. The old saying that your past can come back to bite you in the ass is true, but in this case it was less a bite than a deflowering. His eyes had a few more crow's feet than he'd had her freshman year, his laugh lines deeper than they once were, but she recognized him immediately.

"You've got to be kidding me. Jesus! Callie!"

Callie charged over, and his six-foot-three frame lifted Megan off the stool with as much ease as if he'd picked a feather off the ground. "Let me take a look at you."

"Not too close, it's been a long time." Megan felt her face flush a bit thinking of how long it had been since the two had seen one another.

"You look great, Trouble." He slapped the seat of one of the barstools. "Come on, let's move to a booth. What are you drinking?" He was so excited that he didn't give Megan a chance to answer. He motioned to the bartender. "Two seasonals, Scott."

"Right, boss."

Megan smiled. "Boss? You own this place?"

Callie grinned. "For years I was fighting The Man. Now I am The Man."

The beers arrived just moments later, and they clanked pint to pint. "Trouble McGinn." He shook his head after a drink. "I can't believe you're here. The last time I saw you was graduation night. I was playing the piano, and you and a few other girls were singing out of tune to some song . . . I can't remember."

"I'm never out of tune." Megan sipped her beer.

"Well, not in other places, but you sure were behind a mic." Callie stared at her longer than she preferred. He always had a shit-eating grin on his face. It was disarming to her eighteen-year-old self, so now she both loved and hated it at the same time.

"Yeah . . . "

There's always a moment of an awkward silence when lovers meet up again and both know their lives have taken different paths. The expected benign conversation ensued, but not before Megan had the memory of Callie back in the day.

43

He was the guy who showed up at campus parties wearing a Mets baseball hat backwards, always in a good mood. He'd lean against a wall, usually within arm's reach of the keg. He wasn't the macho guy trying to score girls or start a fight; he was liked by everyone and could be seen by everyone on campus, given his tall frame. Callie could usually be caught rushing to a class he was already ten minutes late for. The single dimple on his left cheek showed itself with even the slightest grin, and it got him out of a few tight spots. He hunched over a little when he spoke to you, partially due to bad posture and partially because Callie had a way of focusing on you when you spoke. It was one of the many things Megan fondly remembered about him from college. What every woman finds sexy: direct, eye-to-eye contact. The kind that made the world around you feel obsolete.

"Mmm. I can't believe you own this place."

"What did you think, I'm working here on a parolee release program?" There were a few instances when Callie and the other guys in Marion Hall ran into problems getting caught gambling, placing bets on the college basketball team. There was a poker game going on somewhere in the dorm every Saturday night.

"There was a time when that looked to be your path," Megan said with a laugh.

"I wish I could argue with that, but"—he raised his hands—"we did like our poker nights back then."

"Wait a minute, I completely forgot," Megan interrupted. "You're from New Jersey."

"Born and raised right down the street, yeah. I was married in the church down the hill."

Megan raised her eyebrows when he mentioned marriage. He wasn't wearing a wedding ring, and there wasn't a tan line from where there was one.

"My wife relieved me of my marital duties a few years ago. She decided—" He rubbed his temple. "How did she put it? Oh yeah. 'I love you, I just don't like or respect you anymore.'"

Megan grimaced at the comment.

"Her work ran her life."

"What does she do?"

"She's a sensitivity trainer."

They laughed.

"No, seriously, she's a doctor, a pediatrician. She fell in love with her partner, actually, and that was that."

"I'm sorry to hear it."

"Thanks. But, enough about me, what have you been up to the last fifteen or so years?"

"A little of this, a little of that."

Callie glanced down at the floor, probably wondering if he should address the purple elephant in the middle of the conversation.

"Life has been pretty boring lately." A bizarre feeling came over Megan when she said that. Suddenly she couldn't stop giggling at the absolute absurdity of her comment. "Actually, I'm renting a place on Lake Hopatcong. I needed some time away from the city." She waved her hand in the air. "A break from it all."

"I was really sorry to hear, or rather read, about what happened. Really sorry."

"Me too." She finished her pint.

"Another drink, Trouble?"

"You asked that a lot during freshman year."

"From what I recall, you never said no."

"What am I supposed to say when a man of your stature twists my little arm?"

He yelled over the bar, "Scott, bring us a sampler." Callie gave Megan a knowing look again, most likely remembering the night they'd spent together when most everyone in the dorm went home for a long weekend break. "So, how long will you be in the area?"

"Not sure. I'm taking it day by day. At least through the holidays, that's a definite."

"Where on the lake are you?"

"Mount Arlington."

"Are you near the water?"

"I'm right on the water. Well, right on the ice."

He laughed and then pointed out the window to the Range Rover. "Is he yours? Tell me, do you still name things? You named your car freshman year. Buck, right?" His tone told her he knew he was right but wanted to impress her.

Megan covered her face with her palms. "How did you remember that?"

"Oh, and I remember you named your leather jacket! Ian, I believe."

She could only nod and smile, thinking she'd forgotten that one.

"So what did you name that beast?" He nodded in amusement toward the window. "Well?"

Megan answered in an Austrian accent. "Arnold."

"Fitting."

———

The young woman had just arrived to Krogh's for work. She entered through the kitchen and donned her apron. Before starting her shift, she peered through the window to see how heavy the lunch crowd was. Much to her surprise, she caught sight of her boss seated with the new woman in town: the New York City detective, the one who'd returned her cell phone.

She watched for a few minutes, paying attention to their gestures, their facial expressions. If she had been closer, she'd have read their lips. His smile was warm, even flirtatious. Her thoughts returned to the detective, wondering why she was really there. The chef asked her to trim some of the entrees being served for the specials on the menu. As she stood over the counter trimming the fat off the pork, she couldn't help but remember the last time she held a knife.

She'd known he was dead, but it still felt powerful, and fair—both an anomaly in her life. She searched her heart to find an ounce of guilt, thinking back to the moment in the great room, but she'd be lying to herself and to God not to admit it felt damn good. The times she daydreamed about his suffering, about getting back at him for her and her mother's pained existence, only brought her to the conclusion that her mother, who she believed was in heaven, had awoken her that early morning hour. So she could enjoy even that slight revenge, even on a dead man.

She finished the prep work and washed her hands before looking back again through the swinging kitchen door. She stared at Callie and the detective. They looked familiar with one another, yet seemed shy in a sweet way. As if it was the first half hour of a blind date, when the chemistry is there but you don't want to get your hopes up. The first time she saw the detective she remembered thinking what a pretty woman she was, except for her eyes. They seemed burdened with sadness. Like her pupils were dark clouds ready to burst rain down her cheeks because the load was just too damn much. Today she seemed lighter.

Her thoughts were interrupted when one of the waitresses motioned for her to go into the dining area and bus some of the tables. She smiled pleasantly.

———

"Callie, are you trying to get me drunk?" Megan laughed.

He shook his head. "Off of three beers? That's an hors d'oeuvre for you, Trouble."

The door to the kitchen swung back, hitting a chair and making Megan turn around to see who'd entered. "Hey, wait, I've seen her. She jogged by the house the other day and dropped her phone. A girl living down the street from where I am told me where I could bring it back to her." Megan turned back to Callie.

"You two have met? Her name is Vivian. She's been working for me for a while now. You know she's deaf, right?"

"I didn't know at first, but I found out later," Megan answered.

"I'll introduce you." Callie waved at a waiter to motion Vivian to come over.

"She can be shy, so don't take it the wrong way." Callie began a slow finger spelling to Vivian, introducing Megan to her.

Megan, knowing no sign language, held out her hand and mouthed *hello* slowly.

Vivian wiped her hands on her apron and reciprocated the introduction.

Callie explained to Vivian that Megan was the one who returned her cell phone. Vivian smiled and in her strongest possible voice, answered, "Thank you." Her voice was muffled, as though she were under water. She then signed to Callie and went back to cleaning tables.

"She seems sweet," Megan said.

"She is. She also hasn't had an easy life. I don't mean just being born deaf, but a very bizarre family situation." Callie grabbed the newspaper Megan had been reading earlier. "See this guy? He's her father."

Megan squinted. "The missing man?"

He nodded. "Missing or murdered…"

"She didn't seem worried," Megan commented.

"I wouldn't be if I were her. He's a son of a bitch." Callie's tone turned callous as he continued. "There's a story, I don't know if it's true or not," he shrugged. "When Vivian was born and her parents found out she was deaf, her father drove and dropped her off at a convent to be raised. He didn't tell her mother. After a few days Vivian's mother threatened legal action. The judge"—Callie pointed to the picture—"that's him, caved in and let her come back home as long as they both lived in a separate wing of the house. He wouldn't have anything to do with her." Callie stared down at the table.

Megan shook her head. "My God, that's awful. Why did the mother stay?"

He lifted his glass, before taking a sip. "People thought for his money. She was a local girl, not highly educated, but very pretty in her day. Some other people thought she had information on him and the judge didn't want those *things* to come out."

Megan stared back at Vivian, in awe of the story Callie just told her. Though it wasn't as if she were unaccustomed to tragedies. "So where is the mother?"

"She died a little while back. The day of the funeral, the judge had all of Vivian's things removed from the wing and placed in the gatehouse."

Megan stared, confused of the circumstances. "Why not just kick her out?"

"He's the kind of guy that wouldn't want a stain on his reputation. Told people it was her choice to move out there."

Megan read briefly through the newspaper about the missing judge. "Where do they think he is?"

He raised his eyebrows. "I don't think they have any idea."

"Well, it's nice of you to help her out." Megan smiled now, returning the knowing look Callie had been shooting her throughout the conversation.

"It's only part-time. She works as a massage therapist the other half. Ya know, she's pretty good. You should have her give you one. She comes to you, brings the massage table and everything."

Megan was thinking she'd rather be getting a massage from the man seated opposite her. And with that fleeting thought she knew it was time to stop the libations and get back to her monastic lifestyle. "I should get going."

Callie looked a little deflated. "Well, I should get back to work. A big dinner crowd is the norm this time of year."

He walked Megan out to the Range Rover. "Don't be a stranger, Trouble."

Megan rubbed her eyebrow, hoping Callie hadn't picked up on the same college-girl nervousness she once displayed and frankly thought was lost forever. "Maybe I won't. Maybe I won't."

———

Megan returned to the lake house feeling a bit nostalgic after running into Chris Callie. She started a fire and sat on the couch, watching the flames jump and listening to the calming noises of the wood crackling. She poured herself a glass of wine and ate half a frozen pizza, remembering that the college years of her life were probably the most serene she'd known: no depressed mothers to tiptoe around, no murders to be solved, no romantic relationships doomed, no unexpected deaths in the family. A part of her didn't want to be reminded of the easier days. It made the current ones nearly impossible to live with. She curled up with a comforter and within minutes was inside a power nap, more from the beer and wine than the relaxing fire.

NINE

THE MAN STARING DOWN on her didn't blink an eye, as if he'd caused Megan to wake on cue and was hardly surprised when she did.

"What the fuck!" Megan yelled before pulling her gun out from the ankle holster. She pointed and slowly moved toward the window. At first she thought a man was standing over her, but she now realized he stood on the deck leering through the window. She jumped over the coffee table with Olympic gold hurdler fashion. She knew the alarm was on, latches secure at each entrance.

The man stood outside holding up one palm as if to say, *it's okay*. There was nothing Megan could think of in that moment that felt okay, especially a stranger on the deck watching her sleep.

"I work for the Macks." His words were mouthed through the window, but the tone in his voice implied that this tedious situation of scaring the shit out of a sleeping woman was an everyday occurrence.

"Yeah, right!" Megan maintained a tight grip on her gun.

"I'm checking on the boathouse and the bubbler."

"At eight o'clock at night? It's pitch black out." Megan grabbed her cell phone, about to call 911 when the thought crossed her mind: *she* was the police. She couldn't bring herself to make the call. Sheer dignity mixed with a whole lot of stubbornness.

"There are light switches in the boathouse, Psycho Sally."

He's offending someone holding a gun on him? What an asshole.

"Check the binder they left you, my name is in it. Jake Norden. They told me they'd leave the renter my number if anything went wrong with the boathouse or dock. I work at the marina in the next cove over."

Megan didn't take her eyes or her gun off of him. She pulled out the binder and went to the maintenance portion. At the top of the page was, in fact, his name. She closed the folder and asked, "Do you make it a point to watch women sleep?"

He was medium height and broadly built, or perhaps he only appeared that way with all the winter gear he was wearing.

"Show me your identification."

He slapped his wallet against the window. "Satisfied?" His voice was gruff, as if he survived only on cigarettes alone.

Megan inspected the unfamiliar Jersey license and reluctantly nodded. "Do what you have to do."

"Try not to shoot me. I'll only be a few minutes." He cupped a hand around a cigarette while lighting it, the wind blowing up against his back. He drew a deep inhale and slowly exhaled the smoke, all the while staring at Megan, moving his eyes up and down her.

She stood and gave him an equally heavy glare.

Once he left the deck, Megan moved closer to the window. "I do not like you, Mr. Norden," she whispered. She watched the entire fifteen minutes as he inspected the inside of the boathouse, testing the bubbler system and the wires leading from it up into the electric sockets they plugged into.

As he was leaving, Jake knocked twice on the side door. In a loud but not shouting voice, he said, "I'm leaving, but I'm sure you already knew that. I'll be back in a week."

He moved around to the street and climbed into a truck. Megan watched as he turned the engine over and was on his way.

Good riddance.

Megan placed another log on the fire, but she was much more alert this time as she lay on the couch. She picked up the coffee table books describing the history of New Jersey. She read for the next few hours before going to bed with her gun beside her.

———

Megan woke and curled herself tighter under the covers, listening to the wind as it mounted the house. There was a curious rhythm to the noise, easily sending her back into a light trance. But she couldn't regain sleep. The bedroom was borderline freezing and her foggy focus now turned to the lack of noise from the furnace kicking on.

She wrapped herself in the down comforter, leaving only her face visible, and waddled to the hallway to check the thermostat. It read fifty.

"Fuck."

Resigning herself to necessity, she went into the kitchen to check the Mighty Mack binder. She found the section on heating and read aloud: *"If the heat goes out, push the red button on the back of the furnace three times, then pray."*

"Oh very funny, Mr. Mack."

Megan had been shown where the furnace was, so she scurried down to the lower level muttering, "Why does heat always go out in the middle of the night? Why not at noon?" She pushed the button three times but didn't pray to God—that was something she'd stopped doing over the course of the last few years. Instead she prayed to the furnace. It turned on in less than a minute. She closed up the back room, walking by the lower level's sliding glass doors. The whistling noise outside prompted Megan to look out. She saw the line of arborvitae trees swaying so strongly they looked as though snapping would be inevitable.

"Damn." She turned, letting the drapes fall back into form, missing the shadow as it moved to the upper deck.

A slight smell of oil filled the house, which was reassuring; the heat was definitely back on. Her only goal was to get back to sleep and not wake until noon. She rechecked the thermostat. The number had already risen a degree. She was relieved until a slam against the side door made her jump. She dropped the comforter as if the air had just shot from fifty to ninety degrees. Her shock quickly turned to anger. "You son of a bitch! Jake Norden, if that's you, this time I'm going to use my gun."

Megan threw on boots and a jacket, then double-checked that her gun was fully loaded. She approached the side entrance door as slowly as walking through a minefield. She lifted the blind. Nothing. Slowly she opened the door, trying not to make a sound as she stepped outside, which was nearly impossible in a house fifty years old. Adrenaline insulated her from the harsh wind hitting her face. She pressed her back up against the house, side stepping toward the back yard. Taking a deep breath, she turned the corner with her gun drawn. The only menacing object within range was the barren magnolia tree. No one. Just Megan, standing in flannel pajamas in the middle of the yard at three in the morning, pointing her gun at a tree. Not exactly a declaration of mental health on her part.

The force slammed into her from behind. She pitched forward face first, hitting the cold frozen ground. He jumped on top of her, pinning her down with the sheer force of his weight. Megan had the wind knocked out of her. She couldn't yell out, not as if anyone would hear her anyway. She searched the ground for her gun. It wasn't in sight. He tore at the back of her head, and she managed to elbow him and turn on her back. He lunged at her again before she had the chance to draw her knee up in hopes of kicking him in the groin.

It was useless. She'd lost the battle.

"Get off of me, you damn dog!" Megan yelled, pushing at his fur-covered chest, trying to gain leverage. "Off!" She pushed again, having little effect on the overexcited pooch. Time for another tactic: "Good crazy dog, good crazy dog," she crooned. The mutt calmed enough to let her sit up.

As a Homicide detective, Megan had dealt with many predators in her work, but none sat after a fight with pointed ears wagging their tail. This dog looked wide awake and ready to play. She opened the gate pointing toward the top of the street. "Go home. Go on. Go." Her attacker whimpered and walked in circles. Megan noticed he had no collar and, after further inspection, no tags. She looked at dog-with-no-name, and then back at the lake house. He again cocked his head. Megan had seen men in the past make the same motion, but they didn't want shelter—they wanted much more. She sighed. "You can't stay out here, you dope; you'll freeze. Come on."

He ran to the door in seconds.

Megan picked up her gun and put the safety lock on. Heading back toward the house, she couldn't help but stop and stare into the dark back yard wondering if an overzealous dog was all that had awoken her.

TEN

WAYNE CLARKE DRILLED A hole through the four-inch-thick ice. The small cove had been frozen over for nearly two weeks, early for the season, but this was the first morning he'd had a chance to do what he loved most: ice fishing. Wayne was fifty-one, but he knew he looked like he was going on seventy. He figured his three ex-wives were responsible—not the two heart attacks, the pack-a-day smoking habit he'd started when he was fifteen, or his love of whiskey.

Wayne led a predictable life, and that's how he liked it. He still lived in the house he grew up in. He worked contracting for the towns surrounding the lake, mainly paving and construction. Every Thursday was pub night, every Saturday was the Elks Lodge. Every Sunday he attended Our Lady of the Lake Catholic Church. The latest service available; it's not as if he were drinking lemonade at the Elks on those Saturday nights. He had a theory that if he attended church at a location on the lake, maybe God would grant him a few good catches. He was a simple man, with simple needs.

He set up his equipment, poured his coffee, added a shot of Jameson into his cup, and lit a cigarette. He wore the necessary gear for a particularly cold early-December day: insulated pants, gloves, boots, bright black and orange checkered winter coat, and the raccoon fur bomber hat an ex-wife gave him for Christmas one year. He couldn't remember which ex, but it was the best gift he'd gotten from any of them and certainly warmed him more than they ever had. All of this would keep his outside protected, but the whiskey, he told himself, is what kept his blood warm, Another one of his self-indulgent theories. He may have been on to something, given the expected high for the day was going to be eighteen.

The lake was filled with an assortment of fish. Trout, bass, largemouth bass, walleye, pickerel. Wayne held the state record a few years ago for a rainbow trout nearing thirteen pounds, but the following year some New Yorker beat his record by a pound or so. Not that Wayne cared, because it wasn't someone from the great Garden State of New Jersey, so to him, it didn't count. It wasn't about the catch today; just being outside, alone, listening to the sound of the wind and the birds pleased him. The patch of ice he fished on was as clear as if he were seated on a sheet of glass covering the lake. The water was nearly still beneath him. Wayne lit another cigarette and checked his watch: a little after nine thirty in the morning. He'd arrived at five, and still no catches. The coffee was long gone, but the whiskey was holding out well. He scratched at the gray stubble on his face, contemplating packing it in and heading to the pub down the street since it opened at ten, when he felt a tug on his fishing pole. Shifting his cigarette to the corner of his mouth, he began to reel his catch of the day in. "About fucking time."

Wayne struggled with the line. The catch was heavy and it fought against the drag of the water. Floating between his legs, four inches under the clear ice, was a man's face, bloated, nibbled on, and staring up at him.

The cigarette fell from the corner of his mouth. "Jesus, Mary, and Joseph."

If they only had fishing contests classed by weight and weren't too picky about the catch having gills or fins, Wayne Clarke would have won that morning. He dropped his fishing pole and ran for shore.

So much for Our Lady of the Lake Sunday prayers.

ELEVEN

MEGAN WOKE TO THE smell of the automatic coffee maker, as well as a quick reminder of her late-night discovery when dog-with-no-name donkey kicked her in the back. He released an exasperating yawn and proceeded to climb over her to jump off the bed.

I wonder if the villa in Mexico is still available.

Two beeps from the kitchen signaled the brewing of the first of many morning coffee jolts was complete. She put on some warm clothes and poured her cup while calling the Macks to let them know about her newfound discovery in their yard. Much to her chagrin, they told her they were huge animal lovers and it wasn't a problem at all to shelter the dog for a while. They added that old dog food, leashes, and pet beds from their own pets still remained in the basement.

Of course they did.

Megan sat down on the couch with her cup of coffee. Dog, as she decided to generically call him, sat beside her on the floor. Megan loved dogs and usually had one growing up, but pet care wasn't high on her priority list right now. She was *not* going to get attached. Dog was definitely black Labrador mixed with something perhaps equine in nature, she thought to herself. He had a white chest with white-tipped paws and breath that reminded her of crime scenes featuring week-old bodies.

"You hit the lottery, Dog, until I find your proper owners."

His ears popped up and he bolted to the bay window. A slow deep growl emerged, and he began to paw at the glass. His snarl quickly turned into barking. "Right. Bathroom break." Megan put on her coat and opened the sliding glass door. Dog bolted out now in full steam down the stairs into the fenced yard.

When Megan walked on to the deck, she saw a far too familiar scene. A few dozen yards away in the cove were policeman, New Jersey troopers, sirens, an ambulance, and a yellow tarp with police tape blowing in the wind.

She closed her eyes, but the images jabbed her memory like an ice pick, tearing her mind apart one more time. Her first scene she was green as a shamrock. Tough as nails on the outside, but terrified to see her first homicide case. It was a stabbing, and never in a million years did she think a human being could hold so much blood. It was obvious the man was dead, but she was told to check his pulse, and that was the first time she'd touched a dead body. The memory haunted her. She'd walked through years of police tape since, not knowing what she'd find on the other side, but she did it because it was not just her job but her calling. She'd thought nothing could be worse than her first case, but her last homicide topped it in every way.

It's not a good thing to have your worst fear topped by a bigger nightmare. It makes you want to escape, and Megan thought she'd done that. Of course her detective brain knew what they were pulling out of the icy water, and it wasn't a bass.

Her coffee had grown as cold as her stomach. "Dog! Come!" Much to her surprise, he did. Animals can sense when someone is serious, and there was zero lilt in Megan's tone. They headed back indoors.

She gave Dog the canine equivalent of a breakfast protein bar: a slice of cold pizza. She went into the basement, found the supplies needed to walk him, and redressed as if she were planning to sign up for the Iditarod.

Before they stepped foot on the driveway, Megan took one last look over at the commotion on the ice in Great Cove. She shook her head. "No."

As soon as they stepped one foot on cement, Dog yanked the leash, dragging Megan up the driveway. Something told her the alpha position was not going to be hers in this temporary arrangement. Every few feet Dog stopped, lifted his leg, released, and then moved on to the next ill-fated target. The street was oddly quiet for a Saturday. There were no signs of any of her neighbors other than cars parked in the driveways. It was as if she was the only inhabitant of McGregor Avenue. Dog urinating against telephone poles was the only noise to be heard. The feeling changed as soon as they walked around the bend in the road.

Dog lunged forward, forcing Megan to let go of the leash unless she wanted to be dragged across the ice and salt on the street. He'd come back when she turned around. Probably. Looking up, Megan saw a woman in a hooded green parka walking a golden retriever.

"Dog! Stop!" It was an exercise in futility; he was already there, planting a few sniffs and attempting to plant something else in the poor unsuspecting dog. Oddly the woman didn't seem surprised to see this massive male canine charge at her. Megan grabbed Dog's retractable leash, attempting to reel him in from his canine lady-love. "I'm really sorry about that. He's not my dog. I just found him and apparently he's not well trained."

"It's okay. He's just honoring his nature." She pushed her hood back, exposing cropped brown hair and a grin that told Megan she was truly humored by the exchange. She looked fifty-something, thin, and fit. "I'm Leigh. I live down the street on the right in that house." She turned and pointed at a white Cape Cod with green trim.

"I'm Megan, I just moved in—" She was about to point down the street.

"To the Macks' place, right?"

Megan looked stunned. "Ah …"

"It's a small town, and an even smaller neighborhood. Actually, the Macks are good friends of ours. They mentioned the last time we had them over for dinner that you were going to rent the place. Mr. Mack has lived on this street since he was three years old."

"He mentioned that to me before they left for Florida. I thought I was the only one here. You're the first person I've seen besides a teenager and a woman jogging by. Vivian, I mean. I met her at the diner later."

"The teenager is Billie, great kid. She house sits when Jo and I are out of town." She turned to look over her shoulder. "Actually, here she comes now. Everyone is buzzing about what's happening on the lake."

"I'm sure," Megan added faintly.

A small ways down the street they both heard, "Hey, wait up guys!" Billie, with her jacket half on and one shoe untied, raced to meet them. "I don't want to miss anything." Billie looked down at Dog with a scrunched up face. "You got a dog?"

Megan held on to the lead as best she could. "Um no, but if you know who owns him, I'd like to take him back to wherever he came from."

Billie and Leigh looked at one another and shrugged, indicating neither knew.

"C'mon Leigh, I don't want to miss this!"

"I'll catch up in a second, Billie, you go on ahead," Leigh said. "It must seem a bit odd for you that people show interest in something like this." Leigh pointed toward the commotion down the street.

Megan had a quiet response. "No, not anymore."

"If you don't have anything going on later, would you like to join Jo and me for dinner? A kind of welcome to the neighborhood," Leigh offered.

Megan was taken aback. She answered without thinking, "Sure, that would be nice."

"Great! Come by any time between six and seven."

At this point Dog had had enough of human socialization and had stopped trying to accost the uninterested female dog. He dragged Megan a few feet away. For a brief moment Megan regretted accepting the invitation, worried there would be too many questions asked about her situation. Then she reminded herself that her life had been splashed all over the news in gory detail, so there was really nothing to be asked.

TWELVE

I STARED OUT THE window at the police, the gawkers on shore, the news vans—basically the sheer chaos of it all—and my only thought was, "I need to get to work later, I hope there's no traffic." It sounds cold, but if you'd known him, it was quite fitting and quite deserved. I glanced over at the Macks' house. I could just barely make out Megan's figure on the deck. I assumed she felt as little about the situation as I did.

———

Megan had just over an hour before she had to walk down to her new neighbors' house for dinner, and she took Dog and a glass of wine down to the dock while it was still light. She'd spent the day zoning out in front of the television, ignoring the activity on the lake. Now the only sign of the earlier commotion was the yellow tarp and police tape, now covering a wider spectrum. A police car was positioned at the shorefront, but there was surprisingly little happening.

Three people parasailing on the ice skidded over the lake. Megan couldn't imagine what speed they were moving, but she was sure they'd reach the other side in no time. She enjoyed the crisp sound that traveled up to her from their sails. It was somehow soothing. Even Dog was relaxed as he yawned and leaned against Megan. She scratched his head and rubbed his ears.

"I need to give you a real name until I find your family. It has to be Irish. My family all has—" She stopped. "*Had* Irish names. My brother Brendan is alive, but the others..." She sipped her wine and reluctantly welled up. But she quickly regained control and put those feelings back up on a shelf. "Let's go back inside, pal."

Megan reluctantly looked over the water at the house Billie had pointed out, the one next to Vivian's gatehouse. Which made it the missing judge's house. She hated the feeling she got staring at the that house. She hated it because her internal compass was moving and pointing straight there. It was the detective hunch she'd learned to hone over the years, which she now shoved onto the same shelf as her family drama.

That shelf is getting heavy, she thought.

———

It was less than a ten-minute walk down to Megan's new neighbor's house, for which she was grateful; it started to snow as she approached the front door. Leigh greeted her with a warm smile. "Come in! Let me take your coat."

Megan handed Leigh her coat and a bottle of red wine. "I brought this." The house smelled spectacular. Megan smiled inside thinking, *This is not a take-out Chinese kind of night.*

"I'll give you a quick tour."

It was interesting to see a different house on the lake other than Chez Mack. Everything here looked state-of-the-art, very modern for a lake house. Leigh explained they had been working on an overhaul for the last sixteen months, renovating the kitchen, bathrooms, and finishing now with the lower level. Just as Megan sat down, she was greeted by the golden retriever she'd met earlier in the day.

"Hey, I remember you." Megan scratched her ears. "I didn't get your name, pretty lady."

Leigh handed Megan a glass of red wine. "This is Lady Sadie."

"You must be royalty then, Lady Sadie."

"She thinks she is!" Leigh laughed, poured herself a glass of wine, and brought out hors d'oeuvres, then sat down on the couch across from Megan. "Dinner will be ready in twenty minutes. Jo just called and she's on her way home. She just finished her last surgery for the day. She's a doctor in Morristown, not too far from here. I guess the roads are getting a little icy. So she's taking her time." Lady Sadie started to get a little amped up, likely smelling another dog on Megan's pants and shoes. "Sadie, in your bed."

Megan's jaw dropped.

"I'm guessing *Dog* doesn't listen quite as well?"

They laughed. "Not in the last twenty-four hours," Megan said.

"So, how are you enjoying our small lake town so far? I know you haven't been here long, but is it what you were hoping for?"

Megan felt a ping of warning in her stomach and hoped the conversation wouldn't turn to her life beyond the last few days. "I'm settling in. It's quiet." She smiled.

"Wait until we get our first real snowstorm; it will get even more quiet. Whatever happened in Great Cove will probably be the most interesting moment until spring."

Megan wanted to say, *I don't think so*, then decided against it.

Moments later the sound of the garage door opening provided a welcome distraction.

"That would be Jo. You get to meet my other half." Leigh placed her hand up to her cheek like a school girl sharing a secret. "Whom I occasionally refer to as General Nightingale."

"Lovey, I'm home," a British voice boomed down the hall.

The sound of keys hitting the kitchen counter echoed before Leigh answered, "In here, hon."

Jo was in her late forties, with typical English translucent skin making her look much younger. She had a confident demeanor, yet Megan could sense a definite kindness, probably due to working with patients. Her mane of tight blond curls was pulled back in a clip. Marching across the room, she gave Leigh a kiss and a hug. She held Leigh's face, looking directly into her eyes.

"How are you feeling, sweetheart?"

"I'm good," Leigh responded.

She raised an eyebrow, giving Leigh a skeptical look. "You're quite sure?" She inspected Leigh's face, muttered something about her color, and gripped her hands. "Are you cold?"

Leigh turned to Megan. "As I was saying, this is General Nightingale."

Jo knocked Leigh's shoulder. "That's a fine way to introduce me to our new neighbor." Jo shook Megan's hand. "Such a pleasure to meet you. Welcome to McGregor Avenue." Jo then excused herself. "If you don't mind, I'm going to go change into something less stuffy."

"Everything is nearly ready," Leigh said before Jo was out of earshot.

"Grand. I'll be down in a bit."

"She cuts into people; I cut into beef, chicken, or fish. Oh, and the 'feeling well' comment was based on a nasty flu I experienced last week. I teach philosophy, and when one of my students comes down with something, it moves through the classrooms like fire."

———

Jo returned, made herself a martini, and proceeded to fill Megan in on some of the characters of McGregor Avenue, which surprised her because she'd yet to see that many people. Jo mentioned the psychiatrist who was just released from the state mental facility; a wife down the street (allegedly) running a call girl ring out of their house while hubby went to work in Manhattan; and then (least interestingly) the kind, small-town people who were really good friends. Leigh mentioned that they had a holiday party every year, which Megan was welcome to join.

Megan was far from ready for heavy socialization, but she thought it was a nice gesture on their part.

Throughout dinner Megan enjoyed watching Leigh and Jo's give and take, finishing one another's stories, easily knowing the other's line of thought. Then the gears switched.

"Is anyone going to bring up what happened in Great Cove today?" Jo blurted. "There were a zillion cars and a big hole in the ice."

Megan began, "I watched the news, but nobody said what they hauled out of the water."

"You're in the Mack house—you probably had a good view of what was going on down there."

And the martinis have kicked in.

"Jo." Leigh tossed a look her way.

"Oh, sorry," Jo offered.

"I've been busy with a dog I found last night, who's temporarily staying with me," Megan said with a forced smile. She didn't want Leigh or Jo to feel badly. "Didn't see much."

Jo was nodding. "Leigh told me about the humping of Lady Sadie."

They laughed and talked about the dogs for several minutes. The conversation, of course, returned to the lake activity.

Jo sipped on her third martini. "I wouldn't be surprised if it was that prick Judge Campbell. What a son of a bitch that man is—hopefully *was*."

"I'm sure everyone is thinking that, but who knows?" Leigh offered.

Megan noted again that whoever this judge was, he was not well liked at all. "I read about it in the paper the other morning. Him being missing, that is, but it didn't really say much. It read more like his resume." She sat back with her drink, knowing she was about to hear mostly the truth with a small amount of innuendo. When someone is hated that much by a large number of people, there is usually a good reason.

Leigh and Jo looked at one another with raised eyebrows. Jo took the lead. "Well. Judge Montague Campbell. Where to start?" She paused to take another sip before blurting, "He *is* a prick."

Megan laughed. "Jo, seriously, don't hold back. Tell me what you really think."

Leigh added, "Can you tell I go for the shy type of woman?"

Jo smiled. "Well, he is!"

"Go ahead, Jo, tell her more about the … prick," Leigh prodded, though you could tell by her pause, she wasn't as comfortable with the expression as Jo was.

"Monty Campbell is one of Morris County's most prominent citizens," she said, adopting a mock reverential tone.

"He comes from old New Jersey money and is a very powerful man in this state," Leigh said.

"So, it's not just because he's a judge that the papers have it splashed all over." Megan folded her arms. "What do they think happened to him?"

"No idea so far," Leigh answered.

Jo topped Megan's glass off. "Apparently, he'd scheduled a trip to go up to his cabin in Vermont, so he put a hold on his mail, his cleaning service . . ." She waved her hand in the air. "All that kind of stuff. Well, ten days later when he was expected at a gala—"

"He was being honored for all the"—Leigh made quotation marks in the air—"*work* he's done for a children's hospital."

"*Work* my English bum, it was just a nod for all the money he'd given over the years." Jo rolled her eyes. "All of his cohorts were to give speeches to rub the prick's ego, if you'll forgive the pun. But he didn't show up."

"At first the police thought he'd been kidnapped, but no ransom call ever came in."

"He lives on the lake. Actually, you can see his house from your place."

"That huge white mansion, at the tip of the cove?"

"It's easy to miss, isn't it?" Jo added sarcastically. "Turn the clock back to a few months ago when Mrs. Campbell died—" She pointed to Leigh. "Tell her what *everyone* in this town was thinking."

"Basically, it was fairly common knowledge the judge and his wife didn't have a *real* marriage, not for a very long time. At least since Vivian was born." Leigh stopped, turning to Jo. "Megan met Vivian at Krogh's."

Jo nodded. "Sweet girl. People in the town keep an eye out for her since her mother's death. A plus to small-town living, I suppose."

Megan attempted to not appear too interested, but she had to ask: "How did her mother die?"

The two women looked at one another, rolling their eyes and answering in tandem, "Good question. Word was she hung herself, but…"

Megan squinted. "There must be a coroner's report, right?"

"She was cremated within an hour of being found. Found by Vivian," Jo answered.

———

As Megan walked back to the Macks' house, it was now clear the light snow had taken a dramatic turn—becoming a storm while she enjoyed dinner. The moment she approached the driveway she regretted not leaving the garage door open so she could use the stairs to get back down to the house.

"Great," Megan moaned. Taking baby steps and keeping one hand on the wall of the garage was as helpful as holding on to a breaking icicle on a steep mountain. Her second step down the driveway was her last. One minute she was standing, the next she was staring up at the evening sky. She flew down the black ice like a hockey puck on its way to the goalie. There wasn't even time to scream it all happened so fast. Moaning from the bounce off the aluminum fence, she groaned. "You bastard. Bastard ice."

After a few moments of ensuring that nothing was broken but her pride, Megan lifted herself up on her elbows. She laughed. "I would give myself a score of nine-point-eight." She sat up, looked around for her wallet. It was still in her fist. "I take that back. Nine-point-nine." She twisted from side to side checking she hadn't pulled anything in her back—nothing wrong, as far as she could tell after a few drinks. She pulled herself up using the fence and was surprised to see the upper level of the judge's home lit. As quick as the light caught her eye, it winked out. Megan stood as still as the freezing night air. Waiting. Watching. Seconds later a light turned on, nothing as overt as the first, moving erratically from room to room. Up, down, in circles. A flashlight.

What are you looking for? she thought. One or two minutes passed by Megan's estimation, and the house turned dark again. Curious. She made her way into the house and called Callie at Krogh's. It took a moment for him to come to the phone.

"Callie? It's Megan."

"Hey, gorgeous. What's up?"

"I just have a quick question, I know you're probably busy."

"Sure, what's up?"

"Is Vivian working tonight?"

"Um, yeah. Why?"

Megan had to come up with something fast. "Oh, good, well, do you mind giving her my number and having her text me when she gets a chance? I slipped on the ice tonight and could really use a massage." Megan stared down at the phone, impressed with her instantaneous fabrication.

Did I lie this easily when I was a teenager? Probably.

"Are you okay? Do you want me to come over?" Callie asked.

"No, it's nothing, but I'm sure I'll feel it at some point."

That actually wasn't a lie, as she was already feeling a tightness in her back. It was a reprieve, in her mind's eye, for lying to a friend.

"Okay, no problem."

Megan gave Callie her cell number and quickly said goodbye. She let Dog out and stood at the door, keeping an eye on Judge Campbell's home. The lights were now off, and they stayed that way until a few nights later, when Megan's curiosity would definitely earn her the nickname Trouble.

THIRTEEN

It was too early to go to bed, not that Megan would be able to sleep. She found not one but two emergency medical kits and, thankfully, a heating pad in the Macks' cabinet. She made use of both. She bandaged a cut on her wrist from her human luge sans sled down the driveway, and plugged in the heating pad. She sat petting Dog and found herself speaking aloud to him while staring into the fireplace.

"I can't do this again. I'm here for peace, to figure out my life. Now I'm getting the same feelings I've gotten on every case in the past, but this can't be my case, okay? It technically *wouldn't* be my case, even if my gut is right. I've lost so much in such a short time. Dad. Momma. I think finding Shannon McAllister's killer killed me. I'm numb inside." She unleashed a self-depreciating laugh. "That's probably why brilliant detective here came to this New Jersey tundra; it's as cold as I've become." She shook her head. "Fuck, what a cliche. I need a break from death. Let someone else do it."

When Megan finished her speech to the now sleeping animal, a faint rap sounded at the door. She gingerly got up and opened the blind. It was Billie.

"Can I come in?" she asked. It was obvious she'd been crying.

"Sure, of course." Megan opened the door to let the teenager in. "Are you okay?"

She didn't answer, but based on her bloodshot eyes and smeared mascara, something was wrong.

Before Megan closed the door, she asked, "Wait, how did you get down the driveway?"

Billie pointed down at her feet. "Traction cleats. They attach to your shoes. I better take them off, though. The Macks have a nice floor and they might scratch."

I seriously need a pair of those, Megan thought to herself as her back throbbed. "Come on in."

Billie climbed up on one of the stools at the kitchen counter.

"Do you want water or tea? I think I have cocoa here, how about that?"

"Cocoa, please." Billie wiped her nose with her sleeve and looked into the living room. "You still have that crazy dog, huh? You gonna keep him?"

Megan shrugged. "I've called a few places and no one has reported a dog with his description as missing, at least not yet, so he's here for now."

"Well, if he's here, you should give him a name. Calling him Dog makes you sound ... weird."

Megan laughed. "I've been trying to think of one. No luck."

"I'm good at these things. Let me take a look at him again." Billie hopped off the stool and went to examine the surprisingly still dog while Megan poured hot water into a mug for Billie's cocoa.

"Clyde."

"Clyde?" Megan said, not expecting that answer.

"Clyde," Billie said with so much certainty. "Now you can stop calling him Dog. He's Clyde."

Megan nodded with much less certainty. "Maybe." She handed Billie the cup of cocoa. They sat petting *Clyde*, for a few minutes before Megan spoke. "Something happen tonight? At home?"

"Well, my mom enjoys her scotch and so do the men she has over. Get what I'm saying?"

Megan recognized the look in Billie's eyes. Fifty years of pain and disappointment trapped within a teenager's body. No matter how much eye shadow and mascara she wore, she couldn't hide it. Billie's countenance was similar to the prostitutes Megan collared in the beginning of her career—worn out too early, too young. "Have any of her boyfriends ever hurt you?"

She stared into the fire and whispered, "No."

Megan wasn't sure she was telling the truth.

"They're too busy beating on my mom, and then she takes them back until the next bottle of scotch arrives. And it always does."

"Where is your biological father?"

Billie shrugged. "I had an older brother. I think he was about six years older than me. Never knew him well. I assume my father took him when he left. If I knew where my father was, I'd be sending him a Father's Day card saying, 'Thanks for the sperm, shithead.'"

"Well, it's the thought that counts." Megan wanted to make her smile. "Stay here for a while."

"They'll be passed out soon." Billie looked down into the cup of cocoa. "What, no marshmallows?"

"What do you think this is, a Jersey diner?"

"It was just a question. Don't get your thong in a bunch." They sat for a few minutes. Then Billie said, "I read about you in the paper."

Megan nodded. "I'm not surprised."

"Does your job—well, is that why you didn't want to see what was going on today in Great Cove with whatever happened?" Billie was nervous bringing up the topic, but she was also clearly curious. She began biting her nails.

Megan was cautious with her answer. "Let's just say I've seen a lot."

Billie whispered, "Me too."

Megan had little doubt the girl had seen a lot, given her tough exterior and sensitive interior. In many ways Billie reminded Megan of herself. Megan, through no fault of her father's, had grown up seeing crime scene photos when she wasn't supposed to and hearing conversations between her dad and Uncle Mike that were not fit for a young girl's ears. Her father couldn't always shield Megan when her mother began having "difficult moments." Those days were imbedded in Megan's mind, and she eventually realized they would never go away. So she tucked them behind the strongest brick wall she could build in her memory. Her mother's worst depression and its aftermath was soul crushing. A girl shouldn't see so much life seeping from her mother.

Megan always looked down and shook her head slightly to shake that memory back behind the brick wall. "So, Billie, may I ask you a question?"

"I'm not sure."

"Why?"

"Because you might not want to know the answer. My aunt always says to never ask a question unless you're ready for the answer, no matter good or bad."

"She's a smart lady."

Billie crossed her legs. "Go ahead," she said with a hint of hesitancy.

Megan could feel Billie building her own brick wall. "Why would your father take your brother and not you? Did your mother fight for you?" Megan was slow with the next question. "Billie, was your dad hurting you? Or maybe your brother hurting you?"

Billie stared into the fireplace, a curious stare, not something Megan was expecting after asking a question like that.

"My brother... I remember him well enough." She looked directly at Megan. "He would never have hurt me. He protected me from the fighting. My dad? I always got the feeling I wasn't his. Sounds weird, right? It was just always a gut feeling. He couldn't stand when I was around, as if I was some kind of reminder. As for my mother, she loves me, but would a woman who fought for me be doing this now? What do you think?"

Megan could tell she was waiting on an answer. "Both my parents are gone now. We had a good family, but there were hard times; they passed. Hold on until you're on the other side of hard."

"Hope that rope is strong enough."

Me too. Me too, Megan thought.

Billie got up and put her mug in the sink. "They should be passed out by now. I'm going to go back." Billie put her traction cleats back on.

"The door is always open, Billie."

"Thanks."

Saying Billie's name made her ask an odd-timed question. "What is Billie short for?"

"Isabelle. My full name is Isabelle Rebecca Saunders."

Megan silently recited Billie's full name. "Your initials are IRS?"

"Wow, thank you for that. I wouldn't have figured it out on my own. Thank God you came to town."

Billie's armor was definitely back in place.

FOURTEEN

THE DIFFICULTY MEGAN HAD getting out of bed the next morning was confirmation that smacking into the fence had taken its toll during the night. She walked over to the full-length mirror to inspect the bruises she was sure would be there. Her shoulder had a nice size black and blue splotch on the back left side, as did the left side of her lower back. She shook her head. "Clyde, no walks today. Settle for the fenced-in yard."

Still in her pajamas, she slipped on boots and went via the garage stairs to get the morning newspaper at the front gate. She unraveled the rubber band and was not the least bit surprised by the front page: LOCAL JUDGE PULLED FROM LAKE HOPATCONG FEARED MURDERED.

Megan looked over at the crime scene tape on the lake and over to the judge's house.

This is going to be a cluster fuck, but not mine.

Megan threw the newspaper on the coffee table, fed Clyde, and double-checked the heat again. It was low but not off, which was a relief. She got dressed, and when she put on her father's favorite cardigan sweater, the image of him in it was just steps away in one of the photographs she'd brought with her. In the photo, Pat sat in his green recliner with pipe in hand. A huge smirk washed over his face. Megan was trying to remember when the photo was taken, but the information seemed locked in her memory, and she had no key.

"Ah, Gint." It was the first time since his death that there wasn't a sinkhole feeling when she thought of him. Perhaps she felt closer to him because she was wearing the same sweater he wore in the photo, or maybe it was his smile. Then reality hit her again: the holidays were nearing, and she would be without both parents for the first time. Last year was so different. Pat and Rose were alive, she was excelling at work, and she was relatively happy. Not the "stop and smell the roses, let's have a group hug" kind of happy, but she was content with how her life was progressing. Megan figured she must have skipped school the day they warned you how life can turn on a dime, and you usually don't get to turn back.

Return to sinkhole mode.

Megan trudged out of the bedroom. She turned on music to listen to in the living room while she read the morning paper. The Macks were obviously classical music lovers, as there wasn't anything else to choose from. Well, that was fine. It's not as if she expected Ozzy Osbourne on their playlist. She stared at the front page of the newspaper. Judge Montague "Monty" Campbell's picture took up three-quarters of the page. The editor, Megan determined, was probably a close personal friend, because the picture was definitely not a recent one. Given his listed age, it was easily fifteen or more years old. Regardless if he was younger or older, Megan didn't like the look of the judge. He certainly wasn't an *un*attractive man. There was just something in the way he smiled that didn't seem genuine, as if mugging for the camera was something he practiced doing in the mirror. As she flipped through the pages, there was little information, which didn't surprise her since his body was discovered less than twenty-four hours ago. The article read more like Campbell's resume once again, focusing on his accomplishments and accolades. This was obviously big news for the area. Hardly any other news was featured.

Megan went to the horoscope section, not because she believed in it, but because she just wanted to read something *else*. She skipped down to her sign, Virgo. There was something about a lunar eclipse in her second house, which she gave little credence to. It went on: "It's best to keep a low profile now as conflict is a possibility."

And then the doorbell rang.

———

A man and woman stood on the deck holding their badges. Megan, of course, was unimpressed.

The female officer asked if they could come in to ask her a few questions. Megan opened the door ushering them in. The female clomped into the home, obviously in alpha mode. "I'm Detective Liz Krause, this is Detective Michalski."

Krause was plain, though not in an ugly sort of way, where a girlfriend might tell a potential fix-up that she had a nice personality. She didn't appear to have that either. She probably did once, but that was a few years ago, Megan assumed. Krause didn't have any one particularly prominent feature that could be deemed her calling card. *Oh, there's Liz, her piercing blue eyes capture your attention.* Nope. She had hazel eyes that were just there to see with. Her demeanor was cold, bordering on rude, and her intention was obviously to push Megan around. Detective Krause would soon learn that would be a mistake on her part.

Megan sized up Krause as they stood in the Macks' kitchen. *This one's all about getting ahead, no matter what.*

Detective Michalski was a different matter. A nice Polish-looking man in the retirement years of his work, friendly, he wore his winter coat a few sizes too big. He was fat, had a kind smile, a gray combover, a ruddy complexion, and a warm manner about him. Megan knew detectives of his type. Nothing insulted nor upset them because they had their eyes on the prize: a retirement home in Florida and a decent pension. He was probably the only man who could handle being frosty Krause's partner.

As the pair walked in, Clyde decided to make his presence known and ran up to the detectives. Michalski knelt down. "Ah, good boy." He scratched Clyde's ears. "You are a handsome fella." Clyde thumped his tail on the wooden floor, whimpering. When Michalski finished, Clyde turned his attention toward Detective Krause. *Amicable* would not be the word for the day. The hair on the back of Clyde's neck rose. He crouched and showed his teeth with a growl Megan had yet to hear from him.

Megan thought animals, especially dogs, knew people better than they knew themselves. They sensed personality and intention, and nine times out of ten, they were right on the money. Had Megan been allowed to show her teeth to Krause, she would have too.

Most people would be nervous when a good-sized dog such as Clyde was showing aggression, but Detective Krause spoke in a detached tone. "Remove him." She repeated it to Megan.

Megan had zero intention of doing so. *Who the hell does she think she is?* "Clyde, stand down." Clyde hesitated then walked over to Megan's side, still humming a growl.

Michalski began, attempting to defuse the obvious growing tension in the room. "We have some questions regarding the body we found yesterday in the cove." He motioned to the newspaper. "Obviously, you've read about it."

"I haven't even been here a week, so I don't see how I can help you," Megan answered.

"We're not asking for your *investigative* help. We know you're renting from the Macks." Krause looked around the room disdainfully. "Temporary leave from the NYPD treats you well."

On second thought, Clyde, don't stand down. "Excuse me?" Megan said aloud and raised her eyebrows. "Do you have questions or not?"

Michalski stepped in. "We were wondering if you've seen anyone suspicious in the neighborhood, anything out of the ordinary. I know you haven't been here long, but anything you could think of would be a help."

Megan thought back to the lights in the judge's house the previous night. "Nope, I can't think of anything." Megan had to ask; it was her nature, and she couldn't break from it: "How was he murdered? What was the method?"

Michalski was about to answer, but Krause interrupted. "That's confidential information, ma'am, but I do have a question. Why was your Range Rover seen in the driveway of Judge Campbell's estate a few days ago?"

Megan laughed. "Oh, *honey*, you have to do better than that when posturing. Didn't the academy teach you anything?" Megan redirected her attention to Detective Michalski. "The young woman who lives in the gatehouse, Vivian, dropped her phone in front of my garage when she was jogging a few days ago. A neighbor told me where she lives and I returned it."

"Vivian Campbell, Judge Campbell's daughter." Krause nodded. "Does she jog by routinely?"

"I wouldn't know."

"Have you had any other interaction with her?" Krause asked.

Megan shrugged. "I was at a restaurant in Sparta on Lake Mohawk where she works. I saw her there."

Krause wrote the information down, pulled out her card, and slapped it on the counter. "Call if you think of anything." She was headed out of the house when she asked, "One more thing. When you saw her at work, did she seem distracted or upset?"

"If I never met her before, how would I know what is distracted or upset for her?" Megan glared. "Bet you aced your behavioral science courses, detective."

Michalski gave Megan a half-hearted smile. "Thank you for your time, Detective McGinn."

"I believe it's *Ms.* McGinn, now," Krause corrected.

Michalski followed Miss Personality out the door with his head down like a child who'd been reprimanded by an angry mother.

The hounding feeling returned the moment Krause and Michalski were gone. Her gut reaction to the activity on the lake, the flashlights flickering in a dead man's house, and now detectives being in contact ...

They'd asked far too many questions about Vivian.

FIFTEEN

THE NUMBER OF VANS *parked in the driveway and the number of people entering the Judge's house was difficult to determine. They carried equipment, boxes, and cameras. They wore jackets that had* CSI *written on the back. I knew it would only be a matter of time before they came to the door. I wondered if they'd find what my mother had found before the Judge tried to give me away. People think I don't know he did that, but my mother told me everything. She wanted me to know why the Judge hated me. I remember the day she told me.*

The day my mother, Victoria, gave birth she knew something was wrong, but medical technology wasn't as advanced as it was today. It took almost a year before anyone else realized something was wrong. Discovered because of a random plate crashing down to the kitchen floor behind me while I sat banging on pots and pans with a wooden spoon. There was no reaction, no crocodile tears, no screaming, not even a glance. Silence. One week later my mother walked into the nursery and I was gone. She didn't panic because she knew he had been a part of it. She walked calmly into the great room, where he sat smoking a cigar, drinking his liquor.

"Monty, what have you done?"

He blew the smoke in her face. "What needed to be done."

My mother had asked again, with a fierceness he was unaccustomed to hearing from her voice. "Monty, what have you done? Where is she?"

He ignored her, but she would have none of it. She turned to leave the room. "She is back in this house by the end of the day otherwise I will make sure everyone knows what I found in your desk." She quickly faced him. "Yes, I know. Get her back now."

"You're not allowed in my office." The Judge glared then, and she described how his right cheek shook, as it always did when he was about to explode. "You are not allowed in there!"

"Get. Her. Back. Now!"

He took an extra long puff from his cigar, figuring, plotting. "Fine, but you're not living in the main house. You and that thing will stay in the east wing. You will maintain your responsibilities as my wife."

"And you will maintain your financial responsibilities toward me and our daughter, or else."

My mother told me she got me back that same night. It was our first night in the east wing, and now I call the gatehouse my home. And I call the Judge dead, as he should be.

———

Megan's cell rang as she emerged from the long hot shower. It was Callie.

"Hey Trouble, how are you feeling this morning?"

"Sore, actually. What's up?"

"I received a text from Vivian. She had a cancellation for a massage today if you want to get in, but after hearing about your steep driveway, I think it would be easier for you to go to her place. Sound good?"

She rubbed her shoulder then twisted from side to side. The motion brought a tight pang running up her back. "I'm going to take you up on that."

"I'll send her a text. Be at her place in forty-five minutes. And, if you like, come over to the restaurant afterward and we can have a bite to eat and continue our conversation."

"Sounds good, I have something to talk to you about." Megan heard a smashing sound in the background.

"Hold on to that thought until I see you. A new waitress just dropped a tray."

Callie hung up without a goodbye.

Megan continued her morning routine and gingerly placed herself in Arnold to drive over to Vivian's. When she arrived a plethora of police and crime scene investigators were running amok on and around the judge's home.

"Shit." Megan looked over at the gatehouse, knowing it wouldn't be long before they hit that too. She walked up and pressed the doorbell. The lights inside flickered and Vivian soon opened the door. Megan smiled, a tad unsure as to how to communicate. Megan knew immediately Callie had been in contact from the note Vivian handed her. It stated Callie told her about the fall she took. She was going in the other room to set up her massage table. Megan nodded, answering, "Okay."

While Megan waited she walked around the gatehouse. She felt a bit intrusive, but her curiosity still got the best of her. The stark outdoor setting was a contradiction to the warm interior. The hacienda-style decor was a warm welcome, with rich colors of orange, red, and yellow on the walls. There was iron lighting and countless candles in the room. A stone fireplace located in the corner had a large plant placed on the hearth. Megan looked over at the coffee table. Pictures of Vivian and a woman she was sure was her mother were placed in a manner Megan wanted to refer to as purposeful—from oldest to most recent—across the top. She could hear Vivian in the next room setting up her massage table when the doorbell rang, again setting off the lights in the gatehouse. Megan looked over at the side pane of glass and could see her least favorite detective standing outside. The look on her face was that of an abused pit bull. She was preparing to lunge.

"That woman's photo should be placed next to the term 'displaced anger' in the *American Journal of Psychology*," Megan whispered to herself.

Vivian came out from the room looking surprised that someone else was at her door. She opened it only enough to show her face. Megan heard Detective Krause introduce herself and her partner in the most insulting way possible to a deaf person: slowly, while using hand gestures and speaking loudly, as if Vivian would suddenly be graced with the power to hear.

Stupid bitch.

The detectives started to walk into the gatehouse, and Vivian shot a look at Megan.

"What's going on here?" Megan asked, not masking her anger now mixed with disgust.

"Well, it didn't take long for you to get over here," Detective Krause snapped. "She your next charity case?"

"You will be in a few minutes," Megan added. "You're trespassing."

Krause pulled out a warrant. "No, we're searching the place."

Vivian looked alarmed now, which made Megan even more determined. "Where is the interpreter? I don't see anyone. You know she's deaf."

"She's deaf, not blind; it's all here in the paperwork."

"I'm sure it is—one of the judge's cohorts signed off on an illegal search. She has a right to an interpreter. You will not go through this home without a detailed explanation to the owner, which is now Vivian seeing as the judge is on a slab somewhere."

"*Ms.* McGinn, apparently I need to remind you once again that you do not have jurisdiction here, or anywhere for that matter," Krause said.

"But I do have a cell phone, and with my current pseudo-celebrity status I can get a film crew over here in one minute while you walk all over Vivian's personal freedom and right to an interpreter. And then I'll find the best lawyer to sue your department, the judge who signed that warrant, and you personally on her behalf. And guess what, *she-man*: she will win."

Detective Michalski whispered to his partner, "Krause, let's go."

"We're coming back, with an interpreter." Krause stared Vivian down before slamming the door.

Vivian went up to the door and opened it, prompting Krause to turn around. Vivian flashed Krause her middle finger.

Megan looked out the gatehouse door. "Do you need an interpreter for that sign?"

SIXTEEN

MEGAN IMMEDIATELY CALLED CALLIE and briefly explained the situation. She asked for him to come over to Vivian's right away. Megan wrote a note telling Vivian what she and the detectives spoke about and that Callie was on his way. Vivian pointed at Megan's chest and then down at the floor. She wanted Megan to stay. Megan shook her head no and continued writing on the notepad while saying it aloud: "I can't stay and shouldn't be here when they return. Callie will be here with you."

She then pointed to herself and the outdoors.

"No, you can't leave. They'll be back soon. You need to stay," Megan said and wrote. "I will stay until he gets here."

It wasn't long before Callie arrived. He flew through the door, slightly out of breath. "Megan, what's going on?" He signed with Vivian asking if she was okay. He continued to sign while speaking to Megan. "Why do they want to search the gatehouse? That bastard stayed as far away from Vivian as he could. What are they looking for?"

"I have no idea. It's probably procedural, given that the gate-house is so close to the main house, but—I don't know. The same detectives stopped over at my place earlier this morning."

"What?" Callie was confused. "Why were they talking to you?"

"They were just asking generic questions about seeing anyone in the neighborhood, things like that. And just so you're aware, the female lead on the case is an absolute piece of work. My advice is to stay out of their way and don't get into any communication without the interpreter."

"Wait, where are you going? You're leaving?"

"Callie, I can't and shouldn't be here." Megan felt ashamed for retreating, but she also knew it was in everyone's best interest. "Listen, I didn't get on well with Krause, the lead working this. Trust me on this one. You want me as far away as possible."

Callie stared at Vivian and back at Megan. He was clearly not happy with Megan's choice. "Okay then."

She placed a hand on his shoulder. "If I didn't think my presence would have a negative impact, I would stay. You know that."

His reaction softened some. "I know, kind of."

"Call me or come over later." Megan turned to Vivian and mouthed, "You'll be okay."

Megan returned to the Macks' house immediately and realized the adrenaline jolt she'd had during her verbal warfare with Krause had temporarily lifted the physical pain she was feeling. She knew it would soon return and so popped a few aspirin. When she noticed the morning paper she'd tossed on the counter earlier, she promptly folded it and threw it in the bin. "Enough, no more."

For the next hour she sat, drank a glass of wine that quickly turned into a half bottle with lunch, fed Clyde, then stared outside as light flurries began to cover the deck. It's not as if she could cauterize her detective instinct out of her mind, but she was pretty certain she could numb most of it.

So little changes in my life, she thought.

Her cell rang. It was Nappa. Megan kicked it to voicemail, not wanting conversation with anyone but Clyde. It was a sure bet he wouldn't speak back, and that was more than fine with her.

The snow was falling with more consistency by late afternoon. Megan looked out the window to see the bubbler system was on in the boathouse, but the red and green lights signaling to snowmobile riders that there was open water were not on. "Lovely." She grabbed her coat. "Clyde, want to go outside?"

He turned and promptly settled into his nook in front of the fireplace. Clyde was no fool.

"Wimp. I'll be right back."

Megan carefully made her way down to the lake and entered the boathouse, avoiding patches of ice as if they were mines as she made her way over to the power box. The wires leading to the outdoor lights had been cut.

"What the hell?" She walked to the front of the dock and looked around but saw nothing except two stomped-out cigarette butts. She knelt down for a closer look. Nothing distinctive about them, just plain old cigarettes. When she stood up, a burlap bag came over her head. The sack immediately tightened around her neck. She pawed at the hands behind her, failing to loosen their grip. She could feel her breath becoming more and more shallow.

Air, need more air, was all she could think, but she couldn't get herself to stop hyperventilating.

Her attacker was strong, strong enough to lift Megan off her feet. He swung her back and forth. Then she felt the hands release her, and her body hit icy water a second later. She tore at the sack, ripping it off her head. The temperature shocked her, and she was unable to tell which direction was up. She gasped, taking in only frigid water. Her boots began to feel like anchors pulling her deeper into the water.

Megan forced her eyes open. The rising bubbles indicated the direction she needed to get to, and fast. Desperation mixed with adrenaline forced her to kick and flail toward the surface. Air exploded into her lungs as she hurled herself through the surface. She stroked clumsily to the dock and grabbed at it, unable to gain a firm hold. She attempted time after time to pull herself up. It was a fruitless effort. The ice on the dock was too slippery, her hands too numb. She continually fell back into the frigid lake.

A figure slowly walked into the boathouse. Too slowly. When the person reached her, he grabbed her jacket with only one fist, easily pulling her up and over to a dry section of the dock.

"You can't be so clumsy, city girl."

Megan rolled over to see the marina owner, Jake Norden. She was shivering violently and thought hypothermia would soon begin, but she was too angry to allow it.

"What the fuck!"

"What is it with you that *that* is always the first sentence out of your mouth when you see me?"

"Could you have fucking walked any slower to help me!" The words set off a barrage of coughs.

"Thought you were a fish." He grinned.

"That's not funny; I could have died!" Megan tried to stand but found it difficult.

"Here, let me help." Jake grabbed her from behind and lifted her by her waist. "You shouldn't be out here if you don't know how to swim, you know."

She snapped out of his grip. "I know how to swim, you mother-fucker!" Megan began to punch at him. The idea that someone had just tried to ice her—literally—fueled her Irish temper. "You fucking asshole!"

Jake held her back. "What? What happened? I just came to check on the bubbler system."

Even with how unnerved Megan was at the moment, she could tell by the sheer shocked look on his face that Jake was not the person who tossed her in. "Did you see anyone?"

"What?"

"Did you see anyone?" Megan stumbled over to the doors and flung them open. "Someone threw me in."

"What are you talking about? I just walked in and you were in the water. There's no one here. It's icy, you gotta watch it." He stared at her as if she was crazy, and for a moment Megan thought she was too—until she saw the burlap sack floating in the water.

"The lights." Megan pointed to the front of the boathouse with a shaking arm. "They weren't on. I came down to check on the lights. The wires were cut."

"What?" Jake went to the power box to inspect the wires and found them neatly cut, as had Megan. He looked around at the adjoining properties; there was not a soul to be found. "Were the lights working last night?"

In between hard coughs, she said, "Yes. Someone pulled that sack over my head, and then I was in the water."

Jake used a rod to fish the sack out and flopped it on the dock. "I'm in this boathouse all the time, and I've never seen this in here." Jake stood up and looked at Megan. "Jeez, you've got rope burns on your neck. You need to see a doctor. We should call the police."

Megan stared out over Lake Hopatcong, desolate and freezing. "I am the police," she answered.

"God, I wasn't even planning on stopping in. I happened to be checking on another boathouse, so that's why I'm here. You better get out of those clothes. You could catch pneumonia. Are you okay?" Jake looked chagrined for his dismissive attitude earlier.

"Yes, I'm fine!"

He raised his eyebrows at her. "I think now is the time you say thank you."

Megan opened the gate to the yard. "Thank you!" She slipped and slid the entire walk up to the house, entering through the lower level. She pulled off her soaked attire in the laundry room. It took longer than usual since she couldn't stop shaking. She put on sweats and a warm sweater, not that she thought she'd ever feel warm again. She was about to sit when a knock sounded at the back door.

This douche bag doesn't take a hint. She swung open the door. "What—do—you—want?"

"I just wanted to tell you I need to go back and get wires. I'll have it fixed in an hour or so." The gate to the deck creaked. Jake turned to see who had arrived. "Hey, Callie. How are ya, man?" The two men greeted one another with a handshake.

"Hey, what's up?" Callie looked to Megan. "Woah, what happened to you?"

Megan was gob-smacked. "Wait, you *know* this guy?"

Jake asked, "You know *her*?"

"Jake and I have known one another since we were kids. Trouble—uh, *Megan*—and I know one another from college. What happened?"

Jake looked at Megan. "Tell him what you told me."

Megan was angry Jake brought it up. Embarrassment had set in as soon as she'd gotten in the warm house. "Someone came up behind me and threw me in the water."

"You're kind of forgetting a few big points in this story." Jake looked at Callie. "I need to go get some wires and fix the lights on the boathouse. I'll be back in a bit. I'll stop by for a beer soon, we'll get caught up."

Callie answered, "Sounds good," but didn't take his eyes off Megan and the redness around her neck.

Megan motioned for Callie to come in. "I need to get in front of the fire."

"Tell me what happened."

She shook her head. "The lights weren't on down at the boathouse. I went down thinking the switch didn't turn over, and when I opened the electric box, I saw the wires had been cut."

"How do you know they were cut?"

Megan was in no mood to be treated like a weak damsel in distress. "Because I have fucking eyes in my head and could clearly see they had been cut."

Callie was quickly put in his place. "Okay, okay. So, then what?"

"I bent over to look at two cigarette butts and then someone pulled a sack over my head and…" Megan hesitated. This hadn't been the first time she'd been attacked; she found herself fighting the past as much as she was trying to handle the present. "He tried to choke me with it. Before I knew it, I was in the water."

"Jake pulled you out?"

Megan nodded.

"Jake didn't do this, if that's what you're thinking. I know he's a little rough around the edges, but all in all, he is a good guy."

Megan lifted her hands into air quotes. "I'm not sure about 'good guy', but I know he didn't do it." She plodded through to the kitchen and poured herself some more wine. The frigid swim had sobered her up faster than she'd planned on. She and Callie sat in front of the fireplace. Clyde moved in between them, close to Megan, as though trying to warm her. "Next subject, please."

"We should call the police."

"No, we should talk about something else now." Megan gave no room for any further discussion on the subject.

After a releasing a frustrated sigh, Callie said, "When did you get a dog?"

"I found him." With little patience remaining, she got to the point: "So, what happened?"

"Oh, they came back. You were right, Krause is one angry bitch."

"Uh-huh." She hesitated to ask more questions but went ahead anyway. "Did they tear the place apart?"

Callie raised his eyebrows. "Surprisingly, no. They seemed to be looking for something very specific."

"Of course they were. The murder weapon."

"The paper didn't say how he was killed so I have no idea," Callie answered.

"Trust me, they don't either. They're on the wrong path."

"What path do you think they should be on?"

Megan wanted to end the conversation regarding the police, warrants, all of it. "Talk about something else." It was a command and not a request.

Callie started to rub Clyde's belly while staring into the fire, but Clyde was miffed at Megan's divided attention, and he settled himself on the floor. "So, today was your first day in the Polar Bear Club. How did it go?"

Megan punched him in the arm. "Ass!"

He pretended to punch back when Megan turned the wrong way, feeling a biting pain. "Damn it."

"From your fall? Let me see." He lifted her shirt. "You did take a tumble. Ice is pretty unforgiving." He rubbed her shoulder. "That means only one thing then."

"What?"

"You'll have to be on top." He gave her the same smile he did freshman year in college. Now, as then, it worked.

Megan had forgotten how soft Callie's lips were. His kisses were slow and filled with intention. "Bedroom?"

Megan nodded in the direction.

"You never got that massage today, did you?"

She shook her head. "You know how to give a massage?"

"Come on." He stood up and took Megan's hand. In the bed-room, he took his time removing her clothes. "I'd forgotten how beautiful your pale Irish skin is. You look exactly the same." Callie removed Megan's hair clip, allowing her damp chestnut hair to fall over her shoulders. He knelt down and separated her legs slowly, massaging her below the waist.

"That's not the massage I thought I was going to get." She stared down at him, running her fingers through his hair.

"I'm just warming up." He stood up and gave her a long, deep kiss. "Lie down on your stomach."

Megan situated herself on the bed while Callie partially dis-robed. "Do you have any lotion or oil?"

"In the medicine cabinet." Callie returned and mounted Megan as she situated her pillow. "This better be good." She smiled.

"Close your eyes and shut up." He used long, gliding strokes up and down Megan's back while intermittently kissing the side of her neck. He whispered in her ear, "I've never forgotten our first time together. You were wild and confident, and sexy, as if you'd been fucking for years. Loved that."

Megan could smell his cologne. The scent relaxed her as much as his touch. When he lightly kneaded the bruised areas, she flinched for a moment, then relaxed as she felt his hardness expand just below her tailbone.

"We went five times that night."

She lightly opened her eyes. "How did you remember that?" She smiled. "That's youth."

"No, that's this"—he flexed his hips into her—"and this"—he moved his oily fingers into her wetness. In one motion, Callie turned on his back, flipping Megan over his groin. "Fits like a glove."

"Shut up, Callie." She leaned over, offering him intense, wild kisses, which earned a much deserved groan. Megan moved her hands to his wrists and placed his arms above his head, holding him down. It was about to become a long, memorable night.

SEVENTEEN

MEGAN TURNED OVER TO find the most pungent smell coming at her. She was relieved it was Clyde's breath and not Callie's. "Hey, boy." She rubbed his ears and he offered a small whimper in return. "You have to go out?" She checked her watch and was shocked at the time. "Oh my God. It's nearly noon. No wonder you're anxious, buddy." Megan slipped on her robe and tiptoed across the bedroom.

"It's okay, I'm awake," Callie said, turning over. "Did you say noon? I need to get to work."

"Towels are in the side cabinet next to the shower door." Megan went and opened the door for Clyde. When she turned to the right, she found Detective Sam Nappa standing on the deck, about to ring the doorbell.

"Hello, McGinn." He looked her up and down. "I take it you didn't listen to my voicemail."

"What are you doing here?" Megan wasn't sure if she was shocked or angered by her partner's arrival. Though she'd only been out of the city for a week, Megan hadn't seen her partner in nearly a month.

Looking at him now prompted a mental trailer of why she'd run away to New Jersey.

"McGinn, it's twenty degrees out here, can I come in?"

She'd forgotten what little manners she still possessed. "Of course, yes, come in."

Nappa walked in and glanced around. "This is a very nice place. Fantastic view." He walked over to the main window. "Boathouse too. Very nice."

There was a bark at the door.

"That's Clyde. He's not mine." Megan let Clyde in and started to pour his food into his bowl. "So, what did your message say?"

Nappa had a way of staring into Megan that wasn't so much disarming as it was heartening. She knew how much he cared and worried for her. After all, as partners in Homicide, they had to have one another's backs.

"I'm here for a few reasons, but first I want to take you out to lunch, and then I ..."

"Hey, Trouble, I'm late. I need to head to the restaurant so—" Callie stopped not just mid-sentence but mid-stride as he was rushing out.

Awkward.

Megan took a deep breath. "Chris Callie, this is my partner, Detective Sam Nappa."

Boxers facing off before the first bell had kinder demeanors. Nappa, being the ultimate gentleman, took a step forward to shake Callie's hand.

"Hello. Sorry, I didn't know you were expecting company," Callie said without the least bit of an apologetic tone.

"Neither did I," Nappa replied.

"I'm late, I have to go. Nice meeting you, detective." He gave Megan a kiss on the cheek and took a quick sip of the glass of water on the counter before his departure. "I'll call you later."

After Callie shut the door, Nappa cocked his head, folded his arms, and gave Megan a small squint. "New friend?"

"Nappa, he's an old friend from college I ran into here." Megan leaned a hand on the counter. "Nothing more, nothing less."

Nappa knew Megan ran hot that way. He got close once, but a case interrupted them from fulfilling their chemistry. "McGinn, go get ready. I drove by a restaurant on the way here. It looked interesting, as long as it's not *his* restaurant." Nappa smiled. "Pub 199?"

"You're safe."

"I'd say he's safe. *I'm* carrying two guns."

"Good point. Give me fifteen minutes."

———

Megan went into the bedroom to change, and Nappa stared down at the glass Callie had just sipped from. He quietly opened a few kitchen drawers before finding a stash of plastic bags. In the moment, he was unsure if it was his gut or jealousy that made him do it. He did it anyway. He used the plastic bag to pick up the glass and placed it in the pocket of his winter coat.

Time will tell, was his last thought before Megan reentered the kitchen.

———

When they walked into Pub 199, there was a much-needed moment for pause. It wasn't the fifteen or more television screens on the wall or the generous-sized bar that stopped them. It was the room beyond the bar. The combination hunting lodge/biker bar/cafeteria-style bingo hall held an array of stuffed animal trophies: coyote, bear, deer, cheetah, elk, even a giraffe. And those were just the animals Megan recognized.

"Oh my God," Megan laughed.

"Have you been here before?" Nappa wondered.

"No, I would have remembered."

The hostess seated them, and they continued to look around the room in awe.

"PETA must be pissed," Nappa commented.

"This is a taxidermist's wet dream," Megan responded. They fell into silence looking over the menu, and both had to admit the prices were extremely reasonable, especially for two people accustomed to the cost of dining in Manhattan. "Fuck, lobster with sides for fifteen dollars. Twenty-ounce New York Strip with sides for thirteen dollars!"

"Let's order, I'm getting both."

"You're a pig, Nappa," Megan joked, but for a moment she had the same thought.

Their waitress had a nametag pinned to her shirt that read DEE. She was a bleach-bottle blonde, her overprocessed hair resembling straw piled high on her head. She didn't smile. Megan thought she'd probably spent a lifetime waiting tables and pouring shots for small-town drunks. She was the type of woman who didn't age gracefully. It wasn't just the obvious tanning booth visits or the smoker's voice. The giveaway was the glint of bitterness in her eyes when a prettier or younger waitress walked by. A harsh reminder that those days were long gone for her.

The cocktails arrived, orders were placed, and now it was time to have what Megan was sure was going to be an uncomfortable conversation.

Nappa met her eyes. "I haven't seen you in a few weeks. That's kind of unusual."

She nodded. "I think it's the longest we've gone since we became partners."

"Just so you know, I tried to give you fair warning I was coming up here. That's hard to do when you don't answer most of my calls. I was surprised you picked up a few nights ago, not that you said much."

"Nappa, you knew I took a leave of absence. I said I needed to get out of the city." She tapped the table. "Press constantly hanging outside of my apartment building, outside my parents' house. Hell, I was afraid I was going to be photographed at the cemetery when I went to say goodbye before I came out here."

"The perp is still in the hospital."

"I don't give a shit," Megan answered.

"At some point you're going to have to come back for depositions and such. You know that." Nappa's brown eyes filled with guilt. He didn't like to be the one to remind Megan of the cold, hard truth of the current circumstances, the reality of their jobs.

Megan chugged her cocktail and flagged down the waitress to ask for another. "Not this week, not next week, probably not until next year. You know that."

"Next year isn't that far away. It's only a few weeks till Christmas; you know how fast that flies by." Nappa caught himself one comment too late when he witnessed Megan's sullen reaction. "Sorry. You of all people know the holidays are coming up."

"No worries." She wanted to make him feel better for the minor faux pas. "Remember last year at the Murphys'?"

"How could I forget that Thanksgiving? I'm the only Italian-American in a room with thirty-five Irish people. Three cooked turkeys, and your father and Uncle Mike pulling me aside every fifteen minutes to do shots. And the two-day hangover! I think that was my favorite holiday ever. I felt at home, it felt like family."

"Nappa, you are family, don't be a jerk."

"Now I feel like family," he laughed, then also ordered another drink. "What about your college buddy? Callie, was it? Is he family?" He smirked.

Megan rolled her eyes. "Oh stop!" The appetizers arrived just in time as far as Megan was concerned. "It will be a quiet holiday season this year. I don't even want to acknowledge it."

"Well, speaking of the Murphys, Uncle Mike really wants you to call him, even if only to hear your voice. Aunt Maureen bought a bunch of warm sweaters, socks, a winter hat, and gloves for you. I have them out in my car. All from the Irish store in the neighborhood, of course."

"They're always doing nice things like that," she said in almost a whisper. Megan cut to the chase. "That isn't the only thing you brought though, is it?" She was clearly speaking of the letter from the mother of one of their most-recent victims.

"It's in my glove box. I'll give it to you before I leave."

"Did you read it?"

"Absolutely not. She brought it in to the station personally," Nappa added. "Now stop eating all the hot wings; your ass is getting big."

A devoured chicken wing was thrown at his head immediately. Megan would never have admitted it, but it was comforting to see

Nappa again. He'd walked with her through the hell that brought her to this place in her life. There was a knowing they had for one another. Most of the time she was comforted by it; in this moment she felt he could read her every thought, though, and she wanted to keep those to herself for now.

"I see you've had big happenings in this little lake town. It made the city news." Nappa smiled. "Fifteen seconds of news, anyway."

"The crime scene was across from my house," Megan said, swigging her second cocktail. "Strange to see police tape again."

"I guess you're not a fan at the moment."

"No." Megan looked away. "I most definitely am not."

The waitress stopped to clear the appetizer dishes from the table. Megan looked at the waitress once again. Dee didn't smile. Megan felt empathy, but she was also afraid of Dee's jaded demeanor. She quietly wondered if she gave off similar vibrations.

"So, who's your new partner?" Megan asked.

"*Temporary* partner. Palumbo. Rasmussen broke his leg falling down subway stairs chasing a perp. He's out of commission for a while, so it's me and Palumbo until you come back."

"Nudge, nudge," Megan replied to his overt hint. "Palumbo's a good fit for you. He's not the pain in the ass I am—was."

"True." Nappa smiled knowing full well he'd prefer his old partner back. "But you smell better than he does."

"Jeez, be sure to speak at my funeral some day. *She was a good cop and she smelled nice.* That's what I want to be remembered for."

———

An hour later they both had, as Megan called it, food babies. Practically waddling out of the restaurant, Nappa drove Megan back to the lake house. He unloaded Aunt Maureen's winter gifts from the car and then handed Megan the handwritten note.

She held the envelope, not wanting to think about what the mother of a murdered woman would have to say to her. And then she realized how much she and Mrs. McAllister had in common. It's not a club anyone ever wants to join.

"Are you going to read it?" Nappa asked.

Megan didn't answer, because she didn't have an answer. "Good to see you, Nappa. Drive home safe."

"Megan?"

It was odd for her to hear Nappa say her first name. It happened only once previously and the context was intimate, sexual, heated. She turned around waiting for him to continue.

He stalled, fumbled for words. "Just, don't be a stranger. And call Uncle Mike."

She nodded, knowing she was isolating herself and that people who cared for her were concerned. "I will." She walked into the house and was given a bold, spirited welcome by Clyde. She felt a rush of warmth—until she realized she had leftover steak in a bag.

"So it's not me you're happy to see so much as the steak you're hoping you'll get later. Touching."

Megan didn't open the letter. Instead, she placed it on the mantel of the fireplace, tucked behind the vase of dried roses. It didn't go unnoticed. Dead roses. Her mother, Rose, dead. There are no coincidences. There was, however, the lingering question as to who had attempted to harm her on the dock.

Eyes in the back of your head, Meganator, as her father reminded her time and time again. *Eyes in the back of your head.*

EIGHTEEN

I was scheduled for lunchtime prep at Krogh's today, so I left for work earlier than usual. I was only ten minutes from work when I drove over a hill to find a fallen tree branch blocking my way. It wasn't huge, something I knew I could move. I placed the shifter in park, put my flashers on, and cleared the road. When I returned to my car, I went to move the gearshift back into drive, but it wasn't moving. I looked down to find my keys were out of the ignition. I searched the floor of my seat. There was no sign of them. It wasn't until I sat back and looked in my rearview mirror that I realized where they'd gone.

He was wearing a motorcycle helmet, a dark-tinted visor concealing his face. He lunged forward from the back seat, covering my mouth with his cigarette-smelling fingers, and handed me a note. It said, "I know you came into the house the night your father got what he deserved. You are to tell no one—whatever you saw."

I shook my head frantically, trying to sign no to the man. On the passenger seat was a pen. I repeatedly pointed at it. The man didn't let

*go of my mouth. He leaned forward and handed me the pen. I scrib-
bled, "Saw no one!!!"*

*The man took back the note, got out of the car, and pushed his
motorcycle out of the bushes. He pulled up next to my car and dangled
my keys in front of me. Then, surprisingly, he handed them back. He
rode off at warp speed.*

———

The woman at the foot of Megan's bed was bruised and blood-
soaked. "Why, Meggie, why? How could you let this happen? My
own daughter."

Megan shot up, her nightshirt soaked, her hair tangled in sweat.
She needed to catch her breath, if that was possible.

One hell of a way to wake up in the morning, she thought to herself and padded through to the bathroom.

She splashed cold water on her face and looked at her reflection
in the mirror. "Momma, I didn't know. I didn't know."

She went into the kitchen, poured a mug of coffee, and sat on the
couch with Clyde. "Tell me something, boy, did you ditch your family or did they ditch you?" Clyde rolled on his back for Megan to
scratch his belly. "Okay. You don't answer and I won't answer. Deal?"

She turned on her cell phone and thankfully had no texts or
voicemails. Enjoying the silence, she thought back to what Nappa
said about Uncle Mike and tapped the Murphys' home number. He
picked up on the second ring.

"Meganator! Good to hear from you, kiddo."

Megan smiled. "Hi, Uncle Mike. How are you? How is Aunt
Maureen?"

"We're fine, just fine. Now, for the bigger question: How are you?"

Megan exaggerated her response and matched his words. "Oh, fine, just fine." She sipped her coffee. "Is Aunt Maureen there?"

"Nope, she just left to do a grocery run. She'll be upset she missed you. How's New Jersey?"

"Cold, quiet." *Liar.* "Which reminds me, Uncle Mike, please tell Aunt Maureen thank you for the winter sweaters and gear. It was really thoughtful of you both."

"I can't take credit. As usual, she comes up with the best ideas." He became more serious. "Well, ya know you can tell her thank you in person if you come home for Christmas."

Megan felt bad because she knew the Murphys were worried about her. "Uncle Mike, I just need to be away from the city. I need time."

"Okay, I can respect that. But let me ask you a question, Megs."

"Go on. As if I could stop you." She smiled.

"Are you running away or are you running toward something?"

Megan tended to twirl her hair with her index finger when she was forced into previously rare moments of self-analysis. Her finger was twirling furiously now. "Maybe a little of both. I'm not sure what the *toward* part would be. Career? Home? Maybe get married, have a few kids?" At this, they both laughed out loud.

"I can see it now. *Come here, little Patricia, let me show you how to load and aim my nine millimeter.* I'm not buying it."

Megan cackled into the phone. "Neither am I."

"Detective Nappa is worried about you. How was your visit?"

"It was good to see him, but please, not one more word about Nappa, Uncle Mike. I'm warning you."

"I relent, kiddo!"

Megan knew Uncle Mike and Aunt Maureen would dearly like to see the two of them get together. It was probably a good thing they'd been interrupted the one time they'd almost given in to their mutual attraction.

"It's good to hear your voice, Uncle Mike. Do me a favor and don't worry so much about me. You know me, I always make it through." Her tone didn't convince her, so she knew it wouldn't come close to convincing him. Thankfully, he didn't press.

"We'll see you soon."

"Love you guys much." Megan's voice started to break, which meant the end of the conversation.

"Love you much, Meganator."

———

Megan took Clyde out into the yard and threw a toy around for him to get some exercise. She certainly wasn't braving the hill hike after that tumble down the driveway. On what could have been the thirtieth throw, her cell vibrated. It was a message from Callie asking her to drive over to Krogh's for lunch with him. She accepted, yet felt a twinge of unexplained guilt after spending time with Nappa the day before. She stared at the boathouse for a few minutes and hated the fact she was uncomfortable walking out there again. The very reason for her to do so, in her mind.

"Clyde, stay. I need to do this," Megan said to herself, and she was right. Facing the moment she was attacked was imperative. As she would ask victims of violence to take her through their trauma step by step in hopes of remembering even the slightest detail, she was now asking it of herself. Megan opened the gate, taking deliberate steps to the front of the dock. She of course made certain the inside of the boathouse was empty, and it was. Every step over the boards creaked. "I would have heard you walking down. There's no doubt." She looked back at the edge of the dock and it hit her. "Son of a bitch. You were already here before I came down." Megan moved beyond the side door to the boathouse, right up to the edge of the turn to the front boating entrance. "You were in my blind spot." She walked over to the exact spot she'd been standing when the burlap sack was pulled over her head, closed her eyes, and replayed the quick action. "You smelled of cigarettes. The bag smelled like mildew and dirt. And then I hit the water."

Armed with her new clue, Megan walked back up to the house with Clyde. She now knew the frustration of people she'd interviewed, and she didn't like it one bit.

Hurt me once, your fault. Hurt me twice, I pull my trigger, bastard.

Driving down the road en route to Krogh's, she noticed Leigh checking her mailbox and stopped to say hello. "Hi, Leigh. How are you?" Megan could tell by her color and demeanor that she was not feeling much better than she had the night they had dinner last week. If anything, she looked worse.

"Hanging in. I'm just grading papers today, taking it easy. Crazy times in these parts, wouldn't you say?"

"So I read."

"Plans tonight?" Leigh asked.

"Nothing on tap."

"I'm flying solo tonight. Jo is working a double shift at the hospital, if you want to come over. Nothing fancy, I was just planning on ordering a pizza and watching bad television." Leigh's smile seemed painfully forced. "Bring Dog. He and Lady Sadie can play."

"Sounds good. Oh, Billie named him Clyde."

"That kid never ceases to surprise me. See you about seven."

Megan pulled into Krogh's parking lot. The wind was strong on Lake Mohawk across from the pub. Whitecaps surfaced where the water had yet to freeze. If the sun hadn't been out accompanied by blue skies, she would have thought a storm was brewing. She should have taken it as a sign. She found Callie in the restaurant speaking to staff and signing off on invoices. He waved her over, and the staff scattered to their various stations.

"Hey, Trouble, good to see you." He went to kiss her and Megan had an awkward hesitancy about returning the affection. "You know I bite, don't be so shy."

Megan removed her coat and Callie just gave her the grin he'd mastered back in college. They sat in the same booth as the last time she was in Krogh's. "So, do I get to hear the specials, or are you just going to stare at me?"

He gave her a comical snarl. "Drinks first. What's your pleasure? Besides me."

"White wine, Chardonnay."

Callie ordered Megan's wine and a Krogh's Gold for himself. "Pecan-crusted tilapia, linguine with clams, and skirt steak are the lunch specials. I suggest the tilapia."

"It's your place—you would know. Sounds good."

"So, that was a bit awkward yesterday when you're partner arrived unannounced," Callie continued in a probing manner. "The tall, dark, handsome detective must be fun to work with."

"Callie, think what you want, but it's only professional." But Megan looked down at her glass when she answered.

"I'm guessing it hasn't always been, but that's none of my business," Callie continued, raising his beer. "Cheers."

"Cheers. Nappa needed to bring me something from work." She waved it off. "Information from a previous case."

"There's this place called the post office. They actually deliver mail right to your home!"

"Sarcasm duly noted," Megan continued. "I didn't see Vivian's car; is she working today?"

"She's in the back doing prep work."

"How is she?"

"Good. I mean, same as usual, though I think the other day definitely threw her for a loop, as it would anyone." Callie was hedging a bit with his next question. "So, do you think you'll be here for a while, in New Jersey?"

"Why do you ask?"

"I had a great time the other night and just wondered if that will happen again, that's all."

"One step at a time, Callie. I'm here to clear my head, so let's keep things one day at a time. Is that okay with you?"

It was a small laugh. Callie knew he wasn't shot down, just winged a bit. "I'm not accustomed to having the ball in someone else's court, Trouble."

"I remember."

While they sat enjoying their lunch together, they stormed through more memories of college and the twist and turns of their lives since then. Megan saw the flashing lights before Callie. She didn't have to guess about the two police cars pulling up.

"Callie." She pointed. "Now I think *you* have trouble."

NINETEEN

Two police cars and an unmarked car parked outside of Krogh's. Megan didn't have to guess who would emerge from the unmarked car: Detectives Krause and Michalski and an interpreter.

I was right about a storm. I just thought it was going to be on the lake, she thought to herself.

They both rose from the table and headed toward the entrance. Krause entered and handed Callie papers. "I believe one Vivian Campbell works here, is that correct?"

"You *know* she does," Megan snarled.

"What do you want?" Callie asked.

"We have a warrant to search Ms. Campbell's car. *And* we have an interpreter."

Megan snatched the warrant from Krause's hands and examined it. She nodded to Callie and said, "It's legit." Megan looked at Krause. "Whatever that means around here. Wait, you searched her home; why didn't you search her car then?"

Michalski, the voice of calm answered, "Yes, we did check her car, but we're back based on an anonymous tip, detective."

Callie reluctantly showed them to the back kitchen, but not without a comment from Krause directed at Megan. "You do realize you have nothing to do with this case, don't you?"

"What I realize is you're not even close to being capable enough to have *anything* to do with this case."

"Ms. McGinn, you will remain here," Krause barked.

"I own this place," Callie cut in. "She is my patron and she will go anywhere she damn well pleases." He clearly wasn't about to be bossed or have Krause boss anyone around in his restaurant.

Vivian was chopping vegetables at the counter with her back toward them when they entered. Callie placed his hand on her shoulder and signed that there were police there to see her, at which point Krause and the interpreter took over communication. Vivian looked confused, on edge. They walked out to her car and she gave the detectives her car keys and was asked to step back. Megan and Callie both paced nervously. Megan knew they wouldn't have come without some kind of knowledge that they would find something.

Megan waited for the other shoe to drop.

One of the officers popped the trunk and pulled back the felt-like fabric, then lifted the board covering the spare tire.

"This is too specific. They're not even searching the rest of the car," Megan whispered to Callie. He could only respond with an even more worried look.

"Detective Krause," the officer said, motioning her over.

She pulled out a pair of plastic gloves and withdrew a knife from the spare tire well. She requested the interpreter to ask Vivian why there was a knife in her trunk.

Vivian signed back that it was not hers, and she only used the trunk to transport her massage table.

Megan felt an eerie calm. She knew what coming next, and it wasn't going to be pretty.

"We're taking you down to the police station." Krause waited for the interpreter to get up to speed. "We're going to ask you questions with the interpreter." She pulled out her cuffs and began to recite the Miranda warning to Vivian through the interpreter.

"Come on!" Callie yelled. "Megan, do something."

Megan knew, as did Krause, that her hands were tied. "Callie, there isn't anything I can do. You need to find the best lawyer in town, someone not affiliated with Judge Campbell." She could tell he wasn't listening to her. "Callie!"

Krause and Michalski placed Vivian in the police car. Callie signed to her that they'd be right down and to not be afraid.

"We'll take my car," Callie said to Megan.

"What? No. I'm not going down there." Megan needed to escape the moment. She wanted to just turn and walk away, get as far away from it as possible. So she did.

Callie followed, screaming her name. She crossed the street, nearly getting hit by a car. Horns were honking, cars screeching.

"Megan, what the fuck? We have to go down there. We have to help."

She was halfway down the boardwalk overlooking Lake Mohawk when she spun around with her finger pointed at Callie. "No, I don't have to help. This is not my problem, and, by the way, it's not your problem either."

Callie was beyond furious. "It *is* my problem, and it *should* be yours. What the fuck kind of cop were you? Where is your fucking heart? You know she didn't do this. You said it yourself—otherwise why start such a pissing contest with Krause? You *know* Vivian is innocent and that bitch only wants to get someone's head on a stake so she can move forward in her career. Are you telling me you're going to let an innocent woman—wait, an innocent *deaf* woman—take the blame for this?"

"Callie! I cannot be a part of this! Why can't you see that?"

Megan turned again, but Callie grabbed her by the arm, jerking her back. "No, I don't fucking see it. Hey listen, I am truly sorry for what you and your family have gone through. I can't imagine anything so awful."

Megan interrupted, "That's right! You can't imagine, so don't even try. What? You think reading about my life in newspapers and what's happened to me, to my family, you suddenly think you have an *ounce* of understanding of my job, my life for the last six months? For the last fourteen years? Well, you fucking don't. You motherfucking don't!"

Callie closed his eyes and took a deep breath. "Megan, you know, *you know*, you can help. I'm asking you, please. Please, just try and do something."

"Do what? I'm on leave. I don't even have jurisdiction here for Chrissakes!"

"You must know people!" Callie pleaded.

"Callie, get her a good lawyer." She again started in the opposite direction then added, "There, I just helped."

Even Megan hated herself for uttering those words.

————

Megan sped home and locked herself in a fortress of guilt and shame. She ran through the possibilities of how the knife could

121

have gotten into Vivian's car. The problem was, there were too many. The car could have gotten broken into; Vivian wouldn't have known, as there's no alarm she would have heard. As she was contemplating the circumstances of the uncovering of the knife, she couldn't help but mutter more questions to herself.

"What the hell are you doing? You said you don't want a part of this. Stop the mental train wreck, now!" She poured a glass of red wine. Clyde stared at her. "Yes, Clyde we humans sometimes talk to ourselves. Go get groomed, we're going over to Lady Sadie's soon." Clyde walked over to the door. "No, not yet, come here, you need to get brushed." While Megan brushed Clyde, he looked up at her with his big brown eyes, as if asking her to change her mind. "Great you, too?"

———

Leigh opened the door before Megan had a chance to knock. "Sadie let me know you were coming down the driveway. Come on in. The pizza should be here any minute."

Megan handed Leigh a bottle of vino.

"What, do you own your own winery?" she laughed.

"No, but I should." Megan let Clyde off his leash and the dogs chased one another around the house before settling in to chew on rawhide bones.

"So, Jo is working a double shift. Does she do that often?"

"Every now and again. After twenty years it doesn't phase me anymore." Leigh poured the wine and started to put together a salad.

"It's good she has someone who's so understanding of her hours." Megan immediately realized how transparent the comment was. "I mean, that's hard to find is all."

Leigh was rinsing the salad ingredients. "I guess you haven't found the someone who can handle your work?"

Megan laughed. "Let's just say they don't stay around long." She motioned to ask if Leigh needed any help cutting the cucumber and tomatoes. "My work is not exactly appealing to most men. And hey, a woman who carries two guns on a daily basis, that just screams for a second date."

"Here's to that!" Leigh clanked glasses with Megan just as the doorbell rang. "That would be the pizza."

They sat and made small talk while both dogs begged for crusts, which both received two times over. Megan couldn't help but notice Leigh looked off. She knew what that was. Eight years ago Aunt Maureen had worn the same burdensome look.

"So, when were you diagnosed?"

Leigh smiled. "I guess it's starting to show." She wrapped herself up in a pashmina shawl. "I'm on my second round of chemo. Breast cancer. Stage two, verging on three, so they say."

Megan remembered when Maureen was diagnosed. Uncle Mike was heartbroken and terrified, even if he didn't say it. Megan's father and mother helped out as much as possible. Rose would go with Maureen to sit with her during chemotherapy. This was, of course, before her mother's memory began to decline. Megan's father was in charge of keeping Uncle Mike centered, strong, and drunk when he needed to be. Aunt Maureen recently celebrated her sixth year cancer-free.

"You're strong. Jo is a great support system. You can beat this."

She nodded. "We all have demons chasing us in one way or another." She sipped from her glass. "I don't have to tell you that."

Megan smiled. "I don't mean to be intrusive; don't feel you need to answer this question, I'm just curious. When you first found out, what went through your mind?" Megan hoped she hadn't crossed any boundaries.

Leigh answered without hesitation. "I wanted to run away. Get as far away from it as I could, but . . ."

"But?"

"But I knew I couldn't do that. I'm a fighter, and also there's Jo. I didn't want to let her down. I knew what I was supposed to do. Step up to the plate and march on. Otherwise, what is it for?"

Megan was hesitant to continue, but Leigh seemed relaxed and open to talking about what she'd been enduring. "Well, what—" Megan sighed, trying to figure out how to phrase the question. "What has it done to your faith, or beliefs? Aren't you angry?"

Leigh nodded. "There are times, yes, I yell and cry and get frustrated. But then I get up, brush myself off. When you first find out, it's like a set of elephant tusks just rammed through every ounce of faith and trust and hope you had for a good, comfortable life. But *good* and *easy* are moments we make. They're earned. I'm not a religious woman—at least, I don't consider myself one. I'd say I'm more of a spiritual person without the organized religion part."

"With everything you're going through, you still have faith?" Megan shook her head and raised her glass. "Leigh, you're an amazing woman."

"Not so amazing, just exercising free will."

"What do you mean?"

"We have a choice as to how we react to the meteorites hitting us in life. This is just my way, most of the time. Hey"—she tapped Megan's glass again to gain eye contact—"I have my bad days. The moments when I'm so sad and angry I just want to hide under my blanket. And I do. The trick is knowing when it's time to get up, and just keep going." Leigh studied Megan as she took in her words.

Megan trailed her finger around the rim of the wineglass. "I'm not ready to come out from under the covers yet," Megan whispered with a crooked smile.

"You're closer than you think." Leigh gave her a warm smile. "Sweetie, it's either faith or fear."

Megan sat for a moment, remembering when fear won. It was now time for faith.

TWENTY

MEGAN CLOSED THE GATE to the deck behind her and Clyde did his last jaunt in the yard for the evening. She fumbled for her keys, dropping them in the snow. Thankfully the sensor lights gave her direction as to where they landed. She was wiping them off when once again a light in Judge Campbell's house caught her eye.

"Come on, Clyde, we're going for a ride." She opened the back door to the truck and Clyde more than willingly jumped in. She was on the judge's street in less than two minutes. As Megan approached, she doused the lights. Vivian's gatehouse was pitch black. Megan assumed that whatever happened earlier, Vivian was probably still at the police station. She waited ten minutes. There was no light, no movement she could discern. She turned the engine over, and the high beams automatically turned on.

Megan was about to put Arnold in reverse when a man ran from the back of Judge Campbell's house into the woods. Megan jumped out of the truck and jogged up the driveway. He was out of sight in seconds. The only light she had came from the truck, so the limitations of running in the dark through the woods proved senseless. The saving grace in Megan's mind was that she trusted her gut, something she thought she'd lost faith in. Even if she was grabbing at straws, that gave her a hint of hope.

"Who are you and what are you looking for?" she whispered.

Megan dialed her cell. She was more surprised at her lack of hesitation than she was that her call went directly to voicemail. "Callie, it's me. I've changed my mind. Call me." She felt a tinge of the old Megan stirring within. The Megan McGinn who was never afraid, not of anyone or anything.

Faith, not fear, she reminded herself.

Megan's phone rang as soon as she returned to the lake house. "Hey," Megan said. "You got my message?"

"Yes," Callie said. "What changed your mind?"

She ignored his question. "Listen, I'm going to do what I can to help, but—and this is the most important part, so you better be listening—I will only help on the down-low." Megan was adamant with her demand. "No one is to know I have any role in this." Her demand was met with silence. "Callie, it's that or nothing."

"Who the hell would I tell?"

"Wrong answer."

"Okay, okay," he rushed to appease her.

"I have one more question, and I want an honest answer."

"What, Trouble?"

"Why are you so invested in this? There's more to it than she's a deaf girl who works for you. Why are you getting involved?"

"Vivian doesn't have anyone. It just seems like the right thing to do. My father was a dick too. Everyone deserves better."

Megan didn't have the experience of a terrible father growing up, so she let it alone. "So, what's the latest? Where are you?"

"At the station. She's basically just sitting in a room."

"They're holding her while they run the knife for prints and blood. Did you find a lawyer?" she asked.

"I've put a few feelers out. Do you really think it's at that point? And shouldn't you be down here?"

"You're sitting in the police station after a knife was found in her car, after her father—bastard or not—was found dead. I think it's far beyond that point. And what about 'down-low' did you not get? Detective Krause will do anything to nail someone for this, and she hates me. How do you think that will help Vivian?"

Callie sighed. "Sorry, you're right. I'm exhausted, I wasn't thinking."

"Get a lawyer down there, now. If Forensics finds even the smallest hair, fiber, print, whatever, they'll work fast on this."

"Okay. What are you going to do now?"

"I have a thought." On that note she hung up on Callie, grabbed a flashlight from under the sink, and picked up her car keys. "Clyde, I'm flying solo on this one."

TWENTY-ONE

"I CAN'T BELIEVE I'M doing this," Megan said to herself as she walked through the snow-covered woods about to break into a dead man's mansion. She'd intentionally parked on a side street about a quarter-mile away. The snow came up to mid-calf, but there were animal tracks enough to mask her footprints. She could feel the cold through her boots and her feet felt like cement blocks, but there was no turning back now. As she approached the back of the house, she thought—actually, more hoped—that the man she witnessed running into the woods would not be there to greet her.

She crossed the cleared stone patio and used the end of her flashlight to knock out a window, which turned out to be in the kitchen area. Noise wasn't an issue; the judge had exactly one neighbor and she was deaf. Megan climbed through and turned the flashlight on, keeping it low. Since she was able to see someone in the house the night she tumbled down the driveway, another person might spy her trespassing, especially given the judge's death was now a high-profile case for the town. Megan walked to the front of the house. There was nothing out of the ordinary—unless you found it ordinary that every photo in every room of the judge's home was of himself. Megan decided it most definitely was not ordinary. "Narcissistic bastard."

She found herself in the great room eyeing the expensive furniture, television, and paintings. "Okay, that guy was obviously not a robber, or most of this would be gone. Every room has expensive items in it, all in tact. So why were you murdered, Judge Campbell? What were you up to?"

Megan walked down the stairs to see headlights coming up the driveway. "Shit!" It was a police car. She flipped the switch on her flashlight, throwing herself up against the wall in between two heavily draped windows.

Now there were two flashlights beaming into the house; she could hear bits and pieces of the policemen's conversation. One asked why they had to do an hourly check on the property. The other complained about it as well, but added it was their job. Megan held her breath as they danced their light beams across the front of the house, then turned back to their squad car. Megan was glad the men did a half-assed job of their hourly inspection. If they had walked around the house, they would have found a broken window in the kitchen. Which would have prompted Megan to bolt out the front door so fast a cheetah would need to stop and use an inhaler in an attempt to keep up with her.

"Dumb asses," she whispered.

She waited until they drove out of the driveway and were halfway down the street before she dared continue her search. She turned on the flashlight, checking her watch. *One more hour. I have to pick up my speed, can't be here when Dumb and Dumber come back.*

Megan found the judge's office and rummaged through his papers and drawers, her thin winter gloves making the work slower than she'd like. She came across nothing out of the ordinary. She stared at a photo on the desk, of him on a hunting trip holding his rifle and a dead turkey displaying his Chiclet smile. She shook her head in disgust.

The clock was working against her. Megan continued her search and reminded herself of the importance of this being an illegal pursuit. If she found anything, she wasn't sure how she would get it into the right hands.

A problem for another time. It might not even matter.

Directly opposite the judge's office was a door she thought was a closet until she noticed a broken latch on it, most likely from the team investigating after his bravura performance as the largest fish bait ever. Megan pulled open the door. One long stairwell led down to a finished basement. She found a light switch and the entire floor lit up.

With no windows anywhere in the lower level, Megan was safe from being caught, at least in the short term. The walls were painted in flat colors to depict stones. Tapestries with the judge's monogram, MXC, sewn into each one covered the walls. The furnishings were decidedly different from the expensive, modern feel of the upper level. This room possessed a Gothic tone. Dark colors, rich reds and browns, and large oak chairs faced a movie screen. A home theater was at the rear of the room with a stacked bar and an additional full kitchen hidden behind a purple drape, also bearing the judge's initials.

Down the hall Megan walked under exposed wooden beams, approaching a large cathedral-shaped door. She walked through it to find what was obviously the gun room, given there must have been at least forty rifles, shotguns, and pistols in sight. Hell, forty had to be a low-ball estimation. Every wall with the exception of one had more self-portraits, and frames from the National Rifle Association and National Shooting Sports Foundation.

It was the bare wall that intrigued Megan. It was too stark given the level of egomaniacal decor in the home. A small wooden coffee table holding gun magazines was the only item within several feet of the empty panel. The room looked unbalanced, like that wasn't a wall at all. She pressed on the wall, felt up and down the sides, Nothing. Her gut feeling that something was off was volcanic now. She checked her watch: thirty-five minutes, tops, before the two policemen returned to perform their stellar mall-cop duty. When Megan looked at the time, her attention was drawn down to her dripping wet boots.

"Some fucking sneak I am." Except the water didn't pool around her feet; it seeped through the joints in the wood floor. "Fucking hell, something is under here."

Megan knelt down, pounding each board under the table. Nothing. She hurled the magazines to the floor and tried moving the table. "You're bolted down? What is going on here?" Megan felt each leg of the table. On all four were silver horseshoe symbols, small, hardly noticeable. She ran her fingers over them and pressed into the end legs until she heard a click. The hardwood floor in front of the empty wall slowly lifted. As Megan raised the end of the table, the sound of hinges opening followed. In one motion the table was on its side and the section of floor underneath now was perpendicular to the ceiling. Another stairwell, another room.

"I think I found your secret, Campbell."

———

Megan used her flashlight. The small puddle from her boots had dripped down onto the first step. Before she began her descent, she double-checked the holster attached to her hip, though she knew her gun was intact—it was second nature. The memory of the ambush on the dock quickly returned, and she pulled her gun out. The moment she reached the last stair, she felt the urge to gag. "Jesus Christ."

The air fresheners plugged into the wall weren't strong enough to cover the stink of old cigars, booze, and sex that filled the room, not to mention the smell of old blood. She found a light switch and was, even for her, surprised when she lit the room. A king-size bed with red silk sheets was positioned in the center of the room. Chairs similar to those in the home theater circled the bed. The sheets were mussed. Megan used her gun to move the top sheet aside. There were multiple stains underneath. Hanging on the wall were five black satin robes with hoods. All of them had a crest of some sort sewn onto the back. The table at the back of the room was filled with what could only be thought of as the Disney World of sex toys: vibrators, leather bed restraints, anal power beads, a strap-on, bondage kits, nipple clamps, sex-slave kits.

"Jesus." Megan looked over at the wall, where a leather whip was hanging. "No home should be without one." She noticed three medicine bottles on the table. The prescription was scratched off, but it was obvious the little blue pills were Viagra. A podium stood in the corner holding a leather-bound book. She flipped through the pages. It read more like a ledger than the sex diary it obviously was.

The boy struggled at first, I overpowered him quickly. The men enjoyed the cat-and-mouse game I played in the beginning. I need to remember it for next time. Note to self, our delayed member deserves two experiences on our next meeting.

"Boy?" Megan looked back to the table. "Oh my God." Now she did feel as though she would retch. "Oh my God."

She didn't know why, but she began taking photos of the room, the robes, the toys, and the leather book. When she took a picture of the podium, she saw two wooden boxes resembling large humidors underneath. One held cigars; the other, DVDs.

"You fuckers videotaped this? Big mistake, assholes." She grabbed three, as she couldn't carry the whole box with her, and she didn't have the time. Her hour was nearly up. She turned off the lights and was about to close off the hidden sex room and then had a better thought. She left the entrance open. "I barely found this. I need to make sure the mall cops find it."

She sprinted up the stairs, grabbed the phone in the kitchen, and dialed 911. She heard the operator ask, "What's your emergency?" then placed the receiver on the counter.

They would trace the call to Judge Campbell's line, see it was broken into, and hopefully be smart enough to search the house.

Megan went back out through the window, DVDs in hand, knowing it was not going to be a popcorn-and-rom-com night when she arrived back at the house.

TWENTY-TWO

MEGAN SAT IN FRONT of her computer holding the DVDs she'd confiscated from Campbell's home. She hedged on viewing them. She knew what she'd find. Willingly going back into the pit, bearing witness to the most appalling, cruel acts by human beings—monsters, really—made her take pause. She needed to remind herself of the many crime scenes when she had to disconnect at a certain point, disengage her feelings from the victim's and their family's. The personal note Nappa brought from her last case was a sore reminder of her failings, which was the very reason it remained unopened. She needed to admit, if only to herself, that emotional compartmentalization was not her strong suit after all.

She loaded the first DVD into the computer.

Four men sat in chairs facing the bed. The hooded robes veiled their faces. There was one chair not spoken for. It was on a step, meant to be higher, more important than the rest.

That has to be Judge Campbell's.

The room was filled with candles. The chandelier above the bed was lit. Megan heard the boy before she was able to see him on screen. He was crying. He looked to be twelve, maybe thirteen, but his whimpers made him sound like a toddler. He swayed back and forth, as if he were drugged or drunk. The leader of the group returned to his seat and removed his hood. His face was covered in a gothic-style black metal mask. The leader ordered the boy to his knees, and in front of each member seated, he was commanded to perform fellatio.

"Jesus Christ!" Megan put her hands up to her head. "You fucking bastards." She had to stand up and look away. Then a scream in the video made her turn back. The boy was being raped now, attacked by the leader while the camera closed in on his face. When his assault was complete, the leader took a candle and lit something. Megan couldn't tell what the object was. The footage was far too dark. The leader ordered the boy to go back on the bed, face down, while two other members held him still. The leader's actions were now in full sight. He was holding a metal rod, glowingly hot. He pressed it to the boy's lower back, just above his tailbone. The young boy wailed in agony.

"Fucking hell." Megan knew those screams would not leave her memory for a very long time, if ever.

She forced herself to watch the other videos. The violence varied from boy to boy. However, each boy's face could easily be seen, especially the tears and the annihilation of their youth.

Megan turned her computer off and sat numb until the walls of the room felt as though they were closing in, ready to crumble around her, pinning her down with the horrific scenes she'd just witnessed. She stood up, needing to steady herself for a moment before walking over to the sliding glass door. She didn't care how hard the snow was coming down. She didn't care how cold it was; she had to get out of the room, away from that computer and those videos. She fell to her knees on the cold deck, leaned forward, and sobbed until there was nothing left. During the last few months her tears were for different, more personal reasons. With what she'd just witnessed, after all her years on the force, not even her last case came close to this level of perversion.

They're so young, so innocent.

Megan let out a deep breath.

Not anymore they're not.

———

Megan took a long hot shower, a modest attempt to cleanse her mind of what she'd witnessed. Two Valiums and a glass of wine were needed to get even a minimal amount of sleep that night. As she double-checked the locks and the alarm on the lake house, she was pleased to see flashing lights at the judge's home.

"You're welcome, asshole."

When she woke, she donned leather gloves, cleaned her finger prints off the DVDs and their boxes, and found a padded brown envelope. All the while she tried to figure out the best way to forward the DVDs to the detectives. She'd checked the morning newspaper wondering if anything had been written regarding suspects in the judge's murder. Nothing, though there was still plenty commemorating the life of that sick bastard. *Which*, Megan thought, *is probably good news for Vivian, for now.* If they had arrested her, it would have received top headlines. She needed to get ready and find Callie, but her first mission was to rid Chez Mack of the grotesque sex tapes. She closed the brown envelope and addressed it to the Mount Arlington Town Police, Attention Detective Krause. She slapped on more than enough stamps to ensure it would arrive and threw the pouch on the passenger seat.

Megan started to drive to Lake Mohawk. Working off little sleep and thinking of the boys in the videos, she couldn't help but be distracted. She missed the turn she was supposed to take and found herself traveling toward Lake Hopatcong State Park. She was looking for a place to turn around when she saw the sign for the Lake Hopatcong Historical Museum. She wasn't about to take a museum tour, but the symbol embossed on the sign made her pull over. She took out her cell phone and opened the pictures application. The symbol from the robes Megan had photographed was an exact match for the symbol of the Lake Hopatcong Museum.

On the other hand, a quick tour might be a good idea.

The museum was a rustic white building more similar to homes on the lake than a museum. An older woman greeted Megan from behind a desk when she entered. The woman seemed happy to have company. She had a warm smile and wore a button-down sweater that had two turkeys embroidered on each side of the chest. Her nametag read HOPE.

Megan was counting on the sentiment of her name. She was near to her last drop of hope, especially after viewing the videos.

"Why, hello there."

Megan fumbled for words in the quiet environment. It's not as if she were preparing herself for loud crowds; this was not going to be an hour at the Metropolitan Museum of Art. There wouldn't be busloads of tourists being dropped off, clicking their cameras in every direction of the museum, or sightseers wearing black socks and Birkenstocks. She didn't need to worry about vacationers displaying confused looks as to what direction they needed to walk, or asking for directions with the kindness of a Rottweiler attacking a toddler. There would be no Manhattanites zigzagging around tourists attempting to decipher streets, bus stops, and subway stations on the maps of the city. No vendors here offered to draw your caricature or sell you *I ♥ New York City* t-shirts, artwork, and the occasional piece of jewelry.

Megan brought her voice down to a whisper. "I'm new to the area and just wanted to look around."

The museum guide stared at Megan strangely and looked around. "Why are you whispering, hon? We're the only ones here. Feel free to walk around."

Megan went to reach for cash. "What's the fee?"

"No charge, hon. It's free admission." She was so kind and had such a sweet temperament. Megan felt as though she was about to walk through another dungeon of secrets, but she was smart enough to know they were lies; this place appeared to be more of a shrine than a museum.

"I can give you a brief tour, if you like?" Hope asked, clearly wanting to have something to fill the next few minutes with rather than sit and pretend she was busy.

"That would be nice. I appreciate it. I do have a question or two," Megan continued. "The symbol on the front of your sign, it's unique. Is it the symbol of the town or something?"

Hope adopted a somber tone. "Oh, well." She crossed her arms. "I'm not sure how long you've been here, but there was a tragedy recently. A wonderful man in our community died suddenly."

Megan noticed Hope had looked away when the expression *died* was used. "Oh, I hadn't known. And it has to do with the symbol, how?"

"Well"—she pointed to a photo of a much younger Judge Campbell—"he paid for the whole museum, out of his own pocket. The only thing he asked was to place a family emblem on the museum's signs. It wasn't much of a request, when you think about it."

Family emblem, my ass. That's his fucking calling card. Son of a bitch.

Megan tolerated a few more minutes of history on the land, the lake, and local business, then she politely excused herself. But not without making a donation to the museum, for Hope's sake.

TWENTY-THREE

They had a translator for me while they searched my car. This fact didn't make it less confusing or startling. I could tell by the look on Callie and Ms. McGinn's face that something was wrong. The only thing I could think about was the man on the motorcycle, his hand around my mouth, unable to scream, and knowing I didn't know how to scream, or even what a scream sounded like.

I sat in the police station for a very long time. Mostly alone, but I knew I was being watched. I may be deaf, but there is closed captioning on television. I've seen the cop shows, which is why, even though I can't speak, I still remained silent. Some people consider this to be my curse. Now silence was my savior.

———

Megan parked in front of Krogh's. Sparta was preparing for the holiday season. Local merchants were decorating their windows. Men on ladders attached holiday lights to the trees overlooking

Lake Mohawk. She remembered a time when she loved the holidays. She, her brother Brendan, and their father would go to the Macy's Thanksgiving Day Parade. Her father would hoist her on his shoulders so she could see Santa when he waved to the crowd as he passed by. Afterward, there was a huge gathering for a Thanksgiving dinner with the McGinns and Murphys all together, but not this year. Three seats were empty at Thanksgiving and would be empty again at Christmas, and the reality of that gutted her.

Megan noticed a mailbox on the corner near Krogh's and dropped the package in. Good riddance. She couldn't get the videos out of her possession soon enough. She knew the brutal images of the assaults, the pure savageness of them, would stay with her forever.

Megan found Callie seated at the bar on his cell phone. He motioned for her to sit beside him and then waved down the bartender for drinks. He soon ended the call and gave Megan a kiss. "Thank you, and I'm sorry for what happened. Our argument."

She nodded, not wanting to say very much. "So, what's going on?"

"I found a lawyer, Phillip Thompson. He's good. Very good."

"That means expensive," Megan commented in a rather jaded tone, which didn't go unnoticed by Callie.

"He's a media whore. It's pro bono. Are you okay?"

"Where is Vivian now?"

"Why are you ignoring my question?"

Megan was anxious as well as exhausted and doing a poor job of masking her mood. "Is Vivian in custody?"

"No, they released her a few hours ago. I took her back to the gatehouse. They impounded her car to do a more thorough search; at least, I think that's why they did. Police were all over Campbell's house when we got back. Do you know why?"

Megan rubbed her forehead and thought aloud. "They didn't arrest her. They know they don't have enough evidence. What time did they release her?"

"What does that matter?"

"Callie, what time did they release her? Jesus Christ, just answer the fucking question!" she snapped at him. She didn't mean to, but she was feeling too much, thinking too much. "Sorry. I had a long night."

"I dropped Vivian at the gatehouse about three or four this morning. Why?"

Megan was hesitant, not wanting to relive what she'd witnessed on the videos. She leaned in close to Callie and barely whispered, "I searched through Campbell's house."

"You broke into his house?" Callie was shocked. "I never asked you to break laws, Trouble; I just wanted your contacts, your influence. What in hell made you do that?"

Megan shook her head. "Don't. Don't." She held up her hand. "You don't get a chance to lecture me or judge my actions. You haven't been where I've been." Megan knew she wasn't talking about Campbell's room when she made the statement; she meant the last six months of her life. "I found a room," she said, signaling for a second drink. "It was a secret room."

"Like a panic room?" Callie asked.

"Maybe for some." She knew it was poor form to say that and shook her head. "It was a—a sex room. It was disgusting."

"How do you know?"

Megan gave Callie a glare. "Callie, I'm not fucking stupid. Jesus, there were a bunch of sex toys and robes. Videos."

"What? Videos?" Callie finished his drink and ordered a second. "Megan, what are you telling me?"

She was just going to say it, hard and honest. "Campbell and others raped young boys. It was some kind of sex cult."

Callie swallowed hard. "You know there were videos? Did you watch them? What ... what happened?"

"It's brutal, and beyond disgusting. I took three out of his home."

"Oh my God. You *stole* things from a crime scene. What were you thinking?"

"They've been returned." Megan stared straight ahead when she answered. "And if you're suggesting I broke a law, think about what that man"—Megan pointed down at the newspaper on the bar, Judge Campbell's picture once again gracing the front page— "and his sick bastard friends did to those boys." She needed to change the course of the conversation. "So, Vivian is back home, for now. That's good. They didn't have enough to charge her, but it also means she's still in the line of fire, even with what the police have uncovered. When do you see this lawyer?"

"*We*. In one hour at Vivian's. We'll take my car since yours is so recognizable."

Neither Megan nor Callie were very hungry, but they needed to kill some of the alcohol in their systems. They ordered lunch to share. Megan couldn't help but state the obvious: "Callie, when all this comes out, this town is going to explode. You know that, right?"

His stare was vacant. "Yeah. How many videos were there?"

"What?" Megan was thrown by the question. "I don't know, why?"

"Do you think Vivian was in one?"

"No. It seemed to be just boys, very scared boys."

"While we were at the police station, I remembered thinking about her car, Vivian's car. She had it in the shop for service a few days ago. So someone else had access to it. What do you think?"

"Anything is possible. I mean, someone could have done it right here, outside the restaurant, but, yes, it's possible it happened at the garage." She turned to Callie. "Wait, why do I have the feeling you want me to somehow look into this garage?"

He squinted. "Didn't you mention that your engine light keeps coming on?" He stared down into his beer, waiting for her to get his shameful suggestion.

Megan ignored the coy attempt. "Where is the garage?"

"Right near Vivian's, around the corner. Actually it's on the way to your place."

"Does a woman run the shop, she pumps gas?"

"Yeah, her name is Lynn. She owns the place, and her son works in the shop."

"I stopped there when I first arrived."

"And you'll be stopping by again." He smiled, nudging her elbow. Then Callie noticed the time. "Let's go to Vivian's. I'm parked out back."

They walked through the kitchen and were nearly out the door when Megan glanced to her right and stopped dead. A burlap sack filled with vegetables was on the counter.

"What's the matter, Trouble, you've never seen vegetables before?"

TWENTY-FOUR

MEGAN WAS QUIET AS they drove to Vivian's to meet with the pro bono lawyer. Seeing the burlap bag in Callie's restaurant forced her to recall the incident on the dock. The memory ran in snapshot mode through her mind as she tried to piece together the event with the clarity she had when working a case. What was the most overpowering were the smells. The pungent smell of the sack, which she was now sure had most likely been filled with onions at some point. The smell of smoke. The cigarettes had dark tips, but there wasn't enough time to see the brand. There wasn't time for anything, except to survive the moment. Survive the moment, as she hoped the boys she witnessed in the sex videos had, though her experiences on the force made her think and know differently. Her gut, as it slowly returned to being the honed tracking device she relied on in her life, didn't leave much hope for those victims. *Still, there's a chance*, she thought to herself.

It was obvious the lawyer had already arrived, given the sleek black Porsche parked in Vivian's driveway. For every pro bono defense Phillip Thompson worked, he surely defended some very rich clients.

"I should have stayed in pre-law," Callie said with an air of jealousy.

"Is it too late for me to marry rich?" Megan asked, giving Callie a gentle elbow jab.

Callie smiled. "*I'd* marry this guy, are you kidding me?"

They rang the doorbell. The lights flickered. Vivian answered the door immediately, signing with Callie.

Phillip Thompson stood up from the couch in the living room. He was not at all what Megan expected. She presumed he'd be tall, cocky. Pitbull lawyers have a way of handling themselves. Megan had seen enough of them in the courtroom. She'd dared even to call some of them menacing—not in regard to their looks but their courthouse style. Phillip Thompson was on the short side, with dark hair and glasses. His eyes were close together with arched eyebrows. His countenance, to Megan, was very jackal-esque. Smart, with laser-sharp attention and ready to pounce on any weakness. In any other circumstance, Megan would have hated him. In this situation, she knew that if anything were to happen to Vivian, this was the kind of lawyer that would be needed.

"I'm Phillip Thompson. No need for your introduction, obviously," he directed toward Megan.

Fucking Oompa-Loompa, Megan thought. She disguised her reaction by biting her lip so hard she was going to morph into Angelina Jolie.

Callie looked Megan's way and mouthed, "Please, don't."

Phillip continued with his introductory speech. "Here is what we have so far, Callie. Would you please translate while I speak?" Phillip didn't wait for a response. "The good news is if they had any hard evidence on Vivian, she would have been arrested on the spot. Now, it doesn't mean they *don't* have anything. They could be holding on to information as they gather more evidence. I don't need to tell you that finding a knife in the trunk of her car goes against her."

"We think it was planted. A setup," Callie said.

"Vivian had her car in the shop for over twenty-four hours this week. Anyone could have had access to it to place the knife," Megan said in a monotone.

Phillip nodded. "I'll need the information on that, name of the garage, who worked on the car, how long it was there."

Vivian was signing back as fast as Callie was translating.

"She says she has all the paperwork of the work done on the car, but it's in the glove box of the car and the car is in the police impound lot. Is there a way to get to it?" Callie asked.

"The garage, I'm sure, has a copy of everything. I'd rather go that route than deal with the red tape to get into the car while in police custody. Small towns have a way of putting up roadblocks, especially in a case involving this particular *victim*."

It didn't take a cast-iron skillet to hit Megan over the head (though many perps she'd locked up over the years would have enjoyed the moment) to make it obvious there had been bad blood between Phillip Thompson and Judge Monty Campbell.

"I'm curious, Mr. Thompson." She noted he didn't ask her to refer to him as Phillip. "Why take on this case? How did Campbell cross you?"

He offered a respectful nod and an ominous smile. "Let's say Judge Campbell impeded certain employment opportunities I was overtly qualified for, and leave it at that."

Megan possessed many attributes—some conflicting and dark, some clear as a crystal vase—but being wrong was usually not one of them. She smiled, gaining another inch in the direction of reclaiming a piece of her broken self.

Broken, not shattered, she reminded herself.

Vivian's signing became faster, so fast Callie had a hard time keeping up with her.

"What is she saying?" Megan asked.

Callie asked Vivian to slow down when Thompson interrupted, "Wait, let's start from the beginning. I need to know everything."

Megan went to get Vivian a glass of water when she caught a glimpse of a photo on the refrigerator. Vivian and her mother were in a boat on Lake Hopatcong. They both had huge smiles. Her mother had her arms wrapped around Vivian. It was obvious Vivian gained all of her good looks from her mother. They shared the same smile, the same glow. She thought back to the photos of her and her own mother, Rose. There weren't many, but the few Megan had meant the world to her, especially now with Rose gone. Photos were the only things remaining, some good memories too. As with the pictures, those were few and far between as well.

Megan looked through the kitchen window at the judge's house and the only thought she could come up with was how impossible it was to think that Vivian's mother would kill herself and leave Vivian with such a monster.

I'm only scratching the surface, Megan thought to herself.

Megan returned to the living room with the water as Thompson began his questioning. He started with the last time Vivian saw the judge. She hesitated signing, and Callie prompted her to answer.

"She's holding back. Callie, tell her we have to know everything," Megan urged.

Callie spoke through each word he signed. He told her it was safe to tell everyone in the room everything, that they were all there to help her. She was still hesitant when Megan picked up one of the framed photos on the coffee table. Pointing at her mother's photo, she mouthed, "Do it for her. Your mother."

"That's a little harsh, don't you think?" Callie snapped at Megan.

Thompson intervened. "No, it's not. She's holding back something. I can't do my job unless we have all of her information, so, no, it's not too harsh."

Vivian stared at her mother's photo, then leaned forward and took it out of Megan's hand. She held it in her lap as she began signing with Callie. She told them of the night she woke up and saw the judge in the great room having an argument with someone. How there was some kind of fight where the glasses were thrown against the window. Vivian abruptly stopped signing, clearly wrestling with the next part.

"Callie, she's hedging." Megan looked at Vivian and mouthed, "It's okay."

Vivian's demeanor suddenly took on that of a wounded doe. She was truly scared, bordering on shamed. Vivian took a steadying breath and told them about entering the house and going into the great room, seeing her father dead on the floor with a knife sticking out of his chest. How he had wounds everywhere. His throat was slashed, his arms were cut, and the knife rested deep inside his loveless heart.

Megan, Callie, and Thompson thought they'd heard everything until Vivian began signing again, explaining that she took the knife out of the judge and plunged it back in. Megan turned away, knowing exactly how bad this was. "Fuck."

Thompson rubbed his forehead and shook his head.

"I don't understand," Callie shouted. "He was already dead! She did this out of anger. He was terrible to her. This should be good news. Vivian didn't murder him." Callie searched Megan's and Thompson's expressions for vindication only to find distressed reactions to Vivian's admission.

Megan spoke in an even tone to a situation that was less than tranquil. "Callie, her prints will most likely be found on the knife when Forensics comes back."

"But he was dead. She said he was already dead when she went into the room." Callie signed to Vivian asking her for the second time if the judge was dead when she entered the great room, and for a second time she answered yes.

"See?"

"I'm sure he *was* dead, but there's really no way for us to prove that in a situation like this," Thompson said.

Callie was starting to unravel. "Okay, then answer me this. How could Vivian move the body some six hundred yards to throw in the lake?" He shrugged his shoulders in bewilderment of Megan and Thompson's lack of enthusiasm toward this obvious obstacle in the case against Vivian.

Vivian was exceptional at reading lips, and even if she weren't, the expressions before her pretty much read like instructions for Things Not To Do at a Crime Scene. She signed she was sorry.

Callie asked Thompson, "So, what do we do now?"

"I would suggest going back to the police and admitting she was in the house and did this. Ms. McGinn is correct. They will find her prints, and then it could get very bad. Was she able to see who was in the house with Campbell? Any description at all?"

Vivian shook her head no.

"Okay, then. We should go. You have somewhere else to go, I believe," Callie said to Megan.

"Wait, Mr. Thompson. There is something else you could use for leverage," Megan suggested.

"What would that be?" He started to pack up his briefcase.

"Judge Campbell was, I believe, in charge of a sex ring. A pedophile sex ring."

"What?! How do you know this? Wait! Don't answer that; otherwise I'm required to answer if I'm asked how I know."

"There were videos of the assaults in a secret room in the judge's house. The police have them. They know," Megan answered.

He shook his head. "This is going to be a nightmare, but you are right. I can use this information to my advantage. Who else knows?"

"I do," Callie answered.

"Does Vivian know about this secret room?"

Callie asked, and she answered no and added that she was never allowed in that part of the house.

TWENTY-FIVE

Megan pulled into the garage. Lynn had just finished filling a car when she got out.

"Well, hello again," Lynn said with a smile.

"Hi, there."

"Need more gas for that tank of yours?"

"Actually, no, not yet anyway. My engine light has been going on and off and I wondered if your son could take a look at it."

"Do you want to leave it?"

"I'll wait if that's okay. It's my only source of transportation, so ..."

Lynn nodded. "Okay. Let me go get him. Could you pull up into the garage for me?"

Megan pulled the Range Rover into the garage, nearly hitting a motorcycle.

"This is my son, Duane. Duane this is—it's Megan, right?"

Now who's the bull-shitter? Everyone in town knows my name.

She nodded while Duane used a rag to clean off his hand before shaking hers. "Pleasure."

"Duane, Megan's engine light is going on and off. Can you run it through the sensor codes on the computer?"

He was tall, with dark hair that could use a haircut. Both arms were covered in tattoos. Each finger also inked. Megan knew it was code for a motorcycle gang. He was hardly the clean-cut type. He wore a white t-shirt under a black vest and a chain hung from one pocket. He stared at her with an intensity that would make most people feel uncomfortable, but not Megan. She returned it.

"Thanks."

"Can you pop the hood for me?"

Megan did so as he lit a cigarette. Same look as the butts she found on the dock.

Interesting, but hardly proof. In the short time she'd been in Mount Arlington, it seemed everyone she met was a smoker.

Megan pointed over to the motorcycle. "I guess that's yours."

"Yep."

Big conversationalist. She looked around the garage. A huge ashtray filled with butts was on a desk, and dirty windows looked out onto Howard Boulevard.

"I thought I was going to knock it over when I drove in."

He spoke over the cigarette dangling from his mouth. "Well, then I guess I'd have to kill you."

"Hasn't there been enough of that going around here lately?"

"Yep."

"A neighbor friend said you just worked on her car recently, so that's why I came here."

"Who?"

"Vivian Campbell. She had to leave it overnight, I think?"

"You ask a lot of questions."

Megan's next thought was that this guy has been interrogated more than once. He knew not to say much.

Duane went to turn over the engine. "No light is on."

"Maybe you fixed it," Megan answered.

"I didn't do anything. You might have an intermittent short in your sensor light."

The icy stare prompted Megan to try another route. "I bet you saw all the action the other day being as your garage is directly across from where Judge Campbell was pulled out."

"Didn't much care. I try to stay away from cops. And detectives."

"Guess that's why you've taken such a shine to me."

He closed the hood. "Guess so."

Dead end. "Well, then how much do I owe you?"

"Nothin'."

"What about labor?"

"Told ya, I didn't do anything."

"Thank you anyway."

"If the light actually does come on, you can bring her back. Can't figure out what's wrong if the light's not on."

She nodded and slowly backed out of the garage because she had a strong sense he wasn't joking about killing her if she hit his motorcycle. Megan sent Callie a text: NOTHING FROM THE GARAGE. CALL WHEN YOU GET A CHANCE.

————

Megan went back home, played with Clyde in the snow, and then attempted to relax in front of the fire, only to find she was failing miserably. She wondered when the videos, the secret room, and

155

the judge's dirty little secrets would hit the news. She knew it would get leaked somehow, and if Phillip Thompson was as good as he thought he was, he'd use it as leverage during Vivian's disclosure of stabbing a dead man.

Her cell rang as she was pouring a drink.

"Hey, it's Callie."

"So, what happened? They had an interpreter there, right?"

"Yeah, Thompson went through the whole story about Vivian being in the house. As slick as he is, he diverted them to the fact he knew about the tapes and the room. They knew they'd lost some of their footing. For now she's not being arrested."

"What about the prints?"

"Nothing has come back yet."

"It shouldn't be taking this long. They're either not finding anything or they're building a case."

"How can they build a case after all the sick shit they found?"

"You'd be amazed what cops can do." Megan hated admitting it, but during her time before going on a leave of absence, she knew cops in her department who played that game—and not always with clean cards.

"Trouble, the news is going to be interesting tonight. I watched the press interview Thompson outside the station."

"I'll look for it."

"You won't have any problem finding it."

TWENTY-SIX

MEGAN MOVED INTO THE television room to search for the latest news, and Callie was right. She had no problem finding the breaking news story about Judge Campbell. It was splashed on virtually every channel. Phillip Thompson stood outside of the police station with countless microphones shoved in his face and was as calm as if he were born to be there. He was bombarded with one question after another. He chose to make a statement that he was representing Vivian Campbell. Vivian had not been arrested and he was certain she would not be. Due to lewd materials found in Judge Campbell's secret sex dungeon involving young boys, he felt confident the case had now gone in a different direction. He went on to disclose it was an anonymous tip that led to the videos to be found by the police and was certain they would make that their number-one priority rather than harass a young deaf woman for a crime she was obviously innocent of. Afterward he walked Vivian to his car and they drove off.

"I hope you're right, Mr. Thompson. There is still something nagging at me with this. I can't put my finger on it."

Megan witnessed countless miscarriages of justice on the job, so it made her uneasy. That troubling feeling just wouldn't go away. She turned the television off when her cell phone rang. Leigh from down the street was calling.

"Hi Leigh, what's up?"

"I just thought you'd want to know. There's an ambulance at Billie's house. Something has happened. She's being taken over to the hospital Jo works at. It looks bad. Her mother and boyfriend are with the police as we speak. I don't know what happened."

"I bet I do." *Another drunk boyfriend and too much booze.* "Tell me the name of the hospital again?"

Leigh told her the name and Megan answered, "I'll go over now. Is Jo working emergency tonight?"

"No, she has back to back surgeries. I would go with you but—"

"No, no. Don't worry. I'll let you know what I find out."

———

The last time Megan had rushed to a hospital, it was for her mother. The feeling didn't seem much different. The adrenaline rush, the hope that things aren't as bad as every terrible thought running through your mind. The nurse directed her to where Billie was in the emergency room. When she pulled back the curtain, her fears were confirmed. Billie had bruises on her eye and lip, and a cut on her forehead. They were stitching up one arm. A soft cast was on one leg.

The busy doctor asked who she was.

"I'm her neighbor. Her mother had to speak with the police and asked me to come."

"We're prepping her for tests to make sure there wasn't any internal damage. I'll be back to get her soon. We just gave her morphine for the pain, so she'll become groggy in a few minutes."

"Thank you." Megan closed the curtain. "So, kiddo, how does the other guy look?"

"How did you find out?"

"Leigh called me."

"And you came down here just for me?"

Megan moved Billie's hair away from her forehead. "Of course. You're my favorite bratty teenage neighbor. Why don't you tell me what happened."

"They were drunk again. Fighting. He slapped her. I got in between them and he pushed me down the stairs." Billie welled up with emotion. "I should have come down to your house. I could feel this time was going to be bad."

"He did this to you before pushing you?" Megan moved her chin slightly. "Those didn't all come from a fall."

"Mom tried to stop him, she did … try. Where is she?"

"She's at home speaking to the police. Do you want me to call your aunt? She'd want to know."

Billie nodded yes and put her hand over Megan's. "Thank you, Det-Megan."

Megan smiled remembering that when she first met Billie, she'd come close to calling herself *Detective Megan McGinn,* and Billie had joked with her about it. "You're welcome, IRS."

Billie slowly fell off to sleep before the doctor returned. "She'll be asleep for some time, probably until tomorrow."

"Is there a social worker available? I need to give them information to call next of kin." Megan was certainly not making that phone call herself. She'd delivered enough bad news for one life-time and wasn't keen to do so regarding Billie. She couldn't help it. She knew Billie was a good kid, even with the wiseass attitude, and she didn't deserve this horrible treatment.

———

Megan sat in her truck for a few minutes, staring out at the hospi-tal parking lot and thinking too many thoughts about Billie, about her recent past. Her own mistakes, her regrets. "Someday, things will go right again. I hope."

She surprised herself by using the word *hope*. She'd lost so much of it within the last year—perhaps there was still some left, some-where. If there was, it was buried deep, deep down inside.

Callie had sent a text asking her to dinner. She declined. Megan wanted the evening to herself, under a warm blanket with Clyde asleep at her side.

TWENTY-SEVEN

Not surprisingly Megan fell asleep on the couch in front of the fire. What was shocking was that she didn't have any nightmares, and actually was able to get restful, quality sleep, which hadn't happened in a long time. Her morning coffee was brewing when she went to check for the paper, but there wasn't one. She checked the local paper online and it was covered with information on Judge Campbell's atrocities.

"The tide has turned for you, asshole." She lifted her mug to the screen in a cheers. "So much for a positive legacy now."

She turned on her cell. While waiting for a signal, she put the morning news on and was shocked to see a different headline. Mount Arlington's mayor had shot himself in the head in the middle of the night. Megan knew it wasn't a coincidence. "Looks like someone was afraid of what was actually on those tapes." She threw some clothes on and did a search for the mayor's home address. "C'mon Clyde, we're going for a quick drive."

When they arrived at the address Megan had found online, a mere three minutes from her current residence, there were plenty of news vans parked outside the home. But what was also outside above the front door was the symbol from the robes in Campbell's basement, the same one on the sign of the museum.

"I knew it. I wonder if that gunshot was really self-inflicted."

Callie called her as she sat there watching the melee. "Hey, your phone was off all night. Is everything okay?"

Megan placed her Bluetooth earpiece on before driving away from the mob scene. "Crazy news this morning. Did you see it?"

"Yeah, I saw it. What do you think?" Callie asked.

"Well, I'm thinking two things. One, he was obviously connected to the men on the tape. What, the guy was late fifties or sixties? He wasn't a victim, he was an abuser."

"And the second?" Callie asked.

"I'm not so sure he killed himself."

"What would make you say that? Of course he did. He knew he was about to get caught, so he offed himself!"

"Callie, in the tapes I watched, you couldn't see the abuser's faces, only hear some of their voices."

"Sorry, Trouble, I'm not agreeing with you on this one."

"Time will tell. Time will tell." Megan's phone beeped. She glanced down at the phone. "I need to take this call, Callie. I'll get back to you."

"Wait—"

Megan clicked over. "Hey, Leigh. Any news?"

"Jo just got home, but she checked on Billie before leaving."

"How is she?"

"Out of it. Jo said Billie will be in the hospital for at least a week, if not more. But she'll make a full recovery."

"Good. Good." Megan was extremely relieved to hear the news. "And the mother? Arrested? Boyfriend arrested?"

"The boyfriend was arrested for assault and battery. The mother has chosen to go to rehab."

"That surprises me, but I'm glad."

"Her aunt is coming today and will stay with her while her mother is away."

"Thanks for calling. Let's hope it works out for both of them." Megan earnestly felt that way.

Maybe that kid will have a chance now.

"Okay, Clyde, time to go back to the house."

———

Megan pulled up to the lake house to find three other cars in front of her garage. She parked and saw fifteen people, at the very least, walking around the deck of the home. She was far from startled because she recognized all their faces.

"Meganator!" Uncle Mike shouted up the driveway wearing the Irish Donegal tweed cap Megan had bought for him only months earlier. Her father's retired Homicide partner and best friend, Michael Murphy, his wife Maureen, and their whole clan were closer to her than most families.

Megan shouted back, "I'll be right down." She couldn't help but notice they each were carrying either a tray or a bowl of some sort, but she had a feeling what they were up to. Uncle Mike got the first hug, then Aunt Maureen. All their kids and their grandchildren followed.

Megan smiled. "What's all this?"

Aunt Maureen chimed in first. "We knew you wouldn't come home for Christmas so an early Christmas has come to you. I hope that's all right."

She was a little overwhelmed but at the same time happy. "Of course. Here, let me open up the house."

One of the grandkids yelled, "Look Grampie, Aunt Meggie got a dog!"

"I see that." Then he mouthed, "You got a dog?" followed by his Irish grin and hearty laugh.

As soon as the Murphys walked in, the usual comments flew out on how beautiful the home was and how spectacular the view was. One comment made by one of the grandchildren made Megan laugh. It was when Joseph blurted, "Oh shit!"

Aunt Maureen corrected that language promptly. "Joseph, more words like that and no turkey." She turned to Megan. "Everything has been cooked and only needs to be reheated."

"Easy enough, I have two ovens." Megan pointed to the back wall.

"Michael Murphy, why do I not have two ovens?" Maureen demanded.

"Because we don't own this lake house!" He opened a box of countless bottles of wine and took out a bottle of Irish whiskey. "Let's pour us a few glasses, Meganator, and you can show me that boathouse." He wanted time to chat Megan up while the kids roamed the house and played with Clyde and the adults set up the tables.

Uncle Mike's eldest son, Michael Jr., yelled for Megan. "Megs, where is the wood for the fireplace?"

"There isn't any, just flick the switch on the side."

Uncle Mike was pouring a glass when the doorbell rang.

Oh great. That better not be the New Jersey detectives, Megan thought to herself.

Aunt Maureen acted suspiciously as if she hadn't heard a thing. Then Megan caught on. "Do you know who is at the door, Aunt Maureen?"

Aunt Maureen didn't look up, answering, "I guess you better see who it is."

Detective Sam Nappa stood at the door with flowers and a dessert. "Hi, partner. Happy early Christmas." He walked in and whispered in Megan's ear, "They made me come. Nearly *threatened* me if I didn't come." A handsome smile followed.

Megan smiled. "It's okay. Get in here. Uncle Mike and I are about to go down to the boathouse to have a drink. Come on."

Uncle Mike, in a rather theatrical tone, said, "Detective Nappa, what a surprise! It's so good to see you. Come join us."

Surprised my lily-white Irish ass. But Megan just rolled her eyes.

They strolled down to the boathouse while Uncle Mike was taking in the view. "Very nice, Meganator, even in winter."

"From what some of the neighbors have said, winter hasn't really started yet, so …"

The three sat in the chairs at the end of the dock and there was the small talk about the children and grandkids. Then Uncle Mike commented, "For a winter respite, you sure did choose a hell of a place, what with that big murder investigation going on." He took a sip of the whiskey. "So, tell me about it."

"I just read what you've read or seen on the news." Megan used to be terrible lying to her father, and now she was terrible at lying to Uncle Mike and Nappa, but it seemed anyone else was fair game.

"Liar."

"It's bad, really—" Megan was about to finish the sentence when one of Uncle Mike's grandsons yelled from the yard.

"Can I come out on the dock?"

In unison all three yelled back, "No."

"Talk to me. To us," Uncle Mike said.

"I wasn't even here a week, and one morning I see police tape over there," Megan said and pointed to Great Cove. "That large white mansion is—was—his. They pulled Judge Campbell out of the lake. He'd been stabbed. An ice fisherman found him."

Uncle Mike interrupted. "I played poker with some buddies a few nights ago and one of them who once worked in New Jersey said he was a bastard."

"Well, the detectives in this town aren't the sharpest. They've been trying to pin it on his estranged deaf daughter, who can't be more than a hundred pounds soaking wet."

Nappa chimed in, "How does someone that small kill Campbell and bring his body down that hill to the lake? Unless she wasn't working alone."

Megan didn't like Nappa's last comment and went on, speaking directly to Uncle Mike. "I ran into an old friend from college here. He owns a restaurant on a nearby lake and Vivian—that's the estranged daughter—she works for him, and he asked me if I could help. Just doing some investigation."

Nappa made an obvious roll of his eyes and added, "Uh-huh. *That's* all it is."

Uncle Mike looked back and forth between the two partners. "I'll skip this part."

"Thank you." Megan gave Nappa a glance. "Anyhow, I had a slip down the driveway and when I got up, there were flashlights roaming around the pitch-black house. Same thing the next night, so I went over to check it out."

"Oh Lord help us. I'm not sure I like where this is going," Uncle Mike said. "Please tell me you didn't break into the house."

Silence is golden sometimes.

"You're just like your father, Meganator."

"Wait, wait. Hear me out. The house was immaculate, which was the first tip. Then I went into the basement. I could feel there was something *off*. So then I moved into the gun room, and I found a secret room—but it was more than a room. A large bed was in the middle with cameras and chairs facing the bed."

Nappa interrupted. "A sex room."

Uncle Mike shook his head. "I know all of us, and God rest your father's soul, we've all seen terrible things on the job, but that has to be the worst thing ever."

"There were these robes with a symbol on them. Like a family crest, but I've come to learn—"

"I bet it was a symbol to let others know they were into this kinky crap," Nappa said.

"One more thing, a big thing. There were all these videos. I watched three and I can't, and don't even *want*, to describe what I saw. The worst part? They branded the boys like cattle, as a sign he's been 'had' by the members of the sex cult. It was on their backs. Their screams were—" Megan shook her head. "It was horrific."

"What I read in the paper today about the mayor killing himself—did he have that symbol anywhere?"

"Yes, outside of his house. I went over and checked this morning. Let me go back a little bit. Before I left Campbell's, I took a few of the videos. Then I left the door open to the secret room, dialed

911, and left the line off the hook so it could be traced. I mailed the videos to the police the next day."

"That is the only part to this story you were smart with. You don't have jurisdiction here. And Nappa told me about what happened in the boathouse." Uncle Mike pointed his index finger her way. "Someone knows you're snooping around. As your father would say, watch your back."

Nappa excused himself. "I'm going to see if they need help in the kitchen. Another drink, anyone?"

Uncle Mike handed him his glass. "After that story, I need one, thanks." He stared out at the cold, mostly frozen over lake. Now that they were alone, it was time to switch gears. "How are you otherwise?"

Megan answered honestly, "Some nightmares. Starting to sleep a little bit better, but I miss Dad and Mom." She took a small swig from her glass.

"What happened to your mom, it wasn't your fault."

She turned her head suddenly. "Yes, it was. I just didn't see it coming."

"You were searching for a killer. You were doing your job."

"Not well, obviously." She offered a wry, self-mocking smile.

Uncle Mike tapped her knee. "You made the right decision to take some time off to clear your head. Though I'm not sure if what you've gotten yourself into is clearing your head, but maybe that's what you need right now."

"To clear my conscience?"

"No, to remind yourself you are a damn good detective. None of the local stooges passing for police around here found that room, did they?"

She shook her head. "Nope."

168

"Well, there you go. Now, let's get up to the house. I'm freezing my butt off and I'm hungry!"

———

It was like old times for Megan, sharing a large dinner with the Murphys, with the exception of the most obvious: her parents not being there. Lots of food, five conversations going on at once, embarrassing childhood stories being told. Megan felt good on the outside and yet there was an impenetrable level of guilt on the inside. She wasn't sure if it was just because she didn't feel closure yet (and she wondered if she ever would) or due to the very distinct memory of viewing the video of the boys being violated. Either way, she wouldn't insult the Murphys by acting down or different than she was in the past. They all put so much effort into coming out to see her, check in on her. Megan may have laughed a little too loud at some conversations, hoping to cover up the difficult time she'd been through, but they were family and family knows. Aunt Maureen caught Megan staring off once or twice and fixed that by piling more food on her plate—a nice medicinal option for the soul, although not necessarily for the body. It was a bandage for her spirit, if only for a few hours.

Aunt Maureen began to clean up the table, to which Megan immediately protested. "No, I won't have it. You brought everything. Nappa and I will clean up. I'll start by putting a pot of coffee on."

"Absolutely," added Nappa.

Megan and Nappa began loading the dishwasher and hand-washing the wineglasses. Standing side by side always felt comfortable for both of them.

"So you knew about this visit all along?" Megan asked.

"What do you think?" He laughed. "You seemed like yourself again. It was good to see." He didn't look at her when he said it.

"In some ways. I'm not sure how long it will last, but the past few hours were good, really nice."

"It's going to take time. I noticed the letter I brought from Mrs. McAllister on the mantel. It hasn't been opened yet." Nappa had whispered his observation.

Megan paused before answering. "Not yet. It's too soon."

He nodded. "I understand. Back in Narcotics I had a father of a dead son send me a note. The kid wasn't doing or dealing drugs. He got caught in the crossfire, needlessly gunned down."

"Why the reason for the note?"

Nappa placed the last wineglass on the drying tray. "I held him. He passed away in my arms. His father thanked me for not letting him die alone."

Silence dominated the conversation until Megan said, "A terrible part of the job."

Uncle Mike shouted over, "Meganator, how's that coffee doing?" He could probably tell Megan and Nappa were getting serious in conversation and wanted to keep the light mood rolling, especially after their conversation down on the dock earlier.

"On the way."

The Murphys and Nappa didn't stay much longer after coffee. It was a good hour back to Brooklyn, not taking into account there could be NFL football traffic en route. It was back to the twenty hugs for a goodbye. Uncle Mike donned his Irish cap again.

"That looks good on you. I knew I picked out a good present."

"I know." Uncle Mike turned to walk out, then stopped. "Meganator?"

"Yeah?"

He threw a shiny coin at her. Of course she caught it. Turned it over in her palm to inspect what it said.

"It's a blessed Irish coin. Carry it with you."

"Thank you."

He smiled, although to Megan it looked like more of a concerned look, the kind her father would give her from time to time. "You're welcome."

TWENTY-EIGHT

Megan was nearly done with the cleanup from the Murphys' visit when there was a knock at the door. It was Callie. When he walked in, he commented, "It smells great in here."

"Family from the city surprised me with an early Christmas dinner. There are a ton of leftovers. I'll make you a plate."

He waved it off. "No, no don't go to the trouble, Trouble. I'm around food all day."

Megan stopped clearing and gave him a look as if to say, *Are you fucking kidding me?*

"Well, I don't want to be rude."

"Uh-huh."

"I'll eat at the counter and watch you play domestic goddess and keep you company." Callie looked tired, run-down.

"Are you feeling okay?" Megan asked after several minutes.

He was finishing a mouth full of food. "Tired. Between every-thing with Vivian and the restaurant and your big mouth," he grinned, "I guess I could use a good night's sleep." He paused, frustrated. He moved his fork in the air as he spoke. "Plus, I still can't understand why you think the mayor didn't kill himself. It seems so obvious to me." He sipped his wine waiting for an answer.

"Maybe he did, maybe he didn't. It's just a feeling. They'll run tests and I'm sure you're probably right."

"You get a lot of gut feelings. What does your gut say about me staying over tonight?"

"Right now, I'm stuffed." Megan threw a few pieces of turkey Clyde's way. He managed to catch both in mid-air.

"You're avoiding answering."

Megan was avoiding. Sometimes sex complicated things, and with Nappa being here recently, she felt as though she were cheating somehow.

"Hold on. I know what's going on here. One of your guests tonight was your detective partner from the city! Mr. I Just Walked Off the Cover of *GQ* magazine." He pointed his fork at her. "Am I right? Yeah. I'm right."

Megan refused to answer. "Are you done? Next topic." She started to wipe down the counters. "How is Vivian doing?"

"So so. She's lost a few massage clients over this fiasco so I'm trying to find more hours at the restaurant for her, but then reporters come in and bother the clientele."

"That's too bad."

Callie shrugged his shoulders. "It will pick up again once this blows over." He stopped and became more serious. "Do you think Vivian is off the police's radar or are they still gunning for her? Maybe she shouldn't have admitted going into Campbell's house. I don't know if it was the best idea."

"You said Thompson was good, one of the best. He enjoyed the camera, that was obvious. I don't think he would have made a decision that ultimately would reflect badly on him." But Megan had a worried look.

"What's the matter?"

"I'm just concerned about Detective Krause. Her head is in a different place. This is all about her career."

Callie stared at Megan, hesitant to ask, yet he still crossed the line. "And you? Were you ever like that?"

Megan didn't like the question, and it was obvious by her glare and cold silence.

"No, it's just a question. Don't take it the wrong way." He knew he'd just made a big mistake. "I'm sorry. Okay? I'm sorry. I wasn't thinking."

"No, you weren't." Megan threw the rag down on the counter and walked out of the kitchen.

Callie knew as soon as the question came out of his mouth that it was the wrong thing to say, to insinuate she was anything less than professional. "Damn it." He followed Megan into the bedroom finding her lying on the bed facedown, staring at her parents' picture on her nightstand.

"I never thought about my career like that." Megan didn't say it in a pouty way. It was more reflective. "In the beginning, because I'm Pat McGinn's daughter, it was more important to be a clean cop. Do the right thing, prove myself."

"I know, I shouldn't have said it." Callie stroked her hair. "I'm sorry."

"You can't imagine the things I've seen. The horrific ways some people hurt one another."

"Worse than the videos you watched?"

"My last case was. It wasn't the same kind of violence but, yes, it was really, really bad."

"What happened?"

"Haven't you picked up a newspaper in the last month or two? I'm not going to talk about it."

Callie surely knew most of the details from Megan's last case. It was all over the news, but his curiosity got the better of him. He wanted to know how Megan got pulled in, but it was quite clear she would not speak of it. Callie put his hand up the back of her shirt, not in a flirtatious manner, just to rub her back. He knew he'd upset her and he remembered it was one act that relaxed her.

Megan began to fade into sleep while staring at the picture of her parents. Early Christmas cheer was now over.

———

They'd fallen asleep on top of the blanket fully dressed, and both stirred around the same time thanks to Clyde whimpering to go out.

"I have an idea," Callie said rubbing his tired eyes. "Why don't we take a few hours. I'll call Jake Norden over at his marina and see if we can borrow two of his snowmobiles. We can go snowmobiling on the lake, maybe get some lunch after. We can have a little time off."

The thought of downtime interested Megan. It was the main reason she came to Lake Hopatcong, but the word *we* slightly annoyed her. She didn't want to be a *we* with anyone right now, and when she was a *we*, she was terrible at it. Relationships never came easily. She'd find a way to screw them up or let her job get in the way. Or the guy would be a jerk and she'd end up feeling guilty somehow. Who the hell needed that? Then she thought Callie was being nice to try to make up for what he said last night and said, "I guess so. Why don't you make some coffee, contact Norden while I take Clyde for a walk."

Megan made it down to Leigh's house with Clyde and was happy to see she was out as well walking Lady Sadie. She looked stronger than the last time they'd met up. "Morning, Leigh." Megan needed to pull Clyde back from Sadie before asking. "How is everything?"

"Well, Billie is more alert today from what Jo said. I was just going to head down to her house and see if her aunt needs anything, give her our number and whatever."

Megan couldn't believe she hadn't thought of Billie's situation since the previous day. Slightly embarrassed, she offered, "I'll go see her again soon."

"I noticed you had quite the crowd yesterday."

"Family came with an early Christmas dinner."

"You're welcome to join us this year if you like."

Megan rubbed her belly. "Oh, I appreciate that, but one Christmas is enough for me. Thanks anyway. I need to head back. I'm getting ready to go snowmobiling on the lake."

Leigh went wide-eyed. "You're brave! Stay away from the boathouses and be careful of the bridges." Now Megan's eyes went wide. "Oh, I don't mean to make you nervous. It really is a lot fun." Leigh looked up at the sky. "Gray clouds rolling in. Hope no flurries today."

"Hope not. See you soon. Oh, and Leigh—you look better today, much stronger."

"Today is a good day."

Megan walked back with Clyde and thought about Leigh's fight with cancer, her own fight with loss, and reminded herself what her grandfather would say: "We all have our crosses to carry, Megs." She was pulled out of the memory when Clyde stopped and stared into the woods. He wasn't growling, but he was extremely focused on an object. Megan rubbed his neck. "What is it boy? What's wrong?" She scanned the area Clyde was centering on. Positioned on a large branch was the hawk she'd seen previously. Megan couldn't figure out why Clyde wasn't barking. After all, the dog barked at wind or dead leaves blowing. "You're okay boy, let's go." As they resumed walking, Clyde continued to stare back at the creature until it took flight over one of the homes and went out of sight.

———

Megan and Callie pulled up to Norden's Marina. Callie explained he'd gotten in touch with him. Jake was in the middle of teaching winter ski lessons about an hour away and said it was no problem to use his snowmobiles.

"Jake said all the gear is in the garage." Callie knew the combination to the home alarm system. They geared up, helmets and all. "Have you ever been on one of these before?" Callie asked patting the seat of the snowmobile.

"Yes, but never on a frozen lake." Megan adjusted her helmet.

"It's pretty similar, a little slicker but not really all that different. Two rules: One is you stay away from the boathouses. Don't get too close. Even though it's daytime some people don't have their bubbler systems on, so the water looks like it's frozen over. And second, don't go all cowboy on my ass and get up to a speed like Taz."

"Who?" Megan had no clue what he was talking about.

"The Tasmanian Devil. From the cartoon?"

"Sure, whatever ... "

They pulled away from the marina going a moderate speed at first, then Callie made the play of racing her to the other parts of Lake Hopatcong, stopping in different spots to give her a bit of a tour. First was the lake house Megan was staying in. She got a kick out of seeing the house from the middle of the lake until she thought about the water pulsating under the more than foot-thick ice. She immediately darted forward and Callie raced to catch up. When they were going around a bend, Megan slowed and asked Callie where they were.

"That's Bertrand Island, though it's not technically an island. It's where the mayor lived. Years and years ago there was an amusement park built there, but they tore it down in the eighties."

"Let's go!" Megan had to admit she was enjoying the change of scenery and the activity. It was a distraction that she needed, not to mention she enjoyed the speed. They covered half the lake with Callie showing Megan the state park, the country clubs, and some of the lakeside restaurants.

After a while, Callie motioned to Megan to check her gas level. She did and it was fine. He pulled alongside her. "Mine is really low. You hang and keep going. I'm going back to fill up."

"I'll follow you back."

"Nah, you're having fun and it won't take me long."

"Are you sure?" Megan wasn't nervous going alone; she was worried he'd run out before he got to refill his tank.

"Yeah, just remember the rules I told you."

"I'm going to go play ice tourist." Megan remembered she'd seen two large islands—Raccoon Island and Halsey Island—on a map of the lake in the Macks' home, so she went north to find them. The homes there were more what she expected from a lake house, given they were on islands. She was sure not many people were year-round residents unless they snowmobiled to work. She was circling around the first island when another snowmobiler appeared directly in front of her. The rider wasn't moving, but his engine was idling. Megan slowed to avoid colliding with the rider. With the dark-shaded helmet, it was difficult to tell whether the rider was male or female. A few seconds later, the rider revved up the engine and charged her like a bull toward a matador.

"Jesus Christ!" Megan swerved and gassed it, going at top speed and nearly losing control of the snowmobile. The snowmobiler came up beside her, inches away from her. The move forced Megan to the right.

Don't go near the boathouses, don't go near the boathouses continued to echo through her mind as she fought to maintain control.

The other rider slammed into her once and she swerved just a few feet from a boathouse with open water. The only solution she could think of was to brake hard, fast. She wasn't sure this was the smartest moved when it propelled her into a three-sixty on the ice. The engine seized up. She struggled to remain upright as she slowed to a stop in the sudden silence. Megan looked around, but the other rider was gone.

"What the fuck?" She focused on restarting the snowmobile when she heard the other sled. Out of the corner of her eye, the other rider reemerged, circling her like a shark.

"Come on baby, start. Start, damn it!" Megan pleaded.

Still nothing.

The other driver slowed down and again pulled up to Megan. This time she was as motionless as her dead snowmobile. She could still see nothing through the face guard on the helmet. The driver pulled out a long silver knife, waving it at her. The knife was only a few inches away when her engine finally turned over. She tore away, heart racing as fast as she was driving. Megan flew down the lake, blind to her surroundings, wanting only to reach safety.

Where the hell is the marina?!

Finally the shoreline began to look familiar and she spotted Norden's. Megan steered her snowmobile toward it. But being on the lake had distorted her sense of speed. The dock seemed to zoom up on her in an instant, and she realized too late that she was going way too fast.

Megan lost control of the snowmobile and slammed into the side of the dock, flying forward. The noise sounded like an explosion. She hit one side of the dock with her arm and went tumbling down onto the frozen lake. The snowmobile went silent. Megan turned over on her back as she heard Callie screaming. He was running from the garage out to the dock.

"Megan! Megan!" He jumped down on the ice and took off her helmet. "What happened? Are you okay? What the hell happened?" He looked down at her arm. Hitting the dock had torn through her gear and cut into her forearm. "Oh my God. You're bleeding really bad. Come on." Callie helped her up and back to shore. "Why were you coming in so damn fast?"

It was difficult for her to catch her breath. "There"—she put her hand up to her forehead, trying to gather her thoughts and stop her heart from coming out of her chest—"there was someone out there. I don't know who. Charging at me, trying to force me off."

"Slow down, okay? Deep breaths."

"The driver was wearing a dark helmet. I couldn't see the face." She looked up at Callie. "Where *were* you?!"

Callie looked confused. "I told you I came back to get more gas. I was in the garage getting the tank."

"The snowmobile stalled. He was chasing me and I turned too fast and it killed the engine."

Deep breath.

"The rider pulled up alongside me and pulled out a knife. A big-ass knife."

Callie ran back to the end of the dock to look around. "I don't see anyone. We were the only ones out there." He whipped around. "I don't even *hear* a snowmobile."

Megan held her injured arm. The blood was now dripping down the ripped coat. "I'm telling you, someone was out there and they had a very clear agenda." Megan went from frenzied to angry. She was more comfortable with angry.

Callie toned down from panic mode into caretaking. "Come on, you're going to need stitches." He moved to help her stand.

"I can do it," she snapped.

TWENTY-NINE

MEGAN SAT WHILE THE doctor sutured her arm. Callie stood by, both not speaking. The doctor attempted to make small talk. "Don't I know you?"

Oh fucking hell.

"No, wait, I *do* know you. You came in to check on that teenager the other day."

Relieved he wasn't going to bring up her time in the news, Megan became more congenial. "Oh, right, yes. I hear she's doing better." The sting of the suture line made her wince slightly.

"Sorry, we're almost done. Yes, given the fall"—he said *fall* in a way that was extremely unconvincing—"you'll be sore for a while but will make a full recovery. I'm just going to get some Steri-Strips to place over the stitches and wrap it with gauze and you'll be all set. But I do want you to wear a sling for a few days."

"Thank you, doctor," Megan replied.

Callie looked confused. "What teenager?"

"A girl who lives on McGregor, down the street from me, was hurt the other night. She's here in this hospital. I came to see her before. I should see her again before we leave, actually."

"How was she hurt?"

"Domestic violence case. Drunk boyfriend of the mother knocked her around and pushed her down a flight of stairs."

Callie flinched at the cause of her injuries. "Man, that's awful. Yeah, we should definitely stop by before we go." He paused. "Are you still up for that lunch? I know this cute restaurant and am good friends with the owner."

Megan was reluctant but consented. "Only if it comes with a few cocktails. My arm is starting to throb. Oh shit, I just realized something: What if the snowmobile is damaged?"

"You had a man—or woman—chase you at top speed around a frozen lake and then threaten you with a knife. Norden will understand. And I can have Duane at the garage fix whatever might be broken."

"Oh, I didn't know you knew him."

"Haven't you figured it out yet, Trouble? This is a small-town area, and almost everyone knows everyone. I don't really *know* him, but I've run into him at Norden's fixing boat engines, quad bikes, stuff like that."

"He makes Manson seem normal," Megan responded.

Callie just rolled his eyes.

The doctor returned, applied the Steri-Strips and the gauze and, for extra protection, an Ace bandage. He handed her a sling. "You're good to go. I want you to wear this for the next few days, just to help keep your arm protected while you heal. You can go to the front desk to see what room Isabelle is in."

They found Billie's room in the small hospital within five minutes, and Megan gave a small knock before popping her head in. "Hey, kiddo, up for a visit?"

Billie gave a big smile, adding a "you bet" through a slight yawn.

"I brought a friend, if that's okay?"

She nodded yes.

"How are you feeling?" Megan asked.

"All right, I guess." Then Billie saw Megan's arm. "Are *you* okay?"

"Just a small cut, no big deal. Here." Megan motioned for Callie to come in. "Billie, this is my friend, Callie."

"Hi. What kind of friend?"

Wiseass teenager has returned. "You're obviously starting to feel better. He's an old friend from college. He owns Krogh's restaurant."

"Oh, hey, I've been there. Great nachos."

Callie laughed. "Thanks."

"So, are you going to share? What happened to the wing?"

"A small bump and scrape falling off a snowmobile. She's kind of a spaz," Callie joked, making Billie laugh.

"Do you know when you can get out of here?" Megan asked.

"A few more tests say maybe a week. I'm not sure I'll be able to make it down your driveway right away, though." Billie laughed, pointing at the soft cast on her leg.

"We'll figure something out." Megan smiled, adding, "You get some rest. I'll see you soon."

Billie smiled. "Okay. Take care of that wing, and your 'college friend.'"

THIRTY

K<small>ROGH'S WAS QUITE BUSY</small> when they arrived, which made Callie happy. "Good crowd today." They walked through the kitchen. Callie asked one of the waitresses to show Megan to a table, give her a menu, and set them up with drinks. "Trouble, I'm just going to check on what's going on in here and see how things have been running. I'll be out in a few minutes."

"No problem." Megan followed the waitress to a booth and made herself comfortable, as much as she could. Her arm felt like it had its own thumping pulse, so she popped a few ibuprofen, knowing a cocktail would ease the slight discomfort faster. While she waited for Callie, she thought of the person on the snowmobile.

Definitely had to be male. Body type rugged, even with winter gear on. Broad shouldered. Big winter gloves means big hands. It was difficult to discern his height because he was seated, but he was possibly six foot, maybe more. What did the knife look like? Think. Think. The knife had a long silver blade with a black handle. Like pretty much every other knife in the universe. But there was something different. Think harder.

"That's all I've got," Megan whispered to herself in frustration.

Callie sat down. "Sorry about that. I needed to check up on things."

"Everything okay?" she asked.

"Running smooth. You looked deep in thought. About earlier?"

"Yeah, something just crossed my mind." Megan was interrupted by a waitress delivering a pitcher of beer and an appetizer of hot wings Callie had ordered. To her surprise, she was suddenly ravenous. "Do you remember what the knife that was found in Vivian's car looked like?"

He shook his head. "We weren't standing close enough. I didn't get a good look at it. Did you?"

"No, but I got a good look at the one today." Megan thought again before adding, "Wait, there was a dip in the side." She got frustrated with herself. "I don't know. Let's eat."

———

I'm sitting in my gatehouse wondering what might happen to me. In most ways, I now regret what I did that night. I read the captioning on the news and look at all the faces and think, am I the only person who knew the Judge was a monster? Then I think, he's been murdered so I wasn't the only one to feel his wrath. Since this has started, I pray to Momma, wondering if she hears me from heaven, hoping she's watching out for me. I think of the afternoon I found her. We'd gone jogging together, as we had every morning. She was a fit, healthy woman. She'd just had an excellent annual check up one month earlier. I can still hear, even though I can't actually hear. I would hear through looking into her eyes, and through sign language. "I will never leave you Vivian. Never," my mother said to me.

They wouldn't let me see her before they cremated her. I know the Judge had something to do with her death, and eventually he would have gotten to me too. So when I pray to Momma and tell her how much I love and miss her, I also pray to whoever killed the Judge. I say thank you.

THIRTY-ONE

"THE RESTAURANT IS GETTING busy. We shouldn't hold a customer's table," Megan said after finishing her cheeseburger. "The owner might get upset." She smiled—with hot sauce on the corners of her mouth.

Callie pointed at Megan's mouth before handing her a napkin. "The owner might need the money too." He looked around for his manager to give him instructions for the rest of the day. "I was thinking of stopping by Vivian's to check on her. Are you up for that?"

"Of course. She's probably feeling confused and lonely."

"I'll send her a text that we're coming over." Callie asked one of his waitresses to put together three appetizers and meals to go. "I doubt Vivian was able to get out much over the last few days."

After the takeout was ready, they walked through the kitchen to go to the car parked behind the restaurant. Megan eyes were drawn to all the kitchen knives hanging above the cutting boards. The prep chefs chopped away and the moment turned into a slow motion walk with her observational detective skills kicking in.

No not that one, not that one, she thought to herself analyzing each knife as she passed by.

Callie noticed Megan staring at the cutlery. "Everything okay?"

"Yeah. It's like being on one of those chef shows. I'm just looking at what they're cooking."

And what they were cooking it with.

———

Vivian greeted them at her door. When she noticed Megan's wrapped arm, she signed to Callie, asking what happened. He told her about the snowmobile accident but not about the knife incident. Vivian asked Megan, via Callie, if she was okay, and Megan smiled and nodded that she was. Callie gave Vivian the bag of food from Krogh's and told her to eat, keep her strength up. She smiled and gave him a hug.

Then they began signing, but this time Callie wasn't translating.

"What are you saying?"

"I'm just asking how she's holding up. If she needs anything."

They were signing back and forth, and Megan felt like someone traveling alone in a foreign country, not knowing the language.

"Ask her if any press or police have been bothering her."

"She said only a few reporters, but police come around more often now to check on the judge's house. There are always two guards in front of the house. "

Megan hadn't noticed anyone when they pulled into Vivian's driveway. There were no police cars outside, but sure enough, when she looked through the window, two policemen were up on the hill near the front door. "They're worried about the backlash because of the latest news," she said.

Callie stopped signing for a moment. "You mean looters?"

"I don't think so, although the judge had some pretty nice-looking firearms in there, and some expensive-looking bottles of wine. I'm sure future evidence is a bigger concern, though. They don't want any tampering. They missed a lot the first time through the house." Megan was edgy, so she took the bags of food to the kitchen. "I'll go put a plate together for her."

She found the cabinet holding the dishes and unpacked an entree of chicken piccata. It was large enough to feed a family of four. The silverware drawer was extremely organized, unlike in Megan's apartment in the city and now in the lake house. Everything here had its place. What caught her eye were the knives. The image of the snowmobiler waving the knife flashed through her brain again. He could have killed her right then.

Why didn't he?

"This isn't making sense," she said.

"I didn't hear you, what did you say?" Callie called.

Megan hadn't realized she'd spoken aloud. "I'm just reheating it a bit in the microwave."

Megan poured a glass of water for Vivian and brought the warm food out for her. Vivian made a sign.

"She said thank you."

"Oh, you're welcome."

Callie told Vivian to enjoy the food and he'd be in touch later—at least, that's what he said along with the hand motions.

"You ready to go home?" he asked Megan.

"Sure. Ask her if she still has my number in her cell, just in case she can't reach you for some reason."

He asked Vivian and she made her best attempt verbally: "Yes, I do."

It was very muffled, but Megan was able to understand her perfectly.

―――

As Callie unlocked the car door, he hunched over the hood. "I have a question for you."

Megan quipped, "No, you're not staying over."

Callie smiled. "That wasn't what I was going to ask even though it's a great thought. You'll probably change your mind later."

"Doubt it," she said as she raised her bandaged arm.

"The question I want to ask is: Why didn't you pull your gun on him, the guy with the knife today? You wear an ankle holster."

Megan stared at Callie, thinking of the best answer she could give him. "Look how far apart we are. I'm here and you're, what? Four or five feet away? Picture us in your restaurant at the booth. The snowmobile guy was closer than the space we shared at lunch. On top of that, the winter gear was covering my holster. In the time it would have taken me to reach for the gun, he could have slashed my throat."

Callie nodded in agreement and then asked, "Why didn't he kill you?"

"You keep putting your foot in it, Callie," she said, looking away in annoyance at his poor choice of words. She climbed into the passenger seat and slammed her door.

Callie scrambled in the driver's seat, cringing. "That came out wrong. Of course I'm happy you're okay, but why go to all that trouble if he hadn't planned on hurting you?"

"I have a better question: How many people knew we were going snowmobiling today? It was impromptu. Answer me that."

"You, me, and Norden," Callie answered, confused as to where she was going with the conversation. He paused. "And Duane."

"Duane? From the garage? Why would he know?"

"When I called Norden while you were walking Clyde, he said he'd call Duane to make a quick run over to confirm the sleds were ready to go."

Megan nodded her head. "Well, isn't that an interesting fact. And when I was at the garage, Duane was smoking cigarettes that looked similar to the ones left on my dock the day someone pulled a burlap sack over my head and threw me into the water."

"That's a bit of a leap. I mean, Duane is very dark, the brooding type, but I don't think he honestly gives a damn about anyone enough to hurt them."

Megan strongly disagreed with Callie's opinion, but for now she'd keep the rest to herself. She'd seen Duane's type countless times on the job, and she'd arrested his sort more times than she could count. So Callie's opinion on what someone like Duane was capable of held no water as far as she was concerned.

"What's Duane's last name?"

"Why?"

She raised her eyebrows. "Just curious is all."

"Baker."

Megan planned on doing some research on Mr. Duane Baker when she returned home. Depending on what she found or didn't find, she'd make a few phone calls.

Having received some frantic phone calls from the new night manager at Krogh's, Callie needed to turn around and go back. He dropped Megan off at the house, which was fine with her. Clyde practically leapt on top of her but then just sniffed at her wounded arm until Megan opened up a can of wet dog food. "Thanks for the concern, big guy."

She turned on the Macks' stereo in the living room, and the classical music that came forth washed a sense of calm over her. Then she had the oddest thought. Megan's mother, Rose, was responsible for instilling the refined tastes of classical music within her brother, Brendan; as hard as she tried, she was never able to get Megan to appreciate it. Now she was gone and Megan sat there enjoying it.

Funny how things turn around, Megan thought.

"Well, Momma, never too late to start."

She opened her laptop to do research on Duane Baker. Clyde finished his meal, then jumped on the couch and continuously nudged at Megan's arm to be petted. He was smart enough to go for the arm that hadn't collided with the marina's dock. Megan plugged in Duane's full name and waited for responses. Nothing relevant showed up besides the name of the garage and his mother's name as owner.

Guess I shouldn't be surprised that he's not on Facebook or LinkedIn.

"Damn it. I hoped I wasn't going to have to do this." She'd left her cell on the mantel when she turned the fireplace on. The letter Nappa brought her remained behind the vase of roses where she'd placed it. She glanced at it and thought for a moment about opening it. She just wasn't ready, and the pangs of guilt swept over her just as they did when she worked her last case. She was unsure if she'd ever be able to face that time in her life, and she worked very hard to push it to the back of her mind; but that rarely worked. Sometimes ignoring things, situations, or even people was the only way to get through it. At least that's what Megan told herself. Most people referred to that as denial; Megan deemed it survival.

She dialed Nappa on his private cell. She didn't want to use his work cell or call on the station's landline. This call was to remain under the radar. There was no surprise when he picked up at the start of the second ring.

"McGinn, is everything okay?"

"Yes, yes," she said as she stared down at her arm in a sling. "Things are fine."

"It was fun the other night, everyone being together."

She wasn't even going to try to deny it. "It *was* a good night. Really nice to see everyone."

"I wasn't sure how you were going to react with the entire Murphy clan arriving without notice."

"Oh, they're family. Not that I wasn't surprised, mind you, but it was a good surprise."

"Now, being I'm your partner—and don't start in with 'not anymore', both you and I know it will happen again—I have this psychic feeling that you have called because you need me to help you with something. How am I doing so far?"

"Not bad. Can you use your psychic powers to look someone up for me? On the down-low, of course."

"Aha! This has to do with the events in your temporary little lake town, I'm sure." Nappa started to turn his upbeat voice to a more concerned tone.

Megan never got upset when Nappa showed this side of himself—that's what partners do for one another. There were many moments she'd shown the same toward him, so she wasn't offended.

"Yes, it does, Nappa. I want you to look up a man named Duane Baker. He lives in Mount Arlington. His mother, Lynn, owns a gas station and car repair shop on Howard Boulevard. He works as the mechanic."

"What do you want to know about him?" Nappa was getting a bit curious.

"I want to see if he has a record." Megan thought about her few minutes talking with Duane Baker in the garage. "Actually, I'm sure he has a record; I want to know what for and how far it goes back."

"Hmm, what makes you so sure he has a record?"

"Oh, you should see this guy. I'm not talking about because of his tattoos or stuff like that. We know better. His *way*. You know what I mean."

Nappa knew exactly what Megan meant. "A bad seed?"

"Maybe. I know this is a lot to ask, Nappa, and I really do appreciate it."

Megan had on occasion taken the back door in her work. For instance, calling people who weren't directly within her department for one thing or another. She'd developed a rapport with a handful of other detectives, technicians, and operators in different divisions. They'd helped her, and when they needed help, she returned the favor.

"I'll run him through NCIC and see what I can find. If he's like you say he is, which I'm sure he is, I'm willing to bet there'll be a rap sheet on him."

"You're the best, Nappa."

"Yeah. Don't be a stranger." He paused. "May I say something?"

Megan rolled her eyes. "As if my saying no would mean anything. You're doing me a favor. Go ahead."

"You're out there for a reason, McGinn. Don't get all wrapped up in this. I want you back rested and ready to go again. Soon."

Wrapped up? You should see my arm, she thought to herself. "I know. Call me when you get something."

THIRTY-TWO

MEGAN HAD HER MORNING coffee outside while Clyde played in the snow in the lower level. She stared out at the area where the snowmobiler had attempted to force her into the open water in front of the boathouses. She knew exactly where he confronted her and wondered not just who it was but why he hadn't followed through with his plan. If his goal was to intimidate her, his success only lasted moments until she was able to get away. She didn't hear the gate open on the side of the house but heard Leigh call for her.

She turned and saw Leigh bundled up like Randy in *A Christmas Story*, the younger brother to Ralphie whose mother would dress him as if he were walking in the Arctic.

Leigh took a look at Megan's arm. "What happened to you?"

Megan glossed over it. "Oh, it's nothing. I took a spill yesterday. I needed a few stitches, but it's not a big deal. Hey, luckily I didn't break anything. Do you want some coffee?"

Leigh seemed a bit puzzled by how blasé Megan was about her accident. "Um, sure, I'd love a cup. And if you need any bandages changed, Jo would be more than happy to do it."

Megan nodded. "Thanks. Let's go in. Clyde! C'mon, we're heading in."

"I see you've taken a real shine to Clyde." Leigh smiled.

Megan laughed through her answer. "Oh he's a pain in the ass, but then again I've heard I am too. So I guess we're a good fit."

Megan poured Leigh a cup of coffee, turned the fireplace on, and asked, "How are you doing today?"

"It's a good day. That's two in a row, so I can't complain. I hope you don't mind me barging in like this. I saw you from the top of the driveway, but you didn't hear me call out your name so I thought I'd stop in."

"No, no, that's fine."

The night before Megan had brought the photo of her parents into the living room. It was a moment to reminisce, mourn. She'd left it on the coffee table before heading to bed. The Murphys' visit, as wonderful as it was, brought up holiday memories of her parents. Her dad and Uncle Mike would sit outside deep-frying two turkeys, drinking beers while her mom and Aunt Maureen attempted to keep all the kids under control and cook at the same time. Until Megan was old enough to know better, her dad would say, "Meggie, come over here and have a sip of my beer, just the foam on top, it's the best part." Rose would catch a glimpse every now and then and yell out the door, "Patrick McGinn, do not give our daughter alcohol!" Megan's father would wave his wife off, knowing it wasn't alcohol really, just the head of the beer.

Leigh noticed the framed picture and couldn't help but comment. "Oh, wow, are these your parents?"

Megan nodded. "Yes. My dad, Pat, and my mom, Rose."

Leigh studied the photo, looking back and forth from Megan to the picture. "You get your red hair from your dad, but your face is identical to your mom's."

It wasn't the first time Megan heard that. It was, however, the first time she was proud of it. "You think so?"

"Oh, yes, absolutely," Leigh answered, holding the photo near Megan's face. "You could be sisters instead of mother-daughter."

"My brother Brendan got mom's blond hair and I guess I should say her more refined tastes. He would go to plays and the opera with Mom while I would go to baseball and hockey games with Dad. Brendan isn't a momma's boy or anything like that, but he's a lot more cultured."

"Is he in Manhattan as well?"

"No, he and his wife and kids live out in Ohio."

Leigh laughed. "So much for being cultured!" She sat back and sipped her coffee, releasing more of a groan than a sigh before stating the obvious: "Well, things have gotten quite interesting around here, but that seems tasteless given the latest news."

"Controversial?" Megan suggested.

"That's putting it mildly."

Megan pulled her hair into a ponytail and put her feet up on the coffee table. She was curious to hear Leigh's response and asked, "Were you surprised at the news of sexual assaults that has come out?" As soon as she asked, Megan realized she may have let it be known she was more aware of certain aspects of the case than what the papers and evening news had reported.

Leigh was not a dumb woman and caught on right away. She stared at Megan with a wry smile, knowing Megan had more information than most, but unwilling to insult her by pressing her for it.

"Well, I can't say much has been made known to the public, but, surprised? Somewhat. I think the whole town knew Judge Campbell was up to something—not as sick as this, but some sort of corruption. Taking bribes, perhaps, or peddling influence or money laundering or something more on the business side of things. But this? Accused of harming young boys? I guess anyone would be shocked at such malevolent acts. Especially from someone we trust to uphold the law—one who is part of the legal system." She looked up at the ceiling in contemplation. "I mean, I teach philosophy, so it's about the fundamental nature of knowledge, of existence. If I had chosen to teach psychology or ethics, perhaps I'd have a firmer grasp on how a person could do something like this." She paused before adding, "But then again, I'm glad I don't because I can be honest and say I would never want to wrap my head around the conscience—or lack thereof—of people who are capable of this. And not only that, but who can maintain an upstanding public persona as a pillar of the community. He must have been a real psychopath. Or is that sociopath? I can never keep them straight."

Megan nodded. "Sociopath, but with a little psychopath thrown in for good measure, I think." She surprised herself by admitting, "I've seen plenty of conscienceless acts. And their fallout." Megan had, since moving to Mount Arlington, been very careful about her confessions. But she felt comfortable speaking to Leigh, which was probably why she let her guard down just a bit.

Leigh stared at Megan and could tell she was running through her mental rolodex of the egregious crimes she'd worked on. "I'm sure you have," she said softly with a hint of sadness for Megan.

Megan offered Leigh more coffee. She wanted to pick her brain a bit. "So, what do you think of the mayor offing"—Megan's detective language seeped in and she quickly self-corrected—"I mean, committing suicide?"

"The timing is weird. Do you know the Appletons down the street?"

Megan shrugged.

"They live in the white house right near mine. Well, Pamela, she goes to yoga with the mayor's wife. They're acquaintances, not so much friends. Pam told me they had a vacation planned for just after the holidays, so I find the timing to be odd. Why would you plan a vacation if you were going to commit suicide?"

Megan moved forward, placing her elbows on her knees and staring intently into the fire. "I didn't know he was married. They didn't say anything on the news about that." She turned to Leigh for confirmation.

Leigh smiled, enjoying the fact that she knew a bit of gossip, and whispered, "Well, there's a reason for that."

Megan had a hunch of what it was and bellowed, "Oh, please don't tell me she owns one of the local news stations!"

Leigh smiled, impressed with Megan's suspicion. She answered, "Something like that. Her brother and cousin are vice president and junior vice president at two of the stations here."

Megan smacked herself in the forehead, falling back into the couch. "Don't take this the wrong way, Leigh, but this town is fucking unbelievable!"

Leigh laughed and stretched a bit. "I should be going. It's time for my next round of meds soon."

Leigh worked harder at making the people around her feel more comfortable about her cancer than she did complaining about it. Megan had the utmost respect for her strength.

"You know if you need anything, I'm around. You and Jo have been so welcoming. If there is anything you need while I'm here, just ask. I can go to the grocery store for you." Megan waved her hand, adding, "Or walk Lady Sadie or if you want me to bring her down here to run with Clyde."

Clyde put in his two cents and rapped his tail on the floor, shaking his bum, obviously excited to hear both dog names in one sentence.

"I might take you up on that."

Megan got Leigh's coat and glanced out at the lake to see a man walking over the ice with a fishing pole and chair. "Leigh, I have a question. Do you know of stores in the area that sell things for winter weather?"

She zipped up her coat. "What did you have in mind?"

Megan scratched the back of her head, trying to remember what Billie called the things she put over her snow boots when she visited Megan. "Cleats? Traction cleats?"

"The only place I can think of is Ramsey Outdoor. They sell everything for outdoors activities—fishing, camping, anything you want. It's in Succasunna, near the Roxbury mall, fifteen minutes away. Do you mind me asking what for?"

"With this driveway, you can't be too careful. I might even take a stroll on the lake, take some pictures of the house from the ice."

"One spill isn't enough?" she asked. Leigh put her winter cap and scarf on. "You just better take care of your arm."

"Yes, mother." Megan waited to make sure Leigh made it up the driveway okay. Then she shut the door and immediately looked up Ramsey Outdoor on the Internet. Then she walked to the window and stared out at Lake Hopatcong. The fisherman was setting up his post with chair, fishing pole, a small cooler and, Megan was sure, hoping there wouldn't be a dead man floating underneath.

Time to get some cleats.

THIRTY-THREE

LEIGH WAS RIGHT. RAMSEY Outdoor was only fifteen minutes away with GPS Sheila giving her directions. The store was the size of a large-scale supermarket. They sold everything you could possibly imagine for the outdoors—canoes, sporting goods, fishing equipment, hunting gear, even clothes. Megan wasn't about to meander around a store this size when she knew exactly what she was looking for. The first salesperson she found led her directly to the area where the traction cleats were sold. She found her size and then headed to the checkout.

Megan smiled at what a terrible shopper she was, and always had been. Her mother practically begged Megan to go on mother-daughter shopping sprees. Megan would only concede if it were a sports shop to get a new baseball glove or a pair of sneakers. She remembered hearing her mother mutter under her breath, "I had to go and have a tomboy. What am I going to do with that girl?"

As an adult, Megan still couldn't stand shopping, especially during the artificially long holiday season. Christmas decorations had gone up the day after Halloween. That fact in and of itself made Megan an anti-shopper.

Thank God for Aunt Maureen and the clothes she had Nappa bring, she caught herself thinking.

The checkout line wasn't too long. She handed the traction cleats over to the cashier as she aimed a look at a locked case behind him filled with knives. One caught her eye. The image of it being waved in front of her rushed in. "Excuse me, may I take a look at a knife in that cabinet?"

The cashier was more than accommodating. "Sure thing. Which one would you like to see?"

Megan pointed at it.

He unlocked the case and took it out to show Megan, then began his sales pitch. His voice sounded like someone pimping wares on QVC. "This is a very popular knife. Mainly used for hunting. Notice the serrated edges and the dip in the body."

"Why are there serrations?" Megan interrupted.

"For a deep cut. This knife can do it in one clean sweep, like a shark bite. Other knives you have to maneuver the blade back and forth. The nickname for this knife is 'the one slice dicer.'"

"Have you sold any this week, or any in the last few weeks? This knife, specifically?"

"Lady, we probably sell three or four of these a day. Do you want to add this to your purchase?"

Megan stared at him momentarily. "Um, no, no thank you, just the cleats, please."

Megan returned home with traction cleats in one bag and rawhide bones for Clyde in another. The pet store was next to Ramsey, so technically it wasn't considered shopping. She felt guilty about how much time she'd spent away from the house lately, so she bought three very large bones for Clyde to keep him occupied while she went for a walk on Lake Hopatcong. When she arrived home, Clyde instinctively grabbed the bag with the bones. Megan reprimanded, "Hey, mind your manners." She reclaimed the pet store bag and gave Clyde one bone, then she proceeded to get ready to hit the ice. The obvious questions surfaced as she was preparing to go out: *What was I thinking? A lake house in winter? I ought to be in Florida or the Bahamas, holding a drink with an umbrella in it. But then I'd be stuck indoors the whole time so I wouldn't get a sunburn. Sometimes it sucks to be so damn Irish. Some decompressing I'm doing.*

What halted the self-doubt was the memory of the vivid brutality forced on the boys in the videos. There was nothing more to think about. She went into the bedroom and pulled out the lockbox where she stored her guns and ammunition. She may have had to hand in her service piece when she went on leave, but she owned two guns privately. Megan felt naked not carrying. As she held the loaded guns, she thought to herself that it was her choice to get involved. There was nothing more to think about. Thinking it was going to be a much more isolating environment, she packed as if she were becoming a survivalist in the woods. She wanted to double-check the box was locked, which it was. She placed one gun in her ankle holster and caught a glimpse of herself in the mirror holding the other loaded gun when the memory of the first time she drew her weapon after joining the force came surging to the forefront of her mind.

Few cops ever have to actually fire their weapon during their time on the job. Some may have to draw them, yes, but firing them is a different story. It's not like television cop shows where they're constantly taking fire and shooting at perps.

The first time Megan took a shot at someone was very clear in her memory. It was one of the hottest summer nights in the last thirty years in New York City. She and her then-partner were investigating a call in Hell's Kitchen from a neighbor complaining about a disturbance next door. They walked into the crime scene to find an older woman hacked to death. They'd swept the apartment to make sure it was clear, and thought it was. Moments later a man charged at them, running down the hall swinging a machete. Her partner had his back toward the man and was about to get his head slashed off when Megan raised her gun and yelled to her partner, "Get down!" She took one shot and to her surprise, the machete-wielding man continued to charge at them. Maybe it was his adrenaline or the fact that he was nuttier than a fruitcake, but Megan took a second shot. He was down for the count.

What amazed her was her response directly afterward. She thought she'd be shaky or feel badly about what had happened, but in that moment, it was all about protecting her life and the life of her partner. There wasn't the slightest tremor in her hands.

The second time Megan drew her gun she had only one regret—that she didn't get a clean shot at Breton Daly. That's a kill she would have been proud of.

She concluded her joyous walk down memory lane. Megan clicked her shoulder holster closed, affirming to herself there would not be a second time she'd be caught unprepared. She did, however, choose not to use the arm sling. Her arm was feeling good enough and she needed the freedom of movement in case there was a need to draw her gun. She'd learned to expect the unexpected living on Lake Hopatcong.

"I'll be back in a little bit, Clyde." Her words fell on deaf ears as Clyde was gnawing at his rawhide like he'd just won the lottery for dogs. Megan went outside to put her cleats over her snow boots, re-membering that Billie had mentioned they scratch wooden floors. They were a bit more difficult to pull over her boots than expected. She had to use quite a bit of muscle to fasten them—not so easy with an injured arm. She walked down to the boathouse. Knowing the bubbler system was about to turn on, she walked over to her neighbor's boathouse. Their boathouse was built on a cement dock so it didn't require a bubbler system and they had stairs leading down to the frozen lake. She was technically trespassing, but the neighbors were away for the winter, much like the Macks, so she saw no harm in it. It's not as if she were breaking and entering a crime scene ... again.

Her initial few steps were similar to a child on his first attempt to walk, wobbling back and forth a bit. After a few minutes, she had it down. The sound of the cleats grabbing into the snow and ice was like someone eating potato chips or popcorn too loudly, but it certainly was a better option than falling on her ass—or worse, through the ice.

She began her walk toward the area where the snowmobiler had stopped her. Megan wasn't sure why she wanted to check it out, but it was like walking back into the boathouse after she was thrown into the icy water. She had to face it.

The lake made sounds like rubber bands snapping. The only moments when she second-guessed her decision to take this trek was when she walked over areas of the lake where the wind had blown the new snow away, showing a clear view of water moving under the ice. "Not comforting."

An ice fisherman was a handful of yards away, so she figured she'd have a small chat with him. He looked to be in his seventies. He had a tranquil demeanor to him. He was a robust man—

someone Megan imagined went to Pub 199 and had both the lobster and steak dinners and always cleaned his plate, washing it all down with a few beers. He nodded to her as she approached.

"Hi there. Catch anything?"

"Only been here for a short bit. I think they're playing hard to get."

Megan nodded, adding as if she knew the slightest about ice fishing, "Uh-huh. They'll come around."

"Out for a winter stroll? Good idea for those cleats—otherwise you'd be slipping around holding on for dear life."

I've been doing that all week, Megan thought to herself. "Do you mind if I ask you a few questions? I'm new to the area."

"Ask away. I have a bit of time on my hands," he said with a husky, guttural laugh, making Megan smile.

"You didn't happen to be fishing here yesterday by any chance?"

"Yes, in fact in this very spot. Didn't catch anything, but I didn't feel like carving out a new fishing hole so I came back here today."

"Did you see anyone on the lake?"

"Well, there was Don Cafferty fishing over near where they found the judge. When I got my things together, there were a few boys playing hockey over there," he answered while pointing in the opposite direction.

"No one else?" Megan asked.

"Actually, now that you mention it, yeah. I was setting up my gear. There were snowmobilers riding so fast you'd think the devil himself was chasing them."

Megan looked up into the sky as flurries were beginning to fall. "Can you point in the direction where you saw them?"

"Well, two were directly in front, over there." He pointed to where Megan and Callie had been. "Then one went on his way and the other headed toward the north end of the lake, and the third ..."

"There were three?"

"Yes ma'am. The third came shooting out of the Casablanca boathouse."

"Casablanca?"

"That's the name the owners gave their lake house. They're New Yorkers, not much here often."

"Would that happen to be nearby?"

"You're right close by. It's about four houses down." He pointed to the left. "You can't miss it, says *Casablanca* on the top of the boathouse."

"Okay. Did you get a look at the driver of the snowmobile?"

"Nope, he got outta here like a bat out of hell."

She nodded. "Well, thank you. I'll let you get back to your fishing." Megan started to walk away when she had one last inquiry. "One more question. That noise, the one that sounds like rubber bands snapping under the ice—should I be worried?"

The fisherman let out a hard, one-too-many-cigarettes kind of laugh. "When you *stop* hearing that noise? Head for shore darlin', or the emergency room, 'cause that's where you'll end up."

Megan raised her eyebrows, not exactly sure how to respond. "Okay. Good to know."

She walked four houses down and found the Casablanca boathouse. It too was built on cement so there was no open water. Snowmobile tracks were still fresh. She walked toward the side of the dock. There were five or six cigarette butts in a pile. "Son of a bitch." She looked out over the lake. "You were waiting for me. Bastard."

THIRTY-FOUR

MEGAN RETURNED TO CHEZ Mack. Looking through the window, she could see Clyde still intent on destroying the bone she'd given him. She turned the corner and saw a brown package up against the side entrance of the house. She removed the cleats and her snow boots, leaving both on the rug at the entrance.

Clyde looked up and gave Megan an *oh, it's only you* look when she entered. She carried the package to the counter, opening it with a pair of scissors. She'd ordered a box set from Amazon only two days earlier and was surprised how quickly it arrived. "Let's see what we have here Clyde—*Basic Sign Language for Beginners, Finger Spelling for Beginners, Start Learning ASL: American Sign Language*. Looks like this is where we start."

For a moment Megan questioned her mental state given that she was now reduced to speaking to a dog who ignored her. She quickly moved past that ego-crippling moment, thinking back to when she was in Vivian's kitchen, frustrated that she wasn't able to understand Callie and Vivian's conversation. She didn't plan on being perfect overnight, but she needed to get a grasp on how to communicate with Vivian, even just on a basic level.

Her cell rang and she saw from the Caller ID that it was Callie. She sent it to voicemail, for no other reason than she just wanted zero communication with anyone. And then Nappa rang.

"Hey," Megan answered.

"How are you, McGinn?" Nappa's tone was oddly suspicious.

Megan turned off the kettle of water she was boiling for her cup of tea and opened the bottle of wine instead. "Did you get anything on Duane Baker?"

"I'll get to that in a moment. I have a question." He paused a tad too long for Megan's patience.

"Yeah?"

"Some hospital in New Jersey called, wanting to set up a follow-up appointment. I was your secondary number on their patient form and they couldn't get in touch with you. Why were you in the emergency room in New Jersey?"

It had never crossed Megan's mind she'd put down Nappa's cell as a contact. Her partner was always her emergency contact. Megan knew this particular tone of Nappa's, and she also knew better than to ignore it.

"I had a small accident on a snowmobile. I was out on the lake, and I ran into a dock."

"More please," Nappa insisted. Megan remained silent. "I'm waiting." Nappa's tone was now stern.

Megan ran her thumb around the edge of the counter, carefully choosing her words. "I had a run-in with another snowmobiler. He was trying to run me off the ice into an open water patch of the lake." Megan could hear Nappa's frustrated sigh. "I'm okay. It was a few stitches, a bruise or two, but I'm fine. As we speak, I'm turning on the fireplace and Clyde is chewing a bone, and I was about to order Chinese when you called. It's a relaxing afternoon on Lake Hopatcong."

Nappa paused, asking with more sensitivity, "Are you sure you're okay? Did you get a look at who it was?"

"No, he was wearing a dark visor on his helmet. I couldn't see his face." Megan shifted gears. "So, what news do you have for me on Duane Baker?"

"Well, you were right. The guy has a long list of priors. There are many stints in and out of jail, ranging from bar brawls to assaulting a police officer to DWIs. He did a short period of time in prison for holding up a liquor store when he was eighteen. He also spent three years in juvie. I don't know that I'm able to find out why, given juvies are sealed."

Megan never liked to give away private contact information, but in this case she knew it was in good hands. "Hmm. I'll text you Clarice Snowden's number. She helps me out with…things. She's a computer expert. Don't ask questions, just go with it. She was a big factor on the McAllister case." Her comment was meant with silence from Nappa. "Anything else?"

"Actually, yes. I ran the glass that your college buddy drank from and—"

Megan whipped into a frenzy. "You what? You did *what*?"

"I don't care if you get mad or not. I didn't have a good feeling about that guy. When you went to get ready to go out to lunch, I took the glass he drank out of and ran his prints."

"What the fuck? Who the…who the fuck do you think you are?" Megan went from zero to completely livid without passing Go or collecting $200.

"Hey, know what? I was looking out for you. You're vulnerable at the moment. You're in a healing stage from a lot of life shit and I have your back, so fucking deal with it."

Nappa rarely, if ever, swore. Megan held the top trophy for that honor. "You had no right." But the wind was coming out of her sails.

"Well, he has no record. He dropped out of law school and he's divorced, but I will say there are a number of years that are unaccounted for. Taxes are paid and—"

"Maybe they're unaccounted for because he's done nothing wrong. Let me know when you find out more on Duane. And I want that fucking glass back. It belongs to the Macks, damn it!" Megan immediately ended the call. "Son of a bitch!"

Megan took the box of sign language DVDs over to her laptop. Speaking again in an all too natural voice to a dog, she said, "Can you fucking believe that Nappa? I mean, what the hell was he thinking?" She tapped her fingertips on the coffee table. "Actually, I'm going to send him a text. He should also check out Norden, the guy from the marina. I have my concerns." Clyde didn't look up. He continued to chew his bone. "God, you're like a crack whore with that thing."

For the next few hours Megan practiced the first disc on finger spelling. It was a repetitive exercise. She surprised herself by picking it up more quickly than she thought she would. She then switched to a harder video of practicing actual signs and promptly felt as though she had two left hands. She should have been prepared for the challenge given her interactions with her last boyfriend, eons ago. She would direct him to turn left but motion to the right. Ambidextrousness was never going to be a part of her future. Funny enough though, give her a loaded gun and her aim was 98 percent on target with either hand.

Callie rang Megan again. This time she picked up. "Hey."

"Hey, Trouble, what's going on?"

The background noise from Krogh's made it difficult to hear Callie. "You sound a million miles away, I can barely hear you."

"Wait a second." Callie opened and closed a door and the din subsided. "What are you doing?"

Megan rubbed her neck, staring at her computer. "I thought I'd learn finger spelling and sign language. Actually, *attempt* to learn would be a more appropriate way to put it."

"It's not easy, I know." Megan could hear Callie's smile. "Tell you what, because I'm such a sweet guy, I'll come over and do what I can to help."

"Callie," Megan sighed, "this isn't a sex romp every time we get together. Everything is getting too complicated and I don't need any more complications in my life. And you are becoming complicated. I shouldn't even be doing what I'm doing in regards to Vivian."

"Trouble, I stayed over the other night and nothing happened. I don't look at you that way. You know me—certainly better than my ex-wife did. I'm not a player."

Megan raised her eyebrows and spoke in a mock shocked tone. "Ha! I'm saying it because I'm familiar with your work."

"Okay, let me say that in a different way: I'm not a player with you."

Megan stared at Clyde thinking, *I really hope you're not all dogs.* Then she remembered Nappa. She knew there were still good guys out there.

"Come on, I won't even hold your hand or try to kiss you. I'll sit at the opposite end of the couch."

Megan intentionally kept silent for an extra moment. "Chinese food. And I'm not putting makeup on or even running a brush through my hair."

"Well, so far it looks like a promising evening."

———

Callie arrived an hour later with the demanded Chinese food. They sat in front of the fire eating while intermittently working on the sign language videos. Megan returned to the first video of finger spelling.

"Before you play it, show me how much you remember of the alphabet," Callie challenged.

Megan waited a moment and went through the entire alphabet, rather slowly, but she aced every letter.

Callie smiled, clearly impressed at how fast Megan had absorbed the information. "That's actually pretty good for a first-timer. You'll get faster and it will come more naturally to you, but good job." He raised his glass to Megan.

"Thanks." Megan was proud of how fast she'd caught on, but she was not looking forward to the next video.

"Now it's time to add the harder bits to this. My suggestion is to first watch the whole video, and on the second go-round go slow, pause, and repeat each sign. But before we start, can I ask you a question?"

"You can ask, doesn't mean I'll answer," Megan said while she was failing at her attempt to get the plastic wrap off another DVD.

"Are…" Callie searched for the right words. "I guess what I want to ask is what upsets you more—your mother dying or the fact that the person responsible is still alive?"

"That's one hell of a multiple choice question." She cleared her throat. "Don't they go hand in hand?" She finally got the plastic off.

"Hopefully, you'll never have to think of what your answer would be in that scenario. That's my answer."

Discussion on that particular topic was now over.

Megan thought for a second. "Wait, how come *you* know it so well? Sign language, I mean."

"Don't you remember in college the kid who lived down the hall from me, Rich? He was deaf and he taught some of us how to sign. I only had a handful of classes with him, but he had this interpreter. She signed like lightning she was so fast. And she was hot. I dated her for a while."

Megan searched back. "Wait, Rich was the tall, lanky guy with the long blond hair?"

Callie nodded. "Yeah, that's him. Nice guy, funny as hell too. He got a lot of girls while he was there, come to think of it."

Megan closed her eyes. "Men." She then remembered, "Wait, he wasn't at Marist the whole four years, was he?"

Callie had a mouth full of food and mumbled, "No."

"What happened to him?"

"He transferred to Gallaudet University in DC."

It was all starting to come back to Megan. "Okay, that's right. That's the private school for the deaf and hard of hearing." She fumbled, using the chopsticks to pick up a fried dumpling. "Why wouldn't the judge send Vivian away to a place like Gallaudet? If he hated her so much, why not just get rid of her?" She stared at Callie waiting for an answer.

"Well." Callie's tone became reflective, bordering on brooding. "Vivian and her mother were very close. From what I could tell, they were like sisters. I don't think Vivian ever wanted to be far away from her mother. And I certainly don't think her mother wanted Vivian that far away." He shrugged. "I've never asked her, but that's how it seemed to me."

"What about her mother's death? Doesn't it seem a little off? I mean, she hung herself? I don't buy it. She's the mother of a challenged daughter. They were thick as thieves, from what I've heard."

Callie set his drink down. "Doesn't everything in this town seem a little off? And if you ask me, the judge had something to do with it. But no one will ever truly know now."

Megan couldn't disagree with Callie's observation. "That's an understatement."

"Do you regret coming out here?" His question was sincere. "I mean not just the town, but everything with Vivian. The judge. Me."

She searched not for the right words, but the most honest response. "Well, I can't say I expected this. I can't say I'm thrilled. My intention in coming here was entirely different." She stared down at Clyde and smiled. "I got a dog out of it anyway. Seriously, though?" She knew her next sentiment would be as much of a shock to Callie as it was to her. "There is a part of me, a part my family instilled in me. Even with everything I've gone through and my family has gone through, I have about three percent of myself left that believes everything happens for a reason. Maybe it was a kind of fate that brought me here. There were plenty of other choices. Warmer choices!"

"Well, *I'm* glad you chose to come here, if that's any consolation."

Megan smiled and switched back to the conversation about Rich. "I wonder where Rich is now."

"He friended me on Facebook about a year ago. He's living in Seattle as some type of doctor working on the research end of a medical study." Callie shrugged. "It looked as though he was doing well. I think he got married too."

Megan smiled but added a squint. "I can't picture you on a computer."

He had a mock look of insult on his face. "Very funny. It's difficult to picture you vertical."

"You're a pig, Callie."

"Hey, I even get the Marist newsletter, but they wouldn't remember you. You never made it to class."

This was certainly not always the case. Perhaps it would ring true on occasion, but Megan never missed her favorite class freshman year. Even if she were still buzzed from the evening before, she'd make the journey across campus at eight o'clock on Mondays, Wednesdays, and Fridays. Professor Paulson drove two hours one-way to teach and Megan had a high level of respect for anyone who would do that for a bunch of rowdy freshman pain-in-the-asses. She also got a kick out of him personally. The first day he walked into the lecture hall he wore sandals, jeans, a Bob Marley t-shirt, and literally did look like Jesus, beard and all. The guy seated behind Megan had whispered in her ear, "Is it just me or ..."

"No," she'd whispered back, "I'm just waiting for the apostles to show up."

"I wonder if he can make water into wine?" the young man asked.

"That would help," she laughed back.

Freshman year philosophy was one of the few classes Megan never missed. It was a fond memory for her. "Hey, I never missed my morning class that year!"

Callie looked at Megan, thought about, and then said, "Actually, you're right, you never did, did you?"

"Nope." She answered with a prideful tone. Clyde whimpered. "You have to go out, boy?" She let him out and Clyde zipped down the deck stairs as if on a mission from God, though Megan was sure a call from Mother Nature was responsible for his rush.

Megan and Callie started the second video for her to watch, as Callie suggested. Halfway through they heard a piercing yelp from outside. It was the kind of noise that was excruciating for any dog owner to hear—pure, agonizing pain. Clyde made the noise three more times. Both Megan and Callie flew off the couch and ran outside without bothering to throw on their coats. Running down the stairs, they bolted left and right into the yard. There was no sign of Clyde until Megan spied his head under one of the bushes in the landscaping. He was on his side, whimpering in pain.

"Clyde! Clyde!" Megan ran over to him. "Callie, he's over here!" She moved her hand over his side. Megan could feel something wet and sticky in his fur. "He's bleeding! Help me pick him up."

Clyde would have been impossible for only Megan to lift with her bad arm. Together, they were able to get Clyde into the living room.

"Jesus Christ, he's bleeding so much. We have to get him to a vet. Where's the closest one?"

"I have no idea. I've never had a pet and this isn't my town." Callie had a look verging on panic.

"Wait, I'll check the book the Macks left for me." This turned out to be a fruitless option. "Shit!"

"Megan, he's bleeding a lot. Think of something!"

"I'm trying, Goddamn it!" She reached for her cell. "Wait, hang on." She dialed and Leigh picked up on the second ring. "Leigh, I need your help, Clyde is hurt. I need the name of your vet. It's an emergency." Megan grabbed a pen and removed the cap using her mouth and spat it out. She wrote down Leigh's instructions. "Okay. Got it." She looked over at Callie. "Do you know where Landing is?"

"Um … yeah."

"Do you or don't you?"

"Off of Lakeside Boulevard."

Megan returned to Leigh. "Okay, we've got it. We're going now. Thanks."

Megan wrapped Clyde in a sheet, and by some miracle they were able to carry him up the driveway to the bottom of the garage. They placed him on the back seat.

"I'll drive. You sit back in the back with him," Callie ordered.

THIRTY-FIVE

It took ten minutes to get to Landing Plaza, yet for Megan it felt like three hours. Callie slammed on the brakes in front of the veterinarian's office. Megan ran in yelling for help and two assistants jetted out. Upon getting a look at Clyde, one yelled, "Get the doctor! This is serious."

Megan followed and went with them into the back room until the vet came in and asked her to stay in the waiting room. She ran her hand over Clyde's head whispering, "You're going to be okay, boy. I'll be right outside." Her voice cracked. "Right outside."

They sat in the waiting room. Megan went from crisis mode to angry mode. It was her natural path, dictated by adrenaline. "What could have done this? A bear? A raccoon? What?" She started to pace.

Callie shook his head. "I don't think a bear. They're in hibernation mode. Just sit down and wait until someone comes out."

Twenty minutes later a vet technician emerged from the back of the office. "Clyde is stable, but we're going to have to do surgery."

"What's going on?" Megan asked.

She held out her hand and showed them three bloodied BBs in a baggie. "There are still two more in, one in his neck and another in his side. The one that hit his neck is what caused the real bleeding. It grazed an artery."

"What? He was shot with a BB gun?" Megan held up her palms and her response bordered on a scream. "I don't understand, he was outside for less than fifteen minutes. It's a fenced-in yard!"

Callie rubbed her back. "Megan, you need to calm down and hear her out."

"We need your permission to perform surgery."

This was an incredibly surreal moment for Megan. "Well, what happens if you don't? What happens?" This was an odd question coming from a Homicide detective, especially Megan. She knew what would happen.

The vet assistant hesitated. "We would then need to put him down. He will bleed out unless we remove the last two BBs."

There was zero hesitancy in Megan's response. "Do it. Do the surgery."

Megan sat with her head against the wall while Callie went to the deli next door to get them coffee. Thoughts zipped like comets through her exhausted mind.

I didn't hear a shot. Or shots? What the hell is going on? Everyone gets hurt around me. People. Animals. Who would do something like this to an innocent animal? Nothing is making sense now.

Callie returned with the coffee. "Here. I couldn't remember how you take it." He placed a bunch of sugar packets and half-and-half pods on the side table.

"Thanks." She sipped the bitter coffee. "This tastes like it was made ten hours ago."

Callie raised an eyebrow. "It probably was."

"Why didn't we hear the BB gun? Multiple shots and we didn't hear anything."

"I was thinking about that too." Callie stopped to add more milk to his coffee, an attempt to give it minimal flavor. "The wind is strong tonight and the house is really well insulated."

"But we heard Clyde." She shook her head. "What am I talking about? I've never even heard a BB gun go off. I'm assuming it's like one of my guns."

"I remember one of my neighbor's boys, when I was still married, that is, had one." He searched for a description. "It's more of a snap. It's fast. It doesn't resonate the way a real gun does."

"Like a snap of the fingers sound?"

He nodded. "Kind of. A little higher pitched, from what I remember."

The next few hours they sat in near complete silence. Megan paced once in a while just to move her nerves around. A few minutes after another mini-lap around the waiting room, the vet technician came out. She had a hesitant look on her face. "Mrs. McGinn?"

"It's not *Missus*. How is Clyde?"

"He lost a lot of blood, but he's going to pull through. We'll need to keep him here for a day, maybe two, but he will be okay."

"Thank God." Megan was relieved beyond measure. "Can I see him? Would it be okay?"

"Of course. The doctor is in with him now. He'll go over everything with you. You can follow me."

"Go. I'll wait here," Callie said with a big smile on his face.

Megan walked into the back area where they were holding Clyde. He had a big bandage around his neck and the other areas where the BBs were removed had been shaved and covered in smaller dressings. There was an IV bag inserted into one paw. The vet took a step back. "Hey, big guy. Your mom is here."

Clyde was groggy and, to Megan, looked basically stoned. "Hey, sweets. How's my guy?" She petted him, sure to not go near where he'd been hurt. Without fail, Clyde's tail thumped on the table. A sound that once annoyed her was now sheer bliss to hear. "You're going to be okay. You'll stay here for a day or two and then come back home." Megan whispered in his ear, "I'll get you your favorite slice of pizza when I pick you up." Clyde proceeded to lick Megan's hand. The word *pizza* apparently was the key ingredient in restoring Clyde's medicinal well-being.

The veterinarian spoke with Megan about some minor details and told her Clyde may even be strong enough to return home at the end of the following day. He asked that she call in the afternoon to check his progress.

Megan returned to Callie and gave him the update as they walked out to the car. Callie felt the need to mention the obvious. "Um, that is going to be one big-ass bill, Trouble."

Megan nodded and said with no uncertainty, "Not as big of a bill the motherfucker who did this will be paying. He wants to fuck with me? Throw me in freezing boathouse water? Try to choke and drown me? Threaten me on a snowmobile? It was a wrong move to fuck with my dog." She hopped into the truck, adding, "Wrong, stupid fucking move. Motherfucker."

If Megan was forced to put a dollar in a jar for every swear word she'd uttered since moving to Lake Hopatcong, the Salvation Army would be making out like bandits this holiday season.

THIRTY-SIX

I wasn't about to be able to sleep after watching hours of news centering on the Judge and the discovery in the main house. I wondered if my mother knew and if that's why he hated us so much, because she found his secret. She was a smart woman—not for marrying him but smart enough to hold something over him to keep her and I together. I know he had something to do with her death, and now I will never know how. All I do know is she's gone and I'm alone. I thank God for Callie. I look out my window at the Macks' house and I see the main light on, and I thank God for Megan too.

———

Callie dropped Megan off. Both were exhausted from the evening at the veterinarian clinic, but Megan just couldn't bring herself to sleep. It was either heat up more Chinese food or have a go on the treadmill in the lower level of the house. She was worried about Clyde and missed his presence. Megan would go swim laps at a nearby gym to de-stress from cases when she was in Manhattan. It cleared her mind and helped calm her. She donned the only set of gym clothes she had packed and remembered how cold the lower level got. She started with just a slow-paced walk, then revved the speed as high as she could go, given her lack of exercise in the last month, if not more. Quite soon Megan broke out into a full sweat, and it felt good. The panting coming from a good run was different from the kind of heavy breathing she'd shared with Callie lately. Most of all it felt good to be alone—with the exception of Clyde's absence, of course. It was nearly an hour before she finished on the treadmill and was soaked through to the bone. Megan sat down for a moment to catch her breath before heading into the shower to wash off her form of meditation.

———

The next morning Megan woke to find a few inches of snow had fallen during the night. Though it looked completely barren of life, there was a beauty to the trees with snow coating the branches. She stood drinking her coffee, and then decided to text Vivian to see if she'd like some company. She assumed she would, and if anyone could help her with the sign language DVD, it would be a deaf woman.

Vivian was very welcoming of Megan's text. Her last lake walk was such a success that she decided to put on the cleats again and walk over to Vivian's via the frozen lake. Megan wasn't in the mood to clean off Arnold and wait for the engine to warm.

Before leaving she put a phone call out to the veterinarian's office, and the report of Clyde having a good night and perking up relaxed her. They told her he'd probably be fine to be picked up at the end of day. Quite relieved, she threw the DVDs in a backpack and headed out.

Megan was less apprehensive walking over the frozen lake this time. There was little if any breeze and the sun shone brightly. She wasn't chilled to the bone as she had often been since arriving at Lake Hopatcong. There were more police at the front of the judge's house than there had been when she and Callie took food over to Vivian's gatehouse the previous afternoon. Detectives Krause and Michalski's car was parked out front, but there was no sign of either. She wondered at the cause of their presence now, when everything in the house had surely been gone through and confiscated.

Unless it hadn't, she thought.

Megan yanked the cleats from her boots when Vivian answered the door. She had been watching the police and saw Megan when she arrived. Megan pointed to her boots and finger spelled, *Off?*

She shook her head no. As Megan walked in, Vivian looked over her shoulder, keeping an eye on the happenings at the big house. Vivian gestured for Megan to sit and then raised a glass of water, pointing back and forth between the glass and Megan. She spelled *no* and couldn't help but notice Vivian's odd stare at her. Megan took the DVDs from her backpack, placing them on the coffee table.

Vivian picked one up and mouthed, "I know sign language."

Megan pointed to herself. "For me."

She raised her eyebrows and shrugged, then wrote on a note pad, "Okay, if you want to try."

Megan took the pad of paper and pencil. She knew her limited finger spelling would take an hour to ask her questions and wrote, "Do you know what is going on over at the judge's house? Has anyone been over here? Bothering you?"

Vivian walked over to the window looking nearly mesmerized. Megan wondered if she was questioning her actions the night her father was murdered. She tapped her on the shoulder, motioning her to start one of the DVDs. Anything for a distraction. They sat for the following two hours practicing different signs, numbers, and small sentences. Then suddenly, Vivian looked saddened, or perhaps frightened. Megan finger spelled, asking her what was wrong.

Vivian took out her laptop and opened a word processor. What she had to tell her must be lengthy, and it would be faster this way until Megan was more proficient with sign language. Vivian typed two paragraphs explaining the day the man in the dark helmet got into her car. She handed Megan the laptop to read and could see Megan's face fill with concern with each sentence she read. Megan typed, asking why she hadn't told anyone and if Callie knew.

Too afraid, no one knows but you and I, Vivian typed back.

Megan had a million questions for Vivian but in the end had only one request: that if she saw the man again, to contact her right away. They were interrupted when Callie texted Vivian checking up on her. She had an odd expression and looked over at Megan, showing her the screen on her phone. Megan read the text: Checking in. I'm over at Megan's. We'll touch base later.

Megan shot up off the couch and looked over at the Macks' house. There was a blind side to the back of the house, so she was unsure if anyone was there. She called Callie immediately. He picked up on the first ring. "Hey, Trouble. I'm on the way over. How is Clyde doing?"

"Oh, well, I'm at Vivian's. I'm on my way back now. Clyde is much better. I think I can pick him up later today, actually. I'll see you in a bit." She hung up without hearing or for the moment caring about his response. She longed for the privacy of her late-night hour on the treadmill. Megan signed *thank you* to Vivian for her tutoring skills and reminded her to lock up after she left, though Megan knew if the man in the dark helmet wanted to get in, he would.

———

As I kept an eye on Megan crossing the lake to go home, the oddest thought came to me. I'm not sure why, but I asked myself: When does she put down her armor? She is so self-protective and suspicious that it comes through in her body language, yet she came over to be helped in learning sign language, something she'd most likely never have to use again. Why? My mother taught me the prayer to the Virgin Mary and I said it for Megan, to protect and guide her. As she neared the house and I felt she was now safely there, I realized we were more kindred spirits than new friends—both going through a different kind of hell that changes you, that changes how you see the world and the people around you.

THIRTY-SEVEN

MEGAN WAS WALKING UP the back steps to the house when Nappa rang her cell. "Hey, Nappa."

"You sound out of breath."

"I'm outside. Did you get any more information for me?" Megan and Nappa had a way of diving right into conversation, though it didn't stop him from making fun of it.

"I'm fine, thank you for asking. Had a small organ transplant this week, but I'm healing."

Megan shook her head. "Great. Oh, wait, don't you want to fill me in on if you're still constipated?"

"Never constipated having you as my partner because you're always taking the shit out of me."

They shared a short laugh over Nappa's coarse sense of humor, which undoubtedly he picked up from her.

"So, anything on Duane Baker's juvie record?"

"That's why I'm calling. Yes, he was in juvie for beating up some councilman when he was young. His name was Collins. When I say *beat up,* I mean the guy went into a coma and had multiple broken bones, including his jaw. You name it and Duane Baker did it."

"Just to this guy?"

"I wouldn't say *just.* The guy never walked again, and he had minor brain damage from the assault."

"In the file was there a reason he gave? Duane?"

"The only thing he said was, 'he had it coming.'" Nappa paused. "Oh, and the marina owner guy, Norden? No rap sheet. He's clean."

Megan stared over at the judge's house. Nappa continued to speak, but there was little seeping in as Megan again mentally replayed the video of the boys being attacked. Sexually mauled. Little doubt, perhaps, that Duane had been a victim and the councilman was one of the robed sons of bitches.

"Okay, thanks Nappa. Gotta go. I'll be in touch."

Megan had long ago mastered the art of hanging up without a *goodbye, ciao,* or even her usual *bite me.* Callie had just pulled in the driveway and she was preoccupied.

He gave a small kiss on her cheek when he closed the front door. "You okay?"

Megan waved it off. "I'm good. I tested out the new cleats again and walked over to Vivian's."

"Oh, okay. I sent her a text and said maybe we'd check in on her later. Tomorrow being Christmas Eve and all."

The comment made Megan stop in her tracks. "Tomorrow is Christmas Eve?" Her heart sank. She visualized Woodlawn Cemetery before leaving for New Jersey, saying goodbye to her parents. Everyone says the first year is the hardest when you lose someone, but after losing both parents within months, nothing felt like it would ever be right again. The sadness, the loss, was the only piece in her that was constant. She hated it, but it felt like her life now. It felt as though it had been her life for a long time.

"What are you doing for the holiday?" Callie asked.

"I already celebrated it." She stared down at her boots. "It's just another day."

Callie was rubbing his hands. "Can we go in? I'm freezing."

They went in and Megan put a pot of coffee on. "I'm making a sandwich. Do you want anything?"

He nodded. "Sure. What were you doing at Vivian's?"

Megan didn't want to mention what Vivian had told her about the man and the motorcycle. Callie barely believed her about the guy on the snowmobile and she didn't feel the need to defend herself. It wasn't enough to disguise everything that was on her mind. She could feel Callie sizing her up, attempting to register her emotions. He didn't know how beautifully she masked them.

Megan's limited culinary expertise resulted a roast beef sandwich with tomato, cheese, and horseradish sauce. She would make one for herself and her dad when they watched a game or one of his favorite Spencer Tracy movies. It was a small memory from the past, but one that had stayed with her.

They sat in silence while eating their small meal when Callie suggested, "If you want, you can come to the restaurant tomorrow. I'll be really busy, but you shouldn't be home alone on a holiday."

Megan wiped her mouth with a napkin. "I'm always alone on holidays. Like I said, it's just another day. You're open on Christmas Eve?"

"We're only closed on Christmas Day and New Year's. You wouldn't believe how many people don't want to cook and are willing to pay a damn high price for a holiday dinner."

"I'm not surprised." Megan paused and then asked, "Say, can you make me a full plate tomorrow? I'd like to take it over to Billie in the hospital. I'm sure whatever she'll have doesn't come close, given hospital food and all."

He shrugged. "Of course. Just send me a text when you want to pick it up and I'll have everything ready." Callie stopped to take another bite of roast beef. "You sure have taken a shine to that kid. I never would have pegged you for the sensitive type."

Megan was only slightly offended because she knew in the past her heartstrings weren't exactly pulled easily. "You're making me sound as frozen as the lake out there."

"I didn't mean to. It's just you with a dog and kind of mentoring this kid down the street… It's just not *you*."

Megan got up and placed her plate in the dishwasher, leaning on the counter. "But helping out a friend of yours when I could lose my badge for it, and putting myself on the line is what?" She said it with the doggedness she used to interrogate perps.

Callie sighed. "Megan, stop. You and I both know how you can be. Or, maybe how you *were*. Don't pretend you weren't that way."

Megan shook her head and proceeded to do what every man so adores in a woman: she slammed her index finger into his chest, "Let me tell you what I had to be to get where I am. Independent. Strong. No one had my back! My dad being a detective meant I had to work twice as hard to prove myself. So if I lose a little of that hard edge along the way to help the victims and their families? It's worth it. Christ, I'm just taking food over to a neighbor. It's hardly sainthood." Megan's phone interrupted her verbal tongue lashing. "What!" She reeled her emotion back in. "Sorry. Yes, this is Megan. So he's okay? For sure? I'll be right over."

Megan looked up at Callie, who was surprisingly unaffected by her rant. "Clyde can come home. I'm going to go pick him up now."

Callie placed his plate in the sink. "I'll drive, and I think I blocked you in. By the way, do you do finger push-ups? My chest hurts from you poking me."

His smart-ass comment broke her mood. "Shut up." It was not God's plan to have Megan write sentimental Hallmark cards.

—————

Callie parked in front of the clinic and kept the engine running. "You go in. I'll stay and keep the truck warm and help you get him in."

Megan jumped out of the truck, more excited than she anticipated on being. "I'm here for Clyde." The receptionist took her credit card faster than a greyhound chasing a rabbit in a dog race. Megan signed every slip and experienced momentary chest pains when she saw the final balance, but when Clyde strutted down the hallway, it was worth every penny. "Come here, boy!" She would deny it until her last breath, but Megan did well up with tears of joy to see the big guy. "How are you?" She scratched his ears and rubbed any areas where there weren't bandages or shaven spots with stitches. The veterinarian handed her ointment for the wounds and gave Clyde an otherwise clean bill of health. He jumped in the back of Callie's truck as if he had just been out for a jaunt at the dog park.

"Well, he's in good spirits," Callie commented.

Then Megan's Irish side came out. "Yes, he is. Now I'm going to find the bastard who did this to him."

"Megan," Callie sighed, "this is hunting season for everything. It was probably just some kids messing around trying to be cool. Adolescent bullshit that went wrong. Something like that."

Megan stroked Clyde's head. "With a fucking BB gun? I don't think so. Drive." Megan wasn't sure, but she could have sworn Callie whispered, "Pain in my fucking ass."

Not the first time, she thought to herself.

THIRTY-EIGHT

MEGAN FELT AS CLOSE as she ever would to bringing home a new-born: Clyde. She allowed him on the couch and fed him, as promised, his favorite pizza. She basically spoiled the hell out of him. Callie told Megan to pick up the Christmas dinners at noon and there would be no charge, given her kind demeanor throughout the night. The sarcasm was duly noted. She sat thinking of the following day and could not quell the feelings of guilt and shame for not acknowledging the impending holiday. She wanted to go back to a time when her parents were alive and smiling. Now, she felt she was dead inside. Clyde must have picked up on her mood; he barked at her and proceeded to maul her with dog kisses.

"Clyde, you are a mush aren't you? I'm going to leave you for a few minutes to go to the mini-mart down the street. I need to get a few things. They're probably going to be closed tomorrow. Be good." Megan climbed up into Arnold, fired up the ignition, and started down Howard Boulevard, gassing it toward the small-town store. It wasn't until she hit the brakes that she knew something was wrong.

She wasn't going fast, but the brakes failed to slow her down one bit. Out of the corner of her eye, she caught a glimpse of an elderly man walking across the lot. Megan started honking the horn repeatedly. He jumped out of the way just in time. Vehicular manslaughter was not a part of her evening agenda. She swerved into a parking lot, tugging at the parking brake handle. Nothing was working.

"Son of a bitch!" She needed to stop the truck, no matter what. Still moving almost thirty miles an hour, Megan turned the steering wheel toward a Dumpster at the far end of the lot. She slammed into it with so much force that Arnold truly became a terminator. Death toll: one Dumpster.

Megan jumped out of the truck and first ran back to the elderly gentleman. He had no injuries, which was a complete relief to Megan. A store owner called the police and within minutes the flashing red and blue lights filled the streets.

How many cops work in a town that is three miles long? Megan caught herself thinking.

At first they accused her of being under the influence, until Megan explained her brakes had failed and she couldn't stop the truck. A beefy, chesty officer went under the Range Rover with a flashlight. "No need for a breathalyzer. The brake line has been cut."

"What?" Megan was dumbfounded. "I just drove this a day or so ago. Let me see." She scooted underneath Arnold and the officer put the light on the brake line. "How does this happen?"

"Lady, this didn't just happen. Look at the evenness of the slice. This was done on purpose."

Son of a bitch.

Megan called Callie, who then called Megan's favorite new friend, Duane Baker, to tow Arnold the short distance to his shop. It was by far not the most social three-minute drive she'd ever taken.

"The Dumpster is history, but they really make those Range Rovers tough. Your truck seems to be fine—except for the fluid lines. They even clipped your parking brake cable. You're really liked, huh?"

Megan stared out the window. "Looks that way."

"Heard someone threw you in the lake. Bag over your head and all. A pretty woman like you needs to be more careful, wouldn't you say? I know about you. City cop. Tough. I watched you on the news. Do you want to know what I see when I look in your eyes?" He didn't wait for a response. "I see a little girl, a little girl who needs to watch her back if she's as smart as she thinks she is."

Megan knew the tone of a thug and did not retreat. "The forty-five I carry around in my shoulder holster is pretty careful, always loaded, and I have eyes in the back of my head."

Douche bag.

Duane had an arrogant smirk as they pulled into his garage. "C'mon in. Callie said he's on his way to take you home and I need to give you some paperwork."

Megan went inside, more to take a look around than to get paperwork or make glorious small talk. Duane lit a cigarette while he fumbled through a file cabinet for forms. "You'll need a copy of the police report for your insurance company." Duane crouched down, the back of his jeans slipping a bit too far, exposing his tattooed back.

Megan stared at the round burn mark on Duane's lower back. No tattoo could hide it, though it looked as though he tried hard enough given how much ink was over his body. For a brief moment Megan felt like she was going to vomit.

I wonder if one of those young boys I saw in the videos was him.

Duane turned to hand Megan the papers "Here. Fill these out." She stared blankly at him. "Um, are you okay?"

She took the papers without answering.

Callie pulled up moments later. Duane said, "Your ride is here. I can get the truck back to you tomorrow."

"Tomorrow is a holiday. No rush."

"I don't celebrate Christmas."

Megan whispered, "Why?"

"Not much to be merry about, I guess. You should know how that feels."

They stared at one another. It was not a romantic stare, not even close. Megan felt frozen. She looked into his eyes, trying to think if there was anything from the videos that would ID him, but the burn mark was enough, and the bastards were smart enough not to film the victims' faces directly. But she knew, and there was a place in Duane that knew as well.

Megan walked out to Callie's car. He had a very concerned look on his face. "Are you okay? How is your arm?"

Megan had such an adrenaline rush that she'd forgotten she still had stitches in her arm. At this point she was impervious to physical pain; it was the emotional heartache that overpowered her when she allowed it to. "I'm fine. Very happy no one was hurt."

"What did Duane say?" Callie began the drive back to McGregor Avenue to drop Megan off. It was a busy night at the restaurant and he said he couldn't stay, though he very much would have liked to.

"He said the truck would be fixed by tomorrow. The brake line was cut, zero brake fluid in the reservoir. Parking brake cable snipped too. Do you know anything about brake lines?"

Callie raised his eyebrows. "Only that they shouldn't be cut, Trouble."

"That's what I was thinking." She paused before getting out of Callie's car. "Something is about to go down. There is a lot I'm unsure of at the moment, but I do know this: something is going down and soon."

Callie stared at her, holding her face in his hands as he kissed her. "Make sure it's not you."

———

Megan woke the next morning on the tip of a dream. She was walking down a path through a park. The trees were green, the sky clear. There was a large picnic table in the grassy field at the end of the path. The table was filled with people eating, laughing, and toasting one another. They welcomed Megan with smiles, motioning for her to sit at the head of the table. Many of the faces were familiar to her, but some of them seemed different: younger, happier than the last time she'd seen them. A woman put a hand on her shoulder. When Megan turned, it was a face she'd recognized immediately. It was her grandmother on her father's side. Megan looked up curiously at her, wondering what the purpose was for all of this. She pointed for Megan to turn around. Pat McGinn stood a few feet behind Megan, doing what he always did at family picnics, manning the grill and smoking his cherry-scented pipe. He looked peaceful and younger than the man she'd buried earlier that year. He smiled at her. Megan walked over, wrapping her arms around him, holding him so very tight. She heard his voice as clear as if he were standing right in the room. "It's time to buck up, baby girl." He turned Megan around and the only person now seated at the picnic table was Rose. Her voice couldn't be heard, but she held up the deaf sign for *I love you*. Megan had learned the sign only one day earlier. In that moment, she felt buoyant. She was being pulled

240

away, as if a bungee cord was tugging her back into her reality and into her loss.

The smell of her father's cherry-scented tobacco filled the bedroom.

THIRTY-NINE

IT WAS ANOTHER COLD morning, and Megan woke with her head facing toward her parents photograph. The dream lingered. She felt so alone and abandoned. Hell, most women her age were on their second or third child, with a stable marriage. Megan made fun of "stable" marriages—she could just picture two horses side by side, eating the same oats and the same hay day in, day out. It was her jaded, cynical side, or perhaps it was her nature. She kept telling herself she didn't much care. Her father brought up Megan and her brother with certain traditions: every birthday, make a list of what you want to achieve in the next year; Thanksgiving was the day to make the list of everything and everyone wonderful in your life, the people who have not just touched you but changed you to make you better; Christmas was the day to spend time with those people and tell them you loved them.

Megan sat up in bed, the sheets and blankets never enough to warm what she was missing. She still tried, then Clyde moaned.

He gave her a nod as if to say, *Not my fault.*

She wondered if there would ever be a time when she said that to herself: *not my fault*. It was a phrase that was hard for her to even utter. She didn't believe it.

Megan went down into the lower level to feed Clyde. As usual she checked that the double doors were locked and she performed a casual glance outside. Empty. Or so she hoped. She opened one of the cabinets for any more doggie goodies and found a red dog vest typically worn by service animals. She said to herself, "It's Christmas Eve, what the fuck."

She looked out the window and saw Arnold parked out front with a note on the window. Megan put on her winter coat over her pajamas and approached the Range Rover, hoping it wouldn't explode when she opened the door. The keys were perched on the visor. The note read: *No charge. Insurance will get this one. Drive safely. D.B.*

Megan huffed out an uncertain laugh. *Comforting.*

―――――

Megan drove over to Krogh's to pick up three turkey dinners. Much to her surprise, Vivian was working, but she was also pleased to see her busy and not alone on the holiday. They signed hello, and Megan was actually surprised to see exactly how busy the restaurant was.

I guess I don't get out much unless it's to funerals or crime scenes.

Megan was sure to place the dinners closer to her than to Clyde in the truck as she drove to the hospital to visit Billie. She dressed Clyde in the service dog vest from the Macks' previous dog, who was, according to the papers Megan stuffed in her coat pocket, an *active canine companion.*

"Clyde, you be good. No pulling on patients' tubes or peeing in the hallways or whatever your imagination could come up with. We're here to see Billie."

Megan walked through the front door with an overly friendly smile and issued the conditional happy holiday gestures, hoping nobody would question Clyde's presence. Not one staff member prevented Megan from walking into the elevator. Clyde was on his best behavior until they entered Billie's room. The television was on mute. Billie stared out the window and was stunned at Megan's arrival.

"Hey, kiddo. Merry almost Christmas." Megan placed the food on her hospital tray.

Billie lit up when she saw Clyde. "Oh my God! You brought Clyde!"

He jumped on the bed and snuggled right next to Billie.

"He's a service dog?"

Megan had a sheepish grin, not wanting many of the staff to overhear their conversation. "He's on a day-pass," she whispered. "And look what I have here—three full dinners, compliments of Callie."

"Your *friend*," Billie smiled.

"Whatever! One for you, one for your aunt, and one for the staff. You always need to take care of the people who are taking care of you."

Billie dug into the tray of stuffing first. "But who takes care of you?"

Megan dropped her usual banter. "See that furry guy who's trying to eat your stuffing? He does a pretty good job."

"Why does he have so many bandages?"

"Porcupine. Dumb luck."

Billie rubbed Clyde's head. "Isn't all bad luck pretty much dumb?"

"Eat your Christmas lunch. Or dinner, whatever it is, wiseass."

Billie looked better than she had the last time Megan visited her. Her color was back to normal and the bruises were fading. They sat petting Clyde while holiday-themed shows ran on the small hospital television.

Megan placed a small piece of turkey on the plates Callie provided. "How are you feeling? Give me an update."

"Well, the leg is sore, but my chest actually only hurts at night or when I try to move. So I guess you could say that kinda sucks."

"You'll be home soon. I mean, with your aunt."

She had a small pout. "Yeah, not with my mom. Ya know, the whole twenty-eight-days thing." Billie was speaking of her mother in rehab.

"Have you heard from her?"

Billie proceeded to feed Clyde from her tray, and he was quite grateful for the indulgence. "No. My aunt said she wouldn't get phone privileges until she's out of detox."

Megan stared at Billie without the acknowledgement that she knew exactly what she was going through. She didn't much want to share the open wound of her youth. "You're prettier without all that crap makeup you wear."

"You really rock at giving out compliments," Billie said, laughing. "So where's your guy?"

"He's not my guy." Megan waited for another smart-ass comment and sure enough she got it.

"He's hot. You better make him your guy before someone else does." She raised her eyebrows. "Get what I mean?"

Megan shook her head. "Just eat and turn the channel, I can't stand cozy, dippy movies."

Billie started channel surfing, but all the local channels seemed to be showing the same newscast.

"Stop," Megan ordered.

Billie turned up the volume. It was a break in regular programming showing Duane Baker being hauled out of his garage in handcuffs. The reporter stood outside in a parka saying Duane Baker was being arrested for the murder of Mount Arlington's mayor, which was determined *not* to be a suicide. There was undisclosed evidence that showed Duane was responsible for the killing.

Megan and Billie said in unison, "Shit."

Billie added, "I've known Duane practically my whole life. Why would he want to kill the mayor? I don't get it."

I do, thought Megan. "Billie, I'm sorry to cut this short, but I have to go."

"Are you going to check this out?"

Smart fucking kid. "No, I'm going to go see a man about a dog." Pat McGinn would always say that to Megan while she was growing up to sidetrack her when he was called to a case. Except this wasn't Megan's case and she wasn't about to share the sordid details with a teenage girl who recently survived a pummeling from her alcoholic mother's boyfriend.

"Come on, Clyde." Megan yanked his leash. He was still too interested in the turkey dinners on the hospital tray. "Text me when you get out, okay?"

Billie had a tense look of concern on her face. "I will as long as you'll be okay."

"I'm always okay."

They both knew Megan was lying.

Megan pointed at Billie's leg in the soft cast. "Take care of that, and rest. That's an order."

After Megan walked out with Clyde, Billie whispered, "You take care. That's an order."

FORTY

MEGAN TOOK CLYDE HOME SO she could watch the full news story. Callie had left three messages on her cell, but her phone's battery had died and she needed to charge it before returning the call. She thought about the newscast and began to doubt its truth, though she wasn't sure why. Duane Baker certainly had a long enough list of priors, certainly had hate inside him, and most likely enough tragedy. Worse, he was victim of the most horrible crime of all: sexual assault.

Megan settled Clyde, then hopped in Arnold and drove over to Norden's Marina. The brakes worked perfectly. *Well, Duane, you may be a scumbag, but you are a good mechanic.* There were no cars in the driveway. No lights on. Megan walked around the outside of the house. It was eerily silent, only a light wind and fog hovering over the frozen water. She walked to the end of the marina dock to find the broken edge where she'd crashed the snowmobile. Megan knelt down to look when she sensed a presence behind her, and she knew. There was no crystal ball needed. She turned and there he stood, his blackened helmet blocking the only exit off the dock. For as hot-headed as Megan could be, her calm resolve was immense when needed, especially when her life was possibly in danger. She stared at the man, knowing she could not positively identify him until he removed his helmet.

"Ms. McGinn. Is there something I can help you with?" Jake Norden asked.

Megan presumably scratched her back while taking the safety off the gun situated in the back of her jeans. "I wanted to see the damage that my ill-skilled snowmobile technique caused so I could reimburse you." Both Jake and Megan were exceptionally unflappable. They stared at each other. "I thought it would be neighborly to make up for it."

He stared at the dock. "It's nothing. Callie said he'd take care of it. Come spring it will be fixed properly. It's nothing for you to worry about. Something tells me you came for another reason."

Megan shook her head. "Not really. I did see your friend on the news. Duane Baker. Sorry about that."

Jake looked down, as if he felt a sense of repentance. That didn't last long, and arrogance quickly showed in his face. "Well, he has a few demons. I'm sure they'll find him innocent eventually."

Megan found that to be an odd statement. Her years of interviewing perps made her keen on body language, and Jake Norden was ice cold, to the point where he could freeze the lake ten times over. "Why do you think that?"

He took another step toward Megan, at which point she teetered on the edge of the dock. "I'm just saying. Innocent until proven guilty, right?"

Megan sidestepped him to move from his path and she was halfway down the dock when he shouted out. "Megan? Or Ms. McGinn?"

Megan turned to see him kneeling by the dock using a knife—a knife she knew all too well—to cut rope from one of the pilings. "Happy Holidays."

She stared at him. More fog rolled in now, masking his countenance. She wasn't sure if it was a grin or a glare emanating from his face, but she knew she didn't like it.

"Sure."

Someone should carve that motherfucker like a turkey, she thought.

As Megan returned to her truck and turned on the lights, she stared into the opened garage and could see four burlap sacks on a bench. She locked the doors immediately, then retreated from what she could only think of as another close call with the icy waters of Lake Hopatcong.

———

Megan was on her way home when she drove near Duane Baker's garage. The CLOSED sign was facing the road, but she saw his mother sitting in the office. She pulled in. Megan knocked on the front door. Lynn didn't respond. Megan knocked again and walked in. "Lynn, it's Megan McGinn. Do you mind if I come in?"

Lynn sat at her desk with a bottle of whiskey, staring at a picture of her son. She shrugged her shoulders. "Don't matter much to me." She took a swig from the dirty glass.

"I, um." Megan sighed. "I saw what happened to Duane, and I wanted to tell you that—"

Lynn interrupted. "Tell me my delinquent son is a murderer? I've gotten enough phone calls and hang-ups today from people who feel that way. Apparently, Christmas Eve is also a day to spread hate in this town."

Megan shook her head. "No, Lynn. That's not why I'm here."

Another shot of whiskey. "My son is no angel. I've known that for a long time. Something turned him when he was a young boy. Not sure what. Maybe when his father ditched us. Who knows what can kill a soul."

Megan was not about to tell Lynn what she'd uncovered. "Lynn." Megan paused. "You and everyone else know I'm a detective. They don't say much on the news about why he was arrested. Maybe I can help."

"You're gonna help me take a second mortgage out on my business to come up with bail money? Or are you gonna make the fact they found Duane's prints on the gun go away?" Lynn finally looked Megan in the eye. "My boy was there that day. The mayor wanted Duane to give him an estimate on one of his cars, thought Duane might be interested."

Megan's first thought, especially with Duane's past was, *He's screwed.* "Are you sure they found prints?"

She nodded. "That's what got him arrested."

Megan sat down. "Lynn, you're his mother. You know if he did it or not."

"Like I said, Duane is a lot of things, but he's no murderer. He's troubled on many levels, but he wouldn't kill anyone. Nope."

Megan chose her next words very carefully. "Did you see him when he came home that day? When he was done working on the mayor's car?"

Lynn threw back another shot. "Sure. He had three other cars to work on. And you saw him too. Ten minutes after he got back, you rolled in with that monster truck. When the light was goin' off."

Megan remembered it clearly. "He was wearing the same clothes he wore when he left for the mayor's house?"

"Yeah. Go figure, his tuxedo was at the cleaners."

Megan knew from dealing with Forensics on her murder cases that shooting someone at close range caused enormous blood splatter. Putting a gun in someone's mouth and blowing their brains out? Duane would have been covered in blood, as well as other bodily matter.

"You know what I've noticed about you, girl?" The whiskey was about to speak. "Nothin' been good since you came to town. The judge is murdered. That poor girl"—she was now waving her very full glass in the air—"that girl down your street is pummeled and in the hospital. Christ, I even heard your damn dog was shot. It sure seems to me that you've got a black cloud over you." Another sip. "And I know what happened to your momma." She nodded. "Yeah, I do read the papers. The first day I put eyes on you I thought to myself, *now there's trouble. Manhattan trouble comin' to our small lake town.* Evil follows you wherever you go. You ever feel cursed? Because it sure seems to me that you are."

Megan allowed the rant. Lynn was hurting and Megan could tell by the bleak, drunk look in her eyes that she probably had been for a long time. No one gets by in this life without pain, but some unfortunate souls carry more of the burden. Megan could tell Lynn was one of them.

It was time to leave Lynn to her bottle and her sadness. Megan looked at her face. Her eyes were filled with so much pain. Megan didn't want to add to it. "If you need anything, let me know."

Lynn returned to her glass full of misery and stared out the window.

252

FORTY-ONE

MEGAN DROVE TO THE local police station looking for Krause or Michalski. Even though it was a holiday, Michalski was churning out paperwork. He greeted Megan with his typical kindness, a smile, and a handshake. "What can I do for you?"

"I was looking for your partner, Krause."

He rubbed his potbelly and looked at his watch. "She would be at the gym about now."

Megan was somehow not shocked given how little professional respect she had for Krause. "With everything going on in this town, she's at the gym? How amateur of her." She spied a countdown tacked to a corkboard above Michalski's desk. In this moment she reminded herself that he was only concerned with getting through the job and hitting retirement.

He saw her gaze. "Seven weeks and three days left," he snorted.

Megan smiled. "Where would this gym be?"

Michalski gave her directions and she thanked him.

"Good luck," he returned with a raised eyebrow.

Megan parked at Black Bear Fitness. She was asked for identification when she walked in, which she immediately ignored, having no temperament for a pimple-nosed college kid. She quickly found Krause in the weight room attempting to prove her manliness. It looked like a military drill. Her personal trainer yelled at her for a few minutes on the treadmill, inserting words of encouragement through every fraction of the workout. After she did a sprint on the treadmill, he made Krause race over to the free weights. Then came sit-ups and jumping jacks. He repeated the steps two or three more times. Megan could tell the training session was over when they bumped fists. Krause sat on the exercise bench drinking water while she watched Megan's reflection in the mirror as Megan approached her.

Krause rolled her eyes. "What do you want? And who told you I was here?"

"No one." Megan didn't want to rat out Michalski. He had enough grievances in his life having her as a partner.

Krause wiped her forehead with a towel. "So, what *sage* advice do you have for me now?"

"I know it would be against your sound moral code to talk about this, but you need to know on the day the mayor killed himself—"

"He was murdered. Or don't you watch the news?" Krause got up and refilled her water bottle at the fountain.

Megan repeated, with great attempt to quell her anger, "The day the mayor died, I saw Duane Baker at the garage ten minutes after he was at the judge's home."

"And I guess his mother told you that. How far in the bag was she?"

Megan held up her palms. "Hear me out. If Duane tried to make it look like a suicide, he'd have been so close that the blood spray would have covered him."

"Uh-huh."

"Do you understand what I'm saying?"

"Duane's mother has been covering for him for years. He's good for this." Krause raised her well-toned arms in the air. "So, what? First you try to help an innocent deaf girl by breaking into and stealing from a crime scene, then forwarding me evidence, and now you're trying to help a loser get away with murder. I'm just curious, when are you up for sainthood?"

"Do you have proof of me doing that?" Megan could match snide with snide. "Any prints on what was sent to you?"

"Your handiwork was all over it. I will give you this though, very smart calling 911 and leaving the receiver off the hook."

Megan leaned against one of the workout machines. "I still don't know what you're talking about."

"Oh get your angelic wings ready, because I will be going after the judge's daughter for his murder when I gather more information."

Megan shook her head. "I don't like you, but you're smart enough to know she wouldn't be strong enough to carry a man nearly three times her weight from the house down to the lake and throw him in."

"She could have had help. And I will find the accomplice. Then she will be going to prison for a very, very long time."

Megan crossed her arms. "Oh, I'm getting this now. This isn't about finding the true perp. This is about you advancing your career in this Podunk town. Tell me, who's promised you what? A promotion? Maybe a steep pay raise, even on the side, so to speak? What would make you go so left of center on this job?"

Krause pointed to her chest. "*I* went left of center? I'm the one who still has a badge! You got people killed, so exactly what lane of the highway were you operating on?"

Megan wouldn't give into her anger, so she smiled. "Someday there will come a time you won't be able to sleep at night. Choosing the wrong path will catch up to you. It always does."

Megan could tell she hit a nerve. She could also feel Krause's glare as she walked out of the gym.

FORTY-TWO

Megan sat with Clyde outside on the lower level. It was an exhausting day that reminded her of too many failures and too much pain. Clouds were moving over the lake and Megan wondered if Lynn was right about her having a dark cloud over her. While Megan wasn't the type to carry a rabbit's foot or find a four-leaf clover, or even win two bucks with a lottery ticket, her own personal dark cloud seemed a bit much. Sometimes truth can be that way.

She heard the gate on the upper level open and saw Callie carrying a large bag, standing over the deck. "Hey, Trouble."

Great nickname.

"Hey." Megan and Clyde walked upstairs through the house. It was a little easier for Clyde to manage the stairs with carpet instead of maneuvering on snow and ice. Megan unlocked the door for Callie. He looked exhausted. "Long day?"

"The restaurant did really well, but my feet and legs feel like lead. I brought more food, mainly because I haven't eaten yet."

"Drag your lazy ass in here."

Callie kicked off his shoes and gave Megan the bag. "How did Billie enjoy the meal?"

Megan didn't mention she hadn't stayed all that long but was quite sure Billie enjoyed Callie's food more than a hospital meal. "What isn't there to like?"

"Why is it I've been working all day and yet you look more exhausted than I do?" Callie asked.

"Thank you for the compliment. I'm always impressed with your gentlemanly skills." Megan smiled. "Yes, I'm a bit tired but pushing through. You're out early for a holiday." Megan took his coat.

"I always plan the last seating for five o'clock so the staff can enjoy their holiday too."

Megan nodded and took out the covered dishes he was thoughtful enough to bring. "And Vivian?"

"More tired than I am. She was very focused and worked really hard today."

"I'm surprised you haven't mentioned the news."

Callie was confused. "What do you mean?"

Megan gave a *duh* look. "Duane Baker? You have four televisions at the restaurant."

"Yeah, and we just set them to stations with Christmas movies. What's going on?"

Megan poured drinks. "He was arrested for murdering the mayor."

"Are you fucking kidding me?" He rubbed his forehead. "But I thought it was a suicide."

"They don't think so anymore." Megan decided to work backwards on the meal and start with pie. "Here, take a look." She clicked the television on.

Callie watched in silence for several minutes. "I guess I owe you an apology. You had a hunch. God, Lynn must be destroyed."

She stared at Clyde. "Yeah." Megan wasn't in the mood to discuss her visit to the garage. It hit too close to what had been on her mind all afternoon. Megan opened the material the veterinarian gave her and knew it was time to change Clyde's bandages. He didn't fight it.

"What about your arm? When was the last time you changed the bandage on your arm?"

"Haven't thought about it. Doesn't hurt so why mess with perfection?" Her smile was forced.

"Come here." Callie washed his hands before removing the bandage on Megan's arm. The Steri-Strips were naturally peeling off. "Looks good. The doctor did a great job. I'm going to put on a little antibiotic cream and you should be good to go."

"When did you get your medical degree?"

"Please, with all the burns and slice-and-dice accidents in the kitchen, I feel like I buy a new medical kit every month." Callie rubbed Megan's arm, but not in a medicinal way. Sensually. He trailed her palm with his fingers. In the moment even though both were exhausted, it didn't temper their attraction and heat. Callie pulled Megan forward and they shared a long, deep kiss. He brushed her hair away from her face and stared into her eyes. "You're beautiful. Do you know that?"

Callie said it with the most sincerity Megan had ever heard come from him. She didn't say anything in response.

"You are," he whispered, then took her hand and directed her to the bedroom. This time was different. It wasn't the hard-core, rough sex they'd grown accustomed to. Callie slowly removed every item of Megan's clothing. He admired each naked part of her body not just with his hands and mouth, but with his eyes. "Beautiful."

It was the first time in a very long time Megan felt she'd made love and not just screwed around. Before falling asleep Megan turned on her side and allowed a single tear to fall down her cheek.

————

Morning felt as though it came in minutes as opposed to hours. She turned over and Callie was fast asleep on his stomach. She threw on jeans and a sweatshirt, leaned over, and kissed him on the back of his neck. The kiss made him stir and turn but didn't wake him, though the sheet and comforter dropped below his hips. And that's when Megan saw the scar. The same round burn mark that was on the boys in the videos. The same mark she'd seen on Duane Baker's back the day in the garage.

Oh my God. Oh my God.

Megan slowly left the bedroom. Her stomach was turning and her face felt flushed. "Outside, Clyde." She walked over to the counter and put her face in her hands. "It all makes sense now," she said to herself.

"Does it?" Callie said from the hallway.

Megan pretended not to understand. "I'm making coffee. Do you have time for a cup?" She pressed her phone while getting the coffee out of the cabinet. "I know I make it too strong but—"

"Answer my question."

"I'm sorry, I didn't hear a question." Megan turned to find Callie pointing one of her guns at her.

"Well, you found out my little shameful secret, but I don't think it could possibly *all make sense.*"

Megan took a step back. "Callie, what are you doing?"

260

He walked up to Megan and rubbed the end of the gun against her cheek. "Now, this was not a part of my plan," he said calmly.

She walked slowly backward into the living room. "Callie, you and the other boys were terribly, disgustingly hurt. Those men were monsters, but that doesn't make you one."

"Oh, so because you watched a few videos of what happened to us, you think you know what we suffered? You think you know the fear and pain?" He started circling Megan. "Those men stole everything from us. They took our youth. They took our trust. They killed us. Don't you get that? Do you want to hear how they got us there?" He didn't wait for a response. "A few of us were doing lawn work for the judge one summer." He twirled the gun in his hand. "I guess the first clue was how much we were getting paid, way too much for young boys. Every few hours one of the staff would bring out lemonade. It was spiked, just a little at a time. I'm not sure with what, but it did the job they wanted it to. I've never felt so vulnerable. Scared."

Callie walked closer to Megan. She didn't move. "The first time"—Callie paused, staring at Megan's sudden surprise—"oh, you think it only happened once? There were more attacks after the first, because after the first time came the threats: If I told anyone, they wouldn't believe me; if I told anyone, they would hurt my mother. Which, looking back, seems almost humorous."

"Why?" Megan asked.

"I'll get to that."

"No, I have no idea the horror you went through. I didn't say that." Megan was unarmed, and she felt naked. "How many were there?"

"Monsters or boys?" The look in Callie's eyes turned so angry, as if he were possessed, which, Megan thought, he probably was to a certain extent. Who ever truly heals from an experience like molestation? So brutal. Pure evil.

"Boys? I don't know. Enough? One is too many. You *know* how many men were involved. You were in the room. You saw the chairs. Why are you asking me so many questions when you have the answers?"

The slow dance around the coffee table continued. "Why try to frame Vivian and Duane Baker?" Megan asked.

"Vivian? I did not try to frame Vivian. Who would go and frame their half-sister? She did that to herself when she came into the judge's house after I killed him and she stabbed the motherfucker after he was already dead. I did have to laugh at that, by the way. She's a tough gal." Callie stared at Megan before snickering. "Now, Duane I did frame. He was so easy for it. When I killed the mayor and all the blood shot out at me, well hell, I've seen enough shows on television to know they could tell it wasn't a suicide." Callie glanced up at the ceiling, tilting his head, then looked back at Megan. "It was nice to hear him beg for his life. I should have taped it." Callie's sinister laugh was unfamiliar to Megan, so unlike the man she thought she'd known.

"What?" Megan was blindsided by Callie's disclosure. "I don't understand. Why didn't you tell me you and Vivian were related?"

"I didn't know until months ago after my mother died. She left me a letter explaining everything. It was a one-night stand that brought me into the world. The only son of that fucking disgusting bastard."

Megan scanned the room for something, anything to arm herself with. There was nothing to aid her. Megan searched her memory of the events that had taken place since her arrival. "You knew for years who did this to you. Why now? Why start your revenge now?"

Callie stared at her, knowing what he was about to do, so he tolerated her questions. "When I found out he was my biological father, it sickened me. But when Vivian's mother died—a very suspicious death by the way; the whole town knows she'd never have left her daughter with that pig—I knew Vivian would be next. She worked for me for a long time before I found out. It would have been only a matter of time before he hurt her too, and I refused to let that happen."

"You—you tried to drown me. That was you, wasn't it? You threw me in the water with the burlap sack over my head."

Callie used the barrel of the gun to push hair away from his face. "I knew you'd get out."

"Then why?"

"You came here like a wounded puppy. Fragile. Hurting. I wanted to make sure you stayed that way."

"A wounded puppy? So you had someone shoot Clyde too? And what about the lake? Were you the one on the snowmobile? "

"Interesting when the pieces of the puzzle start to come together, isn't it? Now, first of all, I don't hurt dogs. I don't hurt animals. That's just cruel."

"You just hurt humans," Megan said in a low voice.

Callie snarled, "The judge and his posse weren't human! Any person who does that to a child—their own child, at that—isn't human. As for Clyde, I had nothing to do with it. It was just an accident. I told you it was probably some kids trying out their first time at hunting, or some teenage bullshit."

"Callie, were you the third snowmobiler?" Megan fought to keep her voice from trembling.

He rolled his eyes. "Megan, that fisherman is drunk ninety-nine percent of the year. There *wasn't* a third snowmobiler. It was just me and you."

"How did you get back to the marina so quickly?"

"I know this lake like the back of my hand, and I'm a better snowmobiler than you. Remember, I grew up in these small towns. I know my way around."

"You know I can't look the other way on this."

"I know, which is why it makes this so hard." And he actually did look upset. "Here's what I'm thinking. Poor Detective Megan McGinn goes on leave from the force. She's so terribly distraught over her family tragedy that she decides life isn't worth living anymore."

"You think that will actually fly?"

"For a woman with a gun pointed at her, you sure do have a cocky side to you."

"Actually, Callie, I think you're in a bit of trouble right now."

"How's that?"

"I never keep any of my guns loaded in the house. Would you like a bullet with that?" Megan sprinted for the door, but Callie grabbed her by the back of her hair. He threw the gun to the floor. Megan elbowed him in the ribs. She kicked him in the shins. She used every effort to injure him long enough to get away. All failed. He was simply too strong.

"Not so fast, Megan." He wrapped his arm around her neck in a chokehold. "Now, Trouble, it seems you're in a *lot* of trouble. The gun won't help me, but this will." He pulled the hunting knife from the back of his jeans and whispered in her ear, "You were the best fuck I ever had." He held up the knife and plunged it into her chest.

The pain was beyond imagining. Her chest felt on fire. All of her senses seemed to work in slow motion, and yet she continued to hold onto Callie as she slid down to the floor. She looked up at him. The room was darkening.

"Goodbye, Trouble."

———

Megan heard people buzzing around her. "Megan, it's Detective Krause. Stay with us. The ambulance will be here soon. Stay with us. Give me that rag," Krause yelled at Michalski. "I need to compress the wound. Jesus Christ, this is a lot of blood."

Megan whispered. Krause had to lean in. "What? Megan, what did you say?"

"My phone."

Then life became pitch black.

FORTY-THREE

Nappa and the Murphys filled the waiting room. Megan was in the operating room for hours before the surgeon came out with an update. The next few hours were critical, he told them. Megan had lost a lot of blood, and the wound was deep. No major organs were damaged, but there was massive internal bleeding that they were trying to stop. She was placed in the ICU. Megan's neighbor, Jo, a doctor at the hospital, gave them updates periodically. Billie made one of the nurses wheel her down to the waiting room, and she sat with all concerned. Detectives Krause and Michalski arrived a handful of hours later with Vivian.

Nappa immediately asked Krause and Michalski what had happened.

Krause answered, "Vivian found her on the kitchen floor. She texted 911. We saw the address and got right over, hopefully not too late. Detective Nappa, I have to hand it to your partner. She's one hell of a savvy lady. She recorded everything on her cell phone. We got a full confession."

"From who?" Nappa and Uncle Mike asked in unison.

"Christopher Callie. He was arrested a few hours ago."

"That son of a bitch," Nappa said.

One of the attendings came in and asked if there were family there. It wasn't as positive as he had hoped. Megan had flat-lined. Though they were able to restart her heart, he suggested it might be time to make peace and sit with her, but only one person at a time.

"Mike, you go," Aunt Maureen said in a weepy voice. "I can't see our Meggie like this."

Uncle Mike cleared his throat. "Sam, I won't be long. You're next."

Nappa nodded, turning toward the window. *Not yet, McGinn. Not yet*, he thought to himself.

The attending walked Uncle Mike into the intensive care unit. He pulled out a handkerchief, wiped his eyes. "Hey Meganator, it's Uncle Mike. We're all here for you, kiddo." He looked at Megan hooked up to so many wires, oxygen. He'd never seen her look so helpless, so weak. "You sure go to an extreme to get a nap in, don't you?" He smiled through the tears running down his face. "Here's the thing. You can't give up, kiddo. You're a McGinn. McGinns don't give up, so you need to fight this. You got that?" He sat and held her hand for a few minutes, but it proved too difficult to see her this way. "Okay, Nappa is here. I'm sending him in." Uncle Mike bent over, kissed her forehead, and whispered, "I love you, Meggie."

Nappa sat down next to Megan just a few minutes later. "Hey, partner." Nappa choked up and said through a shaky voice, "You're not going out like this. Not today. There's a lot more work to do and I can't find another partner that is as much of a pain in the ass as you are. You hear me, Megan?" Nappa sat holding her hand, wondering if she could hear any of what he was saying. A nurse came in.

"Can she feel anything? I mean, is she in pain?" he asked.

"She's heavily sedated. We're making her as comfortable as possible."

Nappa's chin began to quiver. "Okay, thank you."

———

He'd fallen asleep in the chair holding Megan's hand. He felt a small squeeze. It was weak but enough to wake him up. "McGinn, are you awake?"

Nappa could see she was trying to open her eyes, but it was too much for her. She released a small moan, then she went back to sleep. Nappa ran outside to the desk. "We need a doctor in here! We need a doctor!"

Uncle Mike and Aunt Maureen ran out of the waiting room. "Sam, what's going on?"

"Mike, she squeezed my hand! She squeezed my hand!"

Aunt Maureen burst into tears. Everyone in the room began hugging one another as if they'd been friends for years. Doctors and nurses filled Megan's room, shouting orders and medical jargon back and forth. A nurse asked for everyone to return to the waiting area. A half-hour later, the surgeon entered. Hanging on his every word, they listened.

"There is in no clear explanation, but she is beginning to respond." More hugs and tears of happiness flowed. "She seems to have a very strong will to live. She still has a long road ahead of her."

"But you think she'll be all right?" Nappa asked.

The surgeon looked just as shocked as anyone. "I think there is a very strong chance she'll make a recovery."

"Can we go in and see her?" Aunt Maureen asked.

"In a few hours. We gave her more pain medication so she's sleeping right now."

Uncle Mike gave Nappa a bear hug. "Can't keep that girl down!"

FORTY-FOUR

It was a sunny winter day on Lake Hopatcong, cold as usual, but with bright skies. Megan sat on the couch staring out at the beautiful day. Her incision was still very tender, but she was out of the hospital and back with Clyde and over a dozen get-well wishes, flowers, and cards on the mantel. But there was one card she still needed to read and now she felt ready to do so.

Megan gingerly got up from the couch and took the letter Nappa had brought to her when he visited the lake. It was from Mrs. McAllister, the mother of the victim in her last case. She opened it.

Dear Detective Megan,

I hope this note finds you well, though given the painful situation you've just gone through, I'm sure you are in the middle of loss as I was when Shannon was murdered. I wish you all my condolences and prayers. I'm not sure this will help, since I feel I will continue to mourn my daughter until God allows

*me to see her again someday. I want you to remember some-
thing, for when the time is right. We are bigger than our pain.
We are bigger than our suffering. Trust that everything happens for a reason, and know you are loved.*

Best,
MaryEllen McAllister

I know I'm loved, Megan thought to herself, then proudly displayed the card on the mantel.

There was a knock at the front door. Since moving around was still a bit of a challenge and she knew who it was, she yelled, "Come on in."

Leigh and Jo entered. Leigh held another lasagna or stew or one of the many things she'd made for Megan during the weeks following the stabbing. Jo brought medical supplies; she'd put herself in charge of changing Megan's bandages.

"Hey there, patient. How's the pain?" Jo asked as she began feeling Megan's abdomen.

"Sore, but Vicodin is my new best friend." Megan smiled.

Leigh told Megan she'd put the food in the refrigerator.

"I'm not sure there's enough room." Megan wasn't in a comfortable position and had to resituate herself. "Hey, thank you again for taking care of Clyde while I was in the hospital."

"Not a problem. He was a joy," Leigh answered. "Megan, I have a question. I hope it doesn't make you feel uncomfortable."

"Sure. Go ahead."

"Isn't it a little uneasy to be here, considering everything that happened?"

"I guess it was a little at first, but I'm okay with it now. I mean, I can't change what happened and I have this lovely scar to forever remind me, so I had to make peace with it."

They both nodded and Jo said, "That makes sense." She clasped her hands. "You're set. Everything is looking good. I've got to get this one to a doctor's appointment now."

"Thanks for coming by. Hey, how's Billie?"

"I think she'll be getting off crutches next week. She really wants to be able to get down that driveway and see you. We'll check back with you tomorrow, okay?"

Leigh popped her head back into the house before closing the door. "Give us a call if you need anything!"

Megan noticed Jo had left her winter gloves on the coffee table and made a mental note to text her later. Megan remained on the couch flipping through channels on the muted television. She stopped when she saw Phillip Thompson on the screen surrounded by reporters. She knew Callie had retained him for his defense and was a bit surprised he stopped to answer questions. Then she remembered what a media whore he was while working with Vivian. He made a statement that his client was the victim in this circumstance. Megan winced hearing that comment. *Tell that to the stitches in my gut*, she thought to herself.

"He'll plead insanity or PTSD." A part of Megan hoped Callie would, because he was broken. She just never saw how fractured he really was. The easy smile, the amiable nature. It was all a facade. Megan glanced over at Clyde. He was sleeping in front of the fireplace. His fur had begun to grow back where he'd been wounded. Megan recalled that Clyde had never really warmed up to Callie. At the time, she'd assumed he was jealous of the attention Megan gave the man. Dogs really did know best.

There was a knock at the door. Megan figured Jo had remembered she left her gloves behind. "Come on in. It's open. Hey, you forgot your gloves, they're over here."

"Ms. McGinn? Do you mind if I come in?"

Duane Baker.

Megan wanted to rise but knew the sudden movement would be a bad idea. She had not expected this visit. "Oh, um sure, come on in. I thought you were my neighbor from down the street."

"You're not too tired? I won't stay long." He was a bit sheepish entering. "I would have come by sooner, but I knew you probably needed your rest."

She smiled. "That's okay. Have a seat."

Clyde greeted Duane with his tail wagging and nudged his head underneath his arm for the demanded scratching of the head. Megan noted Clyde's approval of Duane.

"Well, I wanted to say thank you, not just for getting me out of jail and taking a knife for it, but for coming by to see my mom when I was arrested. She told me."

Megan remembered the day very well. "You're welcome."

"How's the gut?"

"Sore, but I'm getting there."

There was an awkward silence.

"So, from what I hear, I guess you saw some of the tapes from the judge's house."

She stared at Duane and saw in his eyes the same pain she'd seen in Callie's. "Yes, I did. I didn't see any faces, but yes, I saw the violence."

Duane morphed from tough biker dude to what Megan imagined was the young boy being victimized. His eyes welled and he coughed back his emotion. It was a weak attempt, but he tried. "It was a long time ago. Some days it feels like yesterday. Some days I'm far away from those times, but they're never gone. Ever." He stood up and walked over to the bay window. Staring out at the lake, he continued what seemed like a confession. But Megan knew there was nothing to confess when you're the casualty. "I wonder what direction my life would have taken if that hadn't happened. Maybe I would have turned into a good guy, a better son, not an angry ex-con who does everything wrong."

"Duane, it's not too late. It's never too late to go get help, to make different choices. And it seems to me you're a pretty damn good son. You take care of your mom, her business. Those are good qualities."

He turned to Megan and with a sad sincerity answered, "Something died in me in that room. There are nights when the nightmares are so real I wake up screaming like a little boy."

"Can I ask you something?"

"Sure."

"When it came out that the judge had been murdered, did you think it was Callie?" Megan was nervous she might be overstepping with such a personal question.

Duane pondered Megan's question. "No, actually, I didn't. I never thought he would murder someone, not that the bastard didn't deserve it. Then again, I never thought he was the type of guy to set someone up like he did to me. So what the fuck do I know?"

Megan offered a knowing smile.

"Well, I'll let you get back to whatever it is you do after being stabbed. See you around," Duane said.

"See you around." Megan stopped him before leaving. "Hey, Duane."

"Yeah?"

"For what it's worth, I knew it wasn't you. Not that I didn't suspect it once or twice, but I knew. Call it a gut feeling. And it's not Ms. McGinn, it's Megan."

"I prefer Detective McGinn." Duane shut the door, and Megan whispered to Clyde, "So do I."

———

Megan's cell rang. She didn't recognize the number but answered anyway.

"Detective McGinn?"

Due to the buzz from the Vicodin she'd popped a half an hour previously, Megan had a hard time identifying the voice. This was also the first time Detective Krause had referred to her in a professional manner. "Detective Krause, what can I do for you?"

"Actually, I was just calling to see how you were doing."

High as a kite. "Each day is getting better."

"That's good, that's good."

No matter how stoned Megan was feeling, she could sense the awkward silence while Krause was forming her next sentence.

"Well, we have three out of the five molesters. There are still two left."

"Put pressure on the councilman," Megan suggested.

"I would, but apparently he's pretty much a vegetable. He stroked out a while back. Any thoughts on how to start the search for the last two?"

Megan knew it was a large slice of humble pie for Krause to ask the question, but she still had to give her a hard time. "Well, I would help, but New Jersey is your jurisdiction. I would be overstepping my boundaries by getting involved."

"It didn't stop you before!"

"True." Megan imagined what she would do if she were still working the case. "First, go back to the judge's early life, his college years. These sick bastards bond early. See if any of them have a local connection. I would also check local banks to see if anyone, specifically men, have withdrawn large sums of money as of the date the judge was found in the lake. What you have going for you is they're scared and running. They would have wanted to escape any connection with him and the scandal. Krause, everyone leaves some sort of path, you have that in your favor. I would also—gently—speak to Duane Baker. He might know of other victims besides Chris Callie. If you can find more victims, they might be able to tell you something. They'll fight it, so use your gentle kid-gloves approach." Megan couldn't help but laugh at that last thought.

"Gotcha. Take care of yourself, detective, and please try to be a stranger."

"No arguments on this end."

FORTY-FIVE

MEGAN WAS NEARLY DONE packing up her things when the phone rang. It was Leigh with the great news of her cancer being in remission. It was a high note to end her sojourn in Lake Hopatcong.

She and Clyde walked out onto the deck. He saw a squirrel run across the yard and promptly ran down the steps to defend his property. She leaned on the deck, staring out at the lake, which was now returning to blue water instead of the frozen tundra she'd become so accustomed to. Buds were beginning to sprout on the bushes and trees were turning green again with leaves. She glanced over to the neighbor's house. Poised on the corner of their deck was the hawk she'd witnessed a handful of times. Megan stared at him with a sense of awe. His regal demeanor demanded respect, and she gave it to him. For a moment she was sure he was staring back. Seconds later he took flight, and that would be the last time she'd see him.

Megan took a small box of the personal items she'd brought and put them in the trunk of Arnold. Her trip was going to end much as it had begun. Megan saw Vivian jogging down the street, though unlike at Megan's arrival, Vivian stopped and signed hello and asked Megan how she was feeling.

"Better, thank you," she said slowly as she signed. Her convalescence had made for lots of ASL practice time.

Vivian looked at Megan without signing and said, "Thank you, Megan."

Megan signed, *You're welcome.*

Vivian gave her a hug and began jogging again, but not before turning around and signing one more time: *I love you.*

———

The doorbell rang. To Megan's surprise, it was Billie. She walked in with a small soft cast and only a cane.

"Hey, look at you! You made it to a cane and down the driveway. Congratulations!"

"Thanks. Heard you were leaving soon." It was obvious by the sad look on Billie's face that she wasn't happy to see Megan go.

Megan nodded. "Yep. How are things going with your mom back?"

"She's trying. It has its ups and downs. We both feel bad about how things went down."

"I've been there. You know, Billie, there's one thing I've learned. You can't always see the cracks in everyone else's lives. It's not comforting, because you can always see your own. Wrong choices. Regrets. But it doesn't get better until you let yourself off the hook. Know what I mean?"

She shrugged. "I think so. Why are you leaving now? The Macks don't come back for another month."

"It's time."

"Are you taking Clyde with you?"

Megan smiled, looking down at him. "You bet."

Billie choked back tears. "I'm going to miss you, Megan." Billie moved forward and hugged her. "I really am."

"I'm going to miss you too, sweetie," Megan spoke over her shoulder. "And I promise I'll keep in touch."

Billie pulled back and used her sleeve to wipe her eyes and nose. "So what happens now?"

"I go back."

THE END

© *Anni Nappa*

ABOUT THE AUTHOR

C.J. Carpenter was born and raised in upstate New York. She has spent the majority of her life living in Manhattan and now divides her time between NYC and Philadelphia, where she is currently working on her third novel.